This,
One's
for You

This, One's for You

KATE SWEENEY

VIKING

Also by Kate Sweeney
Catch the Light

VIKING

An imprint of Penguin Random House LLC, New York

First published in the United States of America by Viking,
an imprint of Penguin Random House LLC, 2023

Copyright © 2023 by Kate Sweeney

Viking & colophon are registered trademarks of Penguin Random House LLC.

Visit us online at penguinrandomhouse.com.

Library of Congress Cataloging-in-Publication Data is available.

Printed in the United States of America

ISBN 9780593350270 (hardcover)

1 3 5 7 9 10 8 6 4 2

ISBN 9780593622124 (international edition)

1 3 5 7 9 10 8 6 4 2

BVG

Edited by Kelsey Murphy

Design by Lucia Baez | Text set in Joanna MT Pro

For my boys

PART 1

1
Caspian

SOME MORNINGS, WHEN I'M STILL DRIFTING back and forth between asleep and awake, I think I can hear her voice. She's singing, or maybe she's laughing, and it's the color of sunlight on the back of my eyelids. Orange-gold. Glowing.

It's not her real voice. The human brain doesn't start making memories until the age of two, and she was gone long before that. She died in a time when there was nothing but a half-made, invisible foundation, when my subconscious was still being shaped by experiences that would never be remembered. She shaped me—in the impression of her voice and her touch, and then her absence. But I'll never, ever know her.

If I let them, things with Mom can become an obsession. I'm a detective and she is the case that will make my career. I'm a scientist, and she is the grand, elegant equation that will explain the universe. But the rest of the time, she truly doesn't exist to me.

I run down the front steps and jump on my bicycle, the straps of my helmet dangling down around my ears. My American History final is in ten minutes; I just woke up and I haven't even brushed my teeth.

I begin pedaling furiously up the giant hill that leads away from the cul-de-sac. June gloom is in full force, so I'm not sweating as hard as

I could be by the time I get to the top. Just enough that I feel a trickle at the edge of my forehead.

I fly through the burned-out strip that is downtown El Sobrante, dodging a man who is riding his horse down the street. I pass Santa Shoe Repair, Nerd Crossing, Mountain Mike's Pizza. I barrel into the school parking lot and lock up my bike next to a monstrous hydrangea bush, run down the hallway, and slide into my seat at 8:59 a.m.

Hannah looks over at me and says, "You look . . . interesting. Everything okay?"

She's perfectly neat as always, and there is something deeply calming about her thick golden ponytail, her crisp white T-shirt, the tiny silver H at her throat. I reach up and tug the end of her hair.

"I accidentally slept in."

She raises both hands. "Not my fault."

Then Mr. Henderson walks in, looking sad and rumpled, the human equivalent of a ketchup stain.

"Good morning, seniors! For most of you this will be the last test you ever take at De Anza High. Good luck."

He passes around the test books and pencils and then the next two hours are a fog of essay questions about the Civil War and the industrial revolution. I try, but by the end of it I'm basically propping my eyes open with sticks.

I hand in my test, brush my teeth in the bathroom, and then wait for Hannah and Jake out front. A pack of wild turkeys roams through the parking lot, shitting on cars. I sit on the gate of Hannah's dad's pickup truck, tucked between my bike and the surfboards, my hood cinched over my ears to muffle the chattering birds and the distant highway sounds.

And then we are driving along the Richmond Parkway, my hand on Hannah's knee, Jake whining about being crammed into the back seat of the extended cab. The fog is burning into a smoggy, hazy blue that can't decide if it's dirty or clean. A cormorant corkscrews into the water. Rust-colored fuel cylinders loom on the hillside, blending in to the orange rocks.

We cruise over the Richmond Bridge, past the San Quentin State Prison. Hannah is singing along loudly to the Killers, which she thinks is cool/retro but everyone knows is garbage music. Her voice is slightly off-key, but somehow it's charming.

Hannah is calmly, classically beautiful, with delicate features and soft, pale skin. We've been together since junior year but I liked her for a lot longer than that.

We're heading up to Bolinas, where Hannah and Jake will surf and I'll wait on the beach, and then we'll meet up with a bunch of other kids from school and drink warm beer around a fire under the moonlight to celebrate the great accomplishment of finishing high school.

My phone buzzes on the seat. It's Dad.

Congratulations dude.

> **Thanks. Going up to Bo for the night.**
> **Probably gonna camp out. Good?**

Yep. Just don't drink too much and DO
NOT DRIVE.

> **Got it.**

We stop at the grocery store in town for lunch items: hard rolls, cheese and salami, salt-and-pepper chips. I get a Sprite and Hannah crinkles her nose at me, setting her kombucha on the counter.

"Don't do that," I say, reaching out a finger to push on the freckled end of her nose. "Or I'll make you drink it."

She makes a fake choking noise and watches as I take cash out of my wallet and set it down.

"You guys are disgusting," Jake says. He is clutching an armful of Hostess CupCakes against the front of his UC Santa Cruz sweatshirt. Jake is white, with pale, freckled skin and strawberry blond hair.

"Disgustingly great," Hannah says, lacing her fingers up with mine.

We walk down to the end of the road that leads to the beach. I carry Hannah's surfboard and she carries the food. We find a spot and spread out a big red-and-black quilt, our toes digging down into the dark brown sand that's always a little bit wet, even when the sun is out. We put sunscreen on our arms and ears and noses. It's too cool out to have much more skin exposed than that. Hannah and Jake head down to the water and I lie back and try to read a book about Sun Ra and the Arkestra, the sound of the waves and the soft but relentless breeze rushing in my ears.

I can't focus for long because of the fact of this day: the last day of high school.

I'm done.

I have a scholarship to Cal State East Bay, and my first semester starts in less than three months. Everything is starting. Everything is good. The future is waiting in a neatly wrapped and labeled package. But for some reason I can't really feel it. I never can.

I put down my book and watch Hannah and Jake bobbing up and down in the water like seals. Everything is backlit and the top halves of their bodies are two irregular black shapes, in steady motion on the dark sea.

Hannah is going to school in Ohio, and we are deep into negotiations about what that will mean for our relationship. At any given moment either of us can be found on either side of the argument. We're circling around something inevitable, but no one wants to be the first to let go.

The shadows get longer and longer until it's time to get out, get dry, head to Blake's cousin's house. By the time we park the pickup on the dirt road out front, kids from school have already started gathering.

The house is a California-interior-style wet dream, everything wabi sabi, weathered, reclaimed, decks and steps everywhere. Ceramic sculptures. Glass doors. Cool grass in the twilight, fruit trees sagging under the weight of ripening apricots and plums. It's the kind of house Dad builds for people who have a lot more money than we do.

"I'm hungry," Hannah whines from where she sits on a wrap-around bench on the back deck. She's wrapped up in lavender fleece, white leggings, and Uggs, shivering with wet hair.

"I'm pretty sure Connor is bringing pizza," Jake says, adjusting his baseball cap.

"Yup," I say, "and here he is."

"Hey, bro!" Connor calls from across the yard. He ducks under the crooked branch of a live oak tree, balancing the pizza on one hand. There's lots of hugging and backslapping as we all greet each other. Something about it feels disingenuous, every single time.

More and more kids come, and I start to worry that this is more like a party than a hangout, but by that point the beer is surging through my veins and I feel *good*. Light. Free. This is the way I should feel on the last day of school.

Hannah is over talking to a group of her friends. After a day outdoors, she is this shade of golden pink that is completely enticing. I walk up behind her and wrap my arms around her waist, kissing her neck.

"Excuse me, everyone," I say, winking. "I need Hannah for a minute."

I pull her up the stairs into a bedroom that looks like a perfect replica of a fisherman's bunkhouse with old glass floats and porthole windows, and she pushes me down onto the bed and takes off my glasses and we tangle ourselves up in each other until we get right up to the edge of the line that we are both, for some reason, hesitant to cross. For a while, I lose myself until I'm completely gone, in a way that makes every voice, every thought, everything that isn't the soft blur of Hannah, recede.

Afterward, when we are strung out, breathless, lying limp on our backs, Hannah turns her head to me and says, "Today was the last day of high school, ever."

I nod, slow, rubbing a long strand of her silky hair between my fingers. "So weird."

Suddenly, her aquamarine eyes are overflowing with tears. "Everything is going to change, isn't it?"

The past half hour in this tiny room has sobered me up, made me thoughtful, and for a few long minutes her question swirls around my brain.

She leans over and kisses my shoulder.

"I'm really going to miss you."

"Yeah," I say. "I'm really going to miss you too."

But there's something empty about the words because I can't imagine what it would be like, really missing anyone.

Later, we are back downstairs. I'm loose in a good but dangerous way. Like everything might fall apart at any moment and I might not mind.

I'm sitting on a camping chair next to the fire when I see Sydney Greenfield drifting across the firelit lawn like a fairy. Her black hair is braided into a crown on the top of her head and she's wearing an old black T-shirt that's full of holes and a giant black old-man's cardigan sweater. She's holding hands with a guy I've never seen before. He's white, skinny, and scruffy, and looks like he doesn't belong at a high school party. He tugs her along, both of them looking cool and disinterested. A cigarette dangles between her fingers.

I first met Sydney when we were eight years old, after Dad and I moved from Oakland into the house next door to hers at the end of a dusty cul-de-sac. For years, I followed her everywhere. She introduced me to music and made me dye my hair black and dared me to do a hundred stupid and dangerous things.

But at some point Syd and I drifted apart. Sometimes it felt like she was still and I was moving, and sometimes it felt like I was still and she was moving. Now here we are, on opposite sides of a gigantic ocean. It's weird because for so long she was my twin, the other half of my brain. Sometimes I still wake up at night and expect to find the lump of warmth that is her body in my bed.

The older guy stops for a second to talk to a friend, and Syd stops too, turns her head, looks at me, stares. Her eyes are like exploding stars, the way they suck everything inward. For a second I feel this great missing, this frustrated longing. They pull me in, her eyes, like a swamp.

And then she looks away, turns back to the guy, moves along like a fish in a stream until she's out of sight.

2
Sydney

THIS PARTY IS STUPID. IT'S FULL of the worst kind of normal kids reminiscing about high school. Everyone is singing along to bad music and hugging each other, and all night Robbie's been looking at me in this way where he's trying to tell me that he wants to have sex.

And me? I feel like I'm a human paper cut. There's a sting under my skin that I can't get rid of today.

I look sideways at Robbie, his round blue eyes half hidden under dark, shaggy hair. He's been drinking and smoking pot all afternoon and he smells sad. He's talking to Rich about music in this way he has, basically saying that anything he doesn't approve of is utter trash, and I know he's just moments away from diverting off into a long diatribe about Pantera.

"I'll be right back," I say, dropping his dead-fish hand.

"'K, babe," he says, kissing me on the forehead.

Suddenly, the earth tilts, just a little. That's how I know it's coming. I turn away fast, making my way through the shadowy trees to the back gate, wiping the sweat that's already beading along my upper lip. When I'm out of the yard, in the utter, inky darkness of the street, I sink down to the edge where the curb would be if there were curbs here and let my head fall down between my knees.

My lungs begin to feel like they are full of water, so I concentrate on the feeling of the hard gravel on the backs of my thighs. Three in, six out. Four in, eight out. Six in, twelve out. I do the breathing exercises my therapist showed me in her moldy office. I take two puffs of my inhaler and try to tug the helium balloon of my brain back down to earth.

Then an idle part of me wonders if this isn't really a panic attack at all, if the tightness in my chest is actually killing me. Young people can have heart attacks, right? Every once in a while, it happens. I could die tonight, at this stupid party, on the side of the road in front of some rich hippie's house.

Once, when I was lucky-number-seven years old, I did almost die. At the beach, sucked out too far, my struggle for forward motion turned to a defeated up-and-down bobbing of my body in the ocean, and the waves washed mouthful after mouthful of salt water down my throat. I felt real terror and then an alluring calm right behind it. I knew that it would feel good to surrender. But then my dad yanked me out by the back of my bathing suit and I threw up all over the sand.

I wait for that calm feeling of near death now, but it doesn't come. I can't die tonight. I have to work at Amoeba tomorrow. I have a sound internship at the Fox that starts July 15th. I have a plan. So I draw circles in the dirt with a long stick until the blotches on the backs of my eyelids start to fade. I count and breathe, in and out, again and again.

When I can hear the night birds over the hum of the party, I know I'm going to be all right. I stand up on wobbly legs and start walking.

It's three long, dark blocks to the edge of the mesa, and I pass the time by humming the Roches and rhythmically crunching my feet in the gravel. I light a cigarette and inhale deeply. Something about smoking makes my aloneness feel somehow more alone. Better. Even though the first drag always makes me cough and wheeze.

I crush out the cigarette halfway through and slip the butt into my back pocket. I never, ever litter. Then I walk right up to the edge of the mesa, the edge of the earth, and look down at the calm, moonlit sea, far below in the bay. And I wonder how this perfect calm can be a part of something so turbulent as the ocean.

3
Sydney

WHEN WE WERE KIDS, CASS AND I used to take epic bike rides on the first day of summer. We would ride along the Richmond Bay Trail, chasing birds until our shoulders were burned to a crisp, or head out over rolling farmland to the orchard where we would ditch our bikes in the trees and sneak around the gate, filling up our backpacks with cherries. Once we took BART into the city and rode all the way out to Ocean Beach. I made us go swimming, even though it was cloudy and only sixty degrees outside. Cass insisted on keeping his wet under-wear on when we got out, and his lips were blue the whole ride home. I remember feeling worried about him in this way that I was often worried about him, like I wanted to wrap him up in wool blankets but also yell at him for being such a scaredy-cat.

Today, on the first day of summer, I wake up at noon. I make myself a vegan scramble sandwich and eat it in the kitchen, waiting for my mom to come home from an overnight shift at the hospital. She left me a note that says, *We need to talk,* but I don't feel like talking today.

I sweep the kitchen, listening to a podcast about global atmospheric change and animal populations. The content is pretty much what you'd expect: a thousand elaborate explanations of the myriad of ways in which we are fucking everything up. Carbon dioxide, methane, ozone, chlorofluorocarbons, nitrous oxide. It's like a tragic Greek poem in which everyone is recklessly engineering a slow descent into their own death.

Twenty minutes pass. I wash my dishes and plunge deeper into the dark hole of global doom to distract myself from my own impending implosion. Two marine biologists are talking about dead zones in the ocean caused by changing respiration patterns and a lack of oxygen when I finally hear Mom's car in the driveway. I'm in such a panicked and hopeless mood that I slip out the sliding glass door and hide behind the house.

I stand there for a few minutes, plastered against the back wall, listening to my mother calling for me up the stairs. And then, for some reason, I find myself in the garage, quietly digging my rusty old bike out from a pile of discarded outdoor stuff. The tires are flat, but I figure out how to pump them up and then wipe off the ten million cobwebs clinging to the metal, whispering an apology to the spiders whose homes I've destroyed. My hand-me-down helmet is a revolting, sparkly teal color, but I dust that off too and buckle it under my chin. And then I wheel myself out onto the street, squinting at the rare June sunshine.

By the time I make it to the top of our hill, I'm panting and sweating like a middle-aged man, but then my legs remember the way and I cruise with no hands, all the way down to San Pablo Dam Road. It's the weirdest kind of beautiful here, all rust and garbage and overgrowth. Painted wooden signs, old cars, crumbling churches.

I don't know where I'm heading at first, just following an ancient feeling. I turn onto a side road and after a while the beauty becomes less complicated, more overt. The grass is drying out, so the rolling hills are golden against a deep blue sky. I can hear daytime crickets in the sound of the wind filtering past my ears and all kinds of birds chattering at one another. In the early spring these hills are covered with flowers, but they're mostly dead now.

When I've gone as far as I can pedal, I ditch my bike behind a knobby oak tree, walk halfway up a slope of grass, and flop onto my back in the sunshine. I've forgotten my sunscreen but I don't even care. I need the sun to bring me back to life. I'm a dead wildflower longing for a glass of water, and water is the light. I let it sink into all the tiny little holes in my skin, I let it burn my nose, I let it pull the sweat to the surface.

It's actually working, but then I imagine myself talking to my mother, listening to whatever it is I've done wrong this time. And the dead-zone feeling hits me again. Even out here in this field that is full of oxygen. Then, for some reason, I imagine Cass last night, looking right into my eyes.

For a second, just a second, I let myself miss him. I let myself miss his grass stains and the gap between his teeth, his quiet thoughtfulness and careful observation. No matter how much I hate him, today, in the presence of so much wildness, it feels like he should be here.

Do you feel it? he would say.

I feel it: the heaving of my lungs, the heat of my skin, the scratch of the grass, the thrum of the bugs around me. The vastness of the sky, the dryness of the dirt, the gentle undulation of the hills. I let my awareness stretch outward into the earth, over the dirt and plants and insects, into the sky, into the first day of summer.

4
Caspian

ONCE I'VE SLEPT OFF MY HANGOVER, I meet Hannah at El Trompudo for tacos. It's the spot we go to when we need to talk, and after last night, it feels like we need to.

Across the table from me, Hannah is put together like always, silver necklace hanging gracefully over the neck of the cornflower-blue chunky cotton pullover she hauls around for air-conditioned spots like this. Her eyes are the same color as the sweater.

She unfolds the paper napkin on her tray as if to put it on her lap, then seems to change her mind, refolding it and setting it down next to her plate. She doesn't look at me.

"Are you okay?" I ask, taking her hand across the table. Her fingers are long and delicate, warm to the touch.

She nods decisively and says, "Yes."

I narrow my eyes, studying her face. "Really?"

She sighs, pulling back to her side of the table. "I don't know."

She spears a tiny piece of chicken from her taco with a plastic fork, bringing it to her mouth, where it hovers just out of reach for a while before she sets the fork back on her tray. The four-o'clock sun is slanting in the window, making a long line of light across the table.

"Cass, I'm leaving in four weeks," she says, her face deflating and her eyes filming over with tears.

"I know," I say.

"I couldn't stop crying today," she says. As if to illustrate her point, a delicate tear pushes its way to the edge of her eye, sliding down the curve of her cheekbone. She swipes at it with the back of her hand.

"I can't stop thinking about it either," I say, even though it isn't really true. Lately there's been this emptiness in my head that doesn't really feel like anything at all. It's full of stale, still air and YouTube performances of Bob Weir guitar solos. I look down at the carnitas taco cooling in its handmade tortilla on my tray, wondering at what point in this conversation I'll be able to take a bite. And then I think, *Since when am I such an asshole?*

"I don't think we can stay together," Hannah says. She's finally looking at me, and something about the calm certainty I see in her eyes makes it feel final this time.

I've been anticipating this moment for weeks, imagining what it would feel like when we finally ended things. And now here we are, in our favorite booth, Hannah angelic in the afternoon light. I wait for the wave of emotion to hit.

"Are you sure?" I ask.

She nods, ripping off a small piece of tortilla with her fingers. I wait, but the sadness doesn't come.

"I don't want to be glued to my phone for my entire freshman year," she says, "wondering what you're doing and when I'll get to see you again. I don't think it's healthy."

She stops then, like she's waiting for a response. I lean back and fold my arms across my chest, shaking my head from side to side, willing myself to feel something. I look down at my Styrofoam plate, where a pool of grease is soaking into the tortilla and starting to congeal at the edges.

"Okay," I say, feeling a low level of panic begin to buzz at the edge of my field of vision.

"Okay?" she says.

"Yeah." I tap my fingers on the table. "What else is there to say?"

She nods resolutely, but I can see a tiny wince at the perfectly flat tone in my voice. She reaches for my hand again.

"What do you want to do about Yosemite?"

Fuck. I've been planning this backpacking trip with Jake and Kevin and Hannah for the past six months. We woke up at 5:30 in the morning in the middle of winter just to book reservations on the parks department website. For months, I'd fantasized about seeing the sun rise over Half Dome with my arm slung across Hannah's shoulders. Now it feels like I am seeing that moment for the Instagram selfie it really was.

"It's not a big deal," I say. "You should still come, of course."

"Okay," she says, looking perplexingly hopeful. "I will."

It's a good twenty seconds before I realize that she's still holding my hand and I'm not sure how to get it back.

"Do you want to come over?" she asks.

I think about how easy it would be to throw my bike in the back of her truck, to ride back to her air-conditioned basement with the plush wraparound couch, watch a movie, smell the coconut smell of her hair, let myself forget.

"I don't think that's a good idea," I say.

She nods, suddenly crying again. "You're probably right."

I stand up from the table. "I'm gonna get a takeout box."

I sleepwalk my way to the counter, and the yellow lights and excessive wall decorations and the obnoxious sunshine streaming in the windows suddenly feel way too bright. I shake my head again as if to shake off the incongruousness of it all. Nothing about this moment fits.

When I walk Hannah out to her car, she turns to me and says, "I'll always love you, Cass."

The sentimentality in her voice makes me cringe, so I just nod and close her car door and then watch like a jerk as she drives away.

When I get home my dad is there, reading a book on the couch, drinking the one Lagunitas beer he allows himself every day after dinner.

"How'd it go?" he asks.

I sit on the couch next to him, lacing my hands behind my head. "She broke up with me."

He frowns, the sun lines on the side of his eyes deepening. Dad is tall and thin, with a serious face and dark brown hair that is always a few weeks overdue for a cut. "Ouch. You okay?"

I do an assessment. There's still a faint buzzing in my ears and a numb feeling in my chest right where my heart is supposed to be.

"I think so?" I say. "I mean, I'm sad, but it seemed inevitable."

He puts his book down on the coffee table, in between two abandoned mugs.

"It's rare for high school relationships to last after graduation."

"I know that," I say. "Maybe that's why I don't feel that bad." I look at my feet on the table, the right shoe perpetually untied. "This has been a long time coming."

Even as I say it, I'm not that sure. Is the circumstance making everything stale or is it just me?

"You know," he says, taking a sip of his beer. "Your mom and I met in high school."

Just like that, all the air is sucked out of the room. It's been four years since Dad has mentioned my mom out loud. I've been counting. The last time it happened, we were at a barbecue in Gram's backyard and she said, "Craig, where did you get that awful shirt?" And he said, "Iris," and then turned and walked back into the house.

I'm very still, like I'm watching a deer in the woods, hoping that if I don't say a word, Dad will say something else. I count to ten in my head, waiting. But he doesn't. So I say, "Yeah?"

He adjusts the brim of his baseball cap and says, "Never mind."

I push myself up off the couch and say, "I'm exhausted."

And he says, "That's what you get when you stay up all night."

And I laugh and walk up the stairs, playing my part in the duet we've been working on for as long as I can remember.

5
Caspian

I WAS TEN YEARS OLD THE first time I tried to listen to Mom's records. It was the longest kind of boring and empty afternoon because Syd was away for the weekend and Dad had been out in the garage for hours, working. I was sitting on the couch watching TV, but I wasn't really watching in that way that I don't really do things sometimes because in my mind I'm somewhere else.

The record shelf next to the TV was glowing in the afternoon light, a chunk of sun illuminating the records in the way I used to imagine God would illuminate good Christian people with his presence— waving his hand over their heads with a stream of golden, shimmering light. That's what I always pictured when they described it at Gram's church, God blessing the people like sunlight on dusty old records.

I could see little particles swirling over the titles, regular dust and sawdust, fine and thick. The dust on our records always made me think about the perfectly clean and cared-for records in Syd's dad's basement study, where Syd would pull albums from their sleeves and place them on the player with a reverence I've only ever seen her give to dead things. When Syd put on music, my whole body would fill up with something wild. Syd would start thrashing around, dancing, and I would start thrashing and dancing too, until I couldn't breathe and I knew for sure that I had never felt that good in my entire life.

Up until that afternoon alone in my living room, I had only ever listened to music with Syd. I wondered if it would feel that good coming from my mom's record player, if I could feel like that without anyone else around. So after a while of not watching TV, I got up and shuffled over to the shelf, stood in the light, traced the spines, read the titles. I studied each one until I came to the Beatles, all white with tiny letters.

I pulled the album off the shelf, releasing more dust, then pulled the vinyl out of its sleeve. I put it on the turntable. I felt a tiny thrill race up my spine. I pressed the switch that said On, and the arm of the record player lifted, swept over gracefully, and dropped down.

The speakers crackled and popped, and then music, rock and roll music, started playing, and the one thrill turned into a million tiny chills all over my skin, just like it did in Syd's basement. The beat worked its way into my body and before I knew it I was dancing and playing air guitar all over the living room. I was standing on the couch; I was leaping over the coffee table. I was lost, in the best way. I was listening to music and I was actually listening to music, because I was there. In my mind I was there.

That's when I heard the back door slam and my dad's usually quiet voice, loud but not exactly angry, straining over the music. "Caspian, what are you doing?"

There was an unknowable quality in his voice. I thought, just for a second, that maybe this record could change him too. That maybe he'd feel the sparks in his heart and we wouldn't have to be like this anymore. But as we stood there looking at each other, music blaring, his eyes grew dark and angry, and shame and embarrassment flooded my chest. I fumbled frantically to turn the switch off.

"Nothing, Dad. I was just . . ."

What was I doing?

My dad swept past me in long strides, then stopped and sighed in front of the record player. He lowered his head into his hands, cradled it. Like he had a headache. Like he was sadder than I could ever understand. Then he lifted the record off the turntable and slid it carefully back into the sleeve.

"Don't touch those," he said.

The sharpness in his voice surprised me. Dad was always calm and steady, and I always tried to be good; he'd never talked to me like that before.

I looked down at my toes in the carpet. I said, "Okay."

I always said okay. I still do. And I almost always mean it. But that day, a little part of me broke off from myself and I knew, I *knew*, that I was going to play that record again.

Up in my room, I lie down on my bed, which hasn't been made in days, and I scroll my way through the internet, trying to melt my brain. My thoughts keep leaping forward into the vast, boring expanse of my future, or snagging on the silver H around Hannah's throat.

The fingers of my left hand move up and down the neck of an imaginary guitar, a replica of the one that's hidden in the back of my car.

Normally, when I'm feeling like this, I slip out the back door and head into the city, to my sacred, secret spot in the 24th Street BART station. I play my guitar until my mind is perfectly blank and calm and lost in the rushing stream of people moving up and down the long escalators. But for some reason I can't today, or maybe I don't want to, so instead I do the other thing I do to scratch the itch.

I google *The Darlas*.

Then *The Darlas music*.

And then *The Darlas music Bay Area 1999*.

All I can ever find is a dusty old Myspace page. In the profile picture, my mom is a white blur rocketing around a dark stage. The genre says FIGURE IT OUT and the bio is empty and the music player is broken, so I can't even hear the songs.

I switch over to Instagram and scroll for a while. Lots and lots of blurry, drunken, firelit pictures from last night. Hannah, with her hair swept back, looking placid as ever; Hannah, a dark blur laughing into my neck. I wonder if she knew then that she was going to dump me in the morning.

I swipe over to the search window and type #TheDarlas. About twenty photographs appear, the same ones that come up every time, most of them of random packs of middle-aged women posing in fancy clothes. But today, right at the top is a post that says:

The Darlas Reunion Tour
June 16th: Sacramento
June 17th: Reno
June 18th: Salt Lake City
June 19th: Moab
June 20th: Santa Fe
June 22nd: Austin

June 23rd: New Orleans

June 25th: Athens

June 27th: Charlotte

June 28th: DC

June 29th: New York City

July 7th: San Francisco

The text is written over a black-and-white picture of the band, my mom off to the side, looking out of the frame. My heart lurches. I swipe my fingers over the screen a few times, right at the circle that is her face.

The caption below says: For our collective 40ish birthdays we are getting this smokeshow together again for one last amble across the States. Do not miss.

I click on the username at the top of the photo and scour the pictures for anything band related. Instead, I see beaches, paintings, beautiful blurs that look like two black-haired kids. Then I click back over to the announcement and open the profiles of all the tagged members. Two of them appear to live in Northern California, one in Los Angeles. There are more kids in their pictures, along with friends, families, landscapes, and food shots, but even after hours of the deadliest form of detailed stalking, I find nothing about my mother. Just that one announcement in each of the profiles. For a tour that starts on Saturday night.

I turn off my phone and shove it into a drawer. I hold my pillow over my face until it gets hard to breathe, trying to scrub the picture out of my mind.

My eyelids feel like concrete, but I can't sleep. Instead I think

about how the very day that the Darlas are getting back together, I will step onto the electronic sidewalk of my life: graduation, a summer of partying and double shifts at Ace Hardware, school in August, engineering degree four years later, steady job, house, marriage, kids. It doesn't feel like my life, but I know it's where I'm heading.

The house feels too empty. Too big and too small at the same time. I grab my pedal board from under my bed and head for the front door, quietly, so I don't wake Dad, who is dozing in the evening light. Shoes, keys, wallet. I drive to the El Cerrito del Norte BART station, drumming my thumbs on the steering wheel to the music that is already starting to form in my head.

When I'm on the train riding into the city, rocking like a ship on the sea, surrounded by strangers, guitar case in my hand, something inside me starts to settle and I don't feel so alone.

6
Sydney

ON MONDAY AFTERNOON, I SIT OUT in the yard with Anna and Grace, my older twin sisters who have just finished their second year at UCLA. We've never hung out much, but I don't really feel like being with Robbie today and I also don't want to be alone. I sit on the ground in the shade of the acacia tree, fixing an old Tascam four-track recorder I found on Craigslist and watching a colony of ants wind their way in and out of their nest by my feet.

Anna and Grace are prostrate on loungers in matching gingham bikinis, slathered with coconut oil, baking in the sun. They have barely moved for the past four hours except to occasionally pick up a cell phone.

"You know," I say, looking for a tiny screw that seems to have fallen into the grass, "lying out all day like that is really asking for skin cancer."

Grace sighs dramatically. "Skin cancer is a myth made up by the sunscreen industry. Everyone knows that. I read online that vitamin D deficiency is the number one rising health threat because people are so terrified of the sun."

Grace is a communications major, and ever since she got an A in Psychology of Consumption, she's been an insufferable know-it-all about the stupidest things. Anna, poli-sci, is not much better.

Anna takes a long drink of her LaCroix. "We can't all pull off the undead look, Syd."

"Ha," I say, getting up and dusting off my shorts.

I am the youngest of five near-perfect children. Isabel, Anna, Grace, and Levi could be in the cast of *The Sound of Music*, my mom's favorite movie. They could wear matching outfits made of curtains and sing upbeat songs and bask in the sunshine on a Swiss hillside and look *right* doing it. I would be off to the side, a lost extra from the set of *Beetlejuice*.

I was born prematurely, at twenty-three weeks and two-point-five pounds, and I lived in a plastic box at the hospital for the first couple months of my life. There are all these pictures of me in there, looking ugly and pathetic and small. I've googled it and the survival rate for preemies born that early is only 50 percent.

Having skimmed the line between life and death, I've often felt a sense of camaraderie with dead and dying things. I used to cut articles from Mom's *Nature Conservancy* magazines about climate change and declining animal populations, stories about whole pods of gray whales mysteriously washing up dead on the beach. I'd sit in my top bunk and tape the articles to the wall, surrounding myself with calamity. Something about it was soothing to me.

As expected, my family was troubled by my morbidity. My mother, who had always babied me to the point of nausea, looked on in horror as I dyed my golden-blond hair black and brought home dead spiders and run-over snakes I'd found in the road. Anna and Grace started calling me Grim Reaper. Levi and Isabel, who were too old to really notice or care, just looked at me, faintly puzzled, as if something were out of place.

One morning, not long after they came up with the nickname, I snuck into Anna and Grace's closet with Mom's best scissors and cut long, gaping slashes into their eighth grade promotion dresses. It felt good, ruining something beautiful and beloved. I felt powerful.

A few weeks after that, I poured out every bottle of Anna's glitter nail polish. Then I drew on the sidewalk with Isabel's brand-new thirty-dollar Benefit lipstick. Once, when Mom was at work, I ripped up eight pairs of pantyhose I found in her closet.

"Syd," she would say. "What am I going to do with you?"

My dad started taking me on long hikes in Wildcat Canyon, trying to tire me out as if I were a golden retriever. He had more patience for me than anyone else did. Even when I markered on his brand-new running sneakers, he just sighed, put me into the car, and drove me to the trailhead off Arlington Boulevard.

Anna's phone makes a little chirping sound, and she looks down to check the message. "Hey, Syd, do you have twenty dollars I can borrow? Bryce and I are gonna go get burritos."

I tilt my head to the side, squinting so the sunlight gleaming off her skin begins to blur. I imagine both of them dying at twenty-seven from melanoma. Together to the very end. Mom, crying silently at O'Reilly's Funeral Home on Frontage Road.

"Sure," I say, reaching into my back pocket and dropping a crumpled twenty into her outstretched hand.

"Thanks," she beams. "Love you!"

"Love you too," I say, but it doesn't seem like either of us really means it.

I've ignored Mom's *We need to talk* for two days, but she finally catches me after her Monday evening yoga class while I'm eating leftover pizza in my closet. When she opens the door to my room, despite my not having answered her many knocks, I know I'm trapped.

"Are you avoiding me?" she says. Her arms are crossed and the line between her brows is deep and tired.

"Yes," I reply, looking right into her eyes. They're a crystalline blue that is nothing like my dark brown.

She sits down in my desk chair, already looking defeated. "Why?"

The room is glowing with the gold of the seven-o'clock summer sun, striped with shadows from the redwood branches outside my window.

I look down at the half-eaten slice on my plate. "I just don't really feel like talking."

This is how we begin most of these talks, the ones where she tells me she is concerned about my future and I tell her to leave me alone. She asks a question, I give an unsatisfactory answer, she frowns and finds a subtle way to let me know how disappointing I am.

"Sydney," she says, persevering despite the tiredness of the routine. "You're eighteen years old and you're about to graduate. I think you're overdue for some adult conversation."

I'm silent, trying out the apparent-death strategy. Like a possum caught in a garbage can, I don't move a muscle. Seconds tick by. I can feel my mom's eyes burning a hole in the side of my face.

"Syd, your dad and I are worried about you. You don't have a plan."

I inwardly roll my eyes at her roping Dad in here. I doubt he even remembers what I look like these days.

"I do have a plan," I say, carefully setting my plate down and brushing a crumb from my jeans. This is the moment where I should explain the internship. If I say *the Fox* like one might say *Wells Fargo*, like I'm taking my first baptismal steps into the well of capitalism and not flinging myself into the treacherous ocean of the music industry, if I explain it carefully, she might understand. *John Legend performs there*, I could say. *You love John Legend.*

I play the scene out in my head: the way she'd sit back in her chair, momentarily stunned. It always takes my mom a few moments to integrate new information. *You're just like me*, she'd say when I struggled to understand my geometry homework. *It just takes us a little bit more time.*

But then her face would fall, twisting into that face she makes when she's trying to understand how I turned out the way I did, like I'm a plastic replica of my siblings that got left out in the sun. Levi, Isabel, Anna, and Grace all got straight A's, awards, scholarships. They all chose reputable colleges, sensible futures, without even having to be asked.

All of this plays out in my mind—the conversation, the reaction, the melting Barbie doll—and Mom is just watching me. Then she gets this calculating look on her face, like she's preparing herself, like she wants something. That's when I start to worry.

"I found you a job," she says, smiling a disingenuous smile.

"You what?"

"At the hospital. It's actually a really great program," she says. "Usually they only take college kids on summer break."

It hangs in the air for a second, that term. *College kids.* I am not a college kid.

"You'll get to work in the lab," she continues. "With a mentor and—"

"No thanks," I say.

Mom frowns. "I'm not done explaining."

I shrug. "I'm good."

What I want to say is *Get out.*

"Seriously?" she says.

She scrubs a hand down her face, exasperated, and I see that the moment for bringing up the internship has come and gone.

"Are you going to work at a record store for the rest of your life?" Mom asks. It all circles back to this, really. My mother will never be able to imagine me having higher aspirations than a forever checkout girl. It reminds me of being very young, of my first-grade teacher telling me that I'm not doing it right when my very best work was on the paper. I hung around the Fox every night for months, pestering my way into this apprenticeship. In the world of Bay Area music, the Fox is legendary.

We sit there for a few seconds, eyes locked, neither of us saying anything. Another battle of wills. I make it a point to never lose; I will sit here for hours if that's what it takes.

But then my mom says, "It's not a choice, Syd. It's happening. If you want to keep living here, you're going to take the job."

She stands up, victorious. My blood boils.

"So that's it," I say. "You don't even care if I have a plan already."

She looks at me and takes a breath that is so, so tired. "Sydney, we both know you don't have a plan."

After she leaves, I sit in the closet for a long time. I lean with my back against one wall and my feet pressed against the other. There are dark spots from years of hiding out, one for each foot. The gold light turns into a purple gloom, which turns into shadowy darkness, but I don't turn on my light.

After a while my phone buzzes with a text. It's from Robbie:

Meet me at the Make Out Room at 10:30.

I leave the plate of hard, half-eaten pizza on my desk, throw on my hoodie, grab my backpack, and yell, "I'm going out," on my way down the stairs.

As the train hurtles me toward the city, I think about my mom. She's always insisting that we're alike, but if it weren't for the dramatic circumstances of my birth, I would swear that someone switched me at the hospital.

It's like she can't actually see me at all. I'm a foreign language, a cashmere sweater that shrunk in the wash, that part at the end of the Sgt. Pepper's album where everyone is playing a slightly different note and everything sounds like it's falling into the wrong key. I think it sounds beautiful and scary and strange, but to her it's just a mistake.

But none of it matters because I have a plan. A good, impressive plan. I try not to think about the ultimatum, about how the hell one goes about finding their own apartment in the most expensive city on Earth while working at a record store and spending twenty-five hours a week at an unpaid internship. I try not to think about how tired it makes me feel, and I haven't even started yet.

I get off at the 24th Street station, feeling a little adrift in the crowd. I can hear the screech of the train as it speeds away, layered over the Velvet Underground in my headphones, mixing together to sound like life. As I make my way up the escalator, I hear other sounds, people, muffled announcements from the perpetually broken loudspeaker, music.

Something about the music makes me take my headphones off, sliding them down around the back of my neck so "Sweet Jane" becomes a tinny, faraway sound. In the station, it's just one electric guitar, looping around everything. A little bit thick and distorted. It makes me dizzy.

In a weird sort of trance, I follow the sound around the corner, to the mouth of the big escalators leading to the street. And there, leaning against the wall with his mother's guitar, looking lost and beautiful as ever, is Caspian Forrester.

For a minute I just stand there, mouth agape, my hands gripping the straps of my backpack as people push past me. I feel like a stone being tumbled in the river, up and over the lip of Niagara Falls.

Then he lifts his head and looks right at me, his eyes big and round through his glasses, under the thick shock of dark hair falling across his face. For an imperceptible half second the music stops. Caspian's mouth opens, then shuts. Then the mistake gets turned under a wave of notes that don't seem like they can stop for long. He looks away, down at the fingers of his left hand, and I move along in the river of people and sound, up the escalator and out onto the sparkling, windy street.

I'm shaken, but I start walking, trying to process what I've just seen. Caspian Forrester. Playing the guitar like Keith Richards in the BART station. What the actual fuck? I feel as though the 23.5-degree tilt of Earth has shifted to 24 degrees. Why isn't that empty beer can flying off the street?

It's two blocks to the Make Out Room and the sidewalk is stuffed with people, even on a Monday night. Packs of tech bros weave obnoxiously in and out of the crowd, practically stepping on people who are unhoused while appearing not to notice their existence. Tech bros are my least favorite invasive species. They are the walking version of manspreading, taking up the entire sidewalk while coating everything in the noise pollution of raucous, oblivious laughter.

Levi, my older brother, is a tech bro. He always kind of has been, but recently he got a job at Google—*Google*, my mom had said, like it was the frigging New York Philharmonic—and has since fully blossomed, leaving his lanyard ID card around his neck even at family dinners. We were never that close because he's so much older than me, but it's kind of unbelievable that we are related.

I give the bros of Mission Street the middle finger as I turn left onto 22nd, still a bit dizzy, a little off-key. The glittering sign of the Make Out Room beckons me, but I'm not ready to go inside yet, so instead I lean against the wall and light a cigarette, wheezing as the first drag enters my lungs.

The story of Cass is one I've told myself a thousand times. Cass is a Normal. Capital N, surf-adjacent, party-going, Birkenstock-wearing, studying-for-the-SATs-with-his-blond-girlfriend Normal. It's the reason he ditched me the summer before eleventh grade, after being my best friend for eight years. It's the reason everything turned out the way it did.

I was okay with it because he was no longer adventure material. A true poser, through and through. The Caspian Forrester I know now is nothing like me. He does not have secrets or problems or strange dreams. And he definitely does not play guitar in the 24th Street BART.

"Hey, Syd." Robbie's raspy voice breaks into my thoughts as his hand snakes around my waist and under my sweatshirt. He smells comforting and familiar and is wearing a soft black T-shirt that shows off the tattoo of Mount Tam that ends just above his elbow. He looks down at me with his big blue eyes and I melt a little, until he says, "Feeling casual tonight?"

I look down at my ripped jeans, ratty black chucks. I forgot to put eyeliner on before I left the house, so I'm missing the thick lines that sweep up at the outer corner to add mystery to my otherwise plain face.

"Fuck off. I got into a fight with my mom."

Robbie steps back and puts his hands up like I'm going to shoot. Mom is his all-time least favorite topic. "Just kidding, babe. You look great. Ready to go in?"

Robbie's cousin Drew works the door at the Make Out Room and he's exactly the kind of guy who would let an eighteen-year-old girl into a bar.

"Hey, Syd," Drew says as he tries to make out the shape of my breasts under my sweatshirt. His eyes move back and forth like he's deciphering a secret code.

"Drew." I glower. "Eyes up here."

"Right," he says, rubbing a hand over the stubble on his jaw. He's handsome in a dirtbag sort of way, but something about him makes my skin crawl.

"Thanks, cuz." Robbie, forever oblivious, grabs my hand and pulls me into the crowded bar. He tugs me through the crush of bodies, into the little alcove between the window and the end of the bar, then presses me back against the wall and kisses me. He tastes like PBR and cigarettes, and his cheek is scratchy against my palm. He jumps when I bite his tongue.

"Ouch, fuck. What was that for?"

I frown. "For letting your cousin ogle my boobs."

He shrugs, his mouth unable to decide if it's angry or amused. "What was I supposed to do?"

I roll my eyes. "Figure it out."

Robbie gives me a sweet peck and presses his forehead against mine.

"Sorry. It will never happen again."

I sigh and the tension of the last two hours starts to seep down into the sticky floor. I reach for Robbie's hand, bring his knuckles to my lips, and bite him again.

"It's fine. Buy me a beer?"

Robbie has a wolfish smile and a sheepish smile, and the one he gives me now is a little bit of both.

"I'm out of cash, but . . ." He pulls a little flask out of the inside pocket of his denim jacket and tucks it into my hand.

I sigh, slipping it under my sweatshirt. "I'll be back."

I met Robbie outside of Amnesia on a rainy Wednesday night in

November. I was there with Stasia, my coworker from the record store, to see an experimental noise band from Seattle. It wasn't really my kind of band—a bunch of dudes with long stringy hair, hunched over keyboards and mixers, acting like what they were doing was somehow revolutionary. Robbie came over to bum a cigarette, made a wry joke, batted his eyelashes, and I guess I thought it was charming. Or maybe I just liked the way he looked at me.

Robbie is from New York and had just started his first year of art school when we met. He seemed very mysterious and cool for a good long while, and for the first few months, I was head over heels.

But sometimes, especially lately, being with Robbie feels a little lonely. He never seems to notice any of the details. Not about me, anyway.

I weave through the crowd and make my way into the bathroom. Of course there's a line. Groups of girls are sort of bunched in the middle, so it's impossible to tell how long it will actually take to get inside a stall. Luckily I don't have that much pride, so I walk right up to the edge of the mirror by the sink, avoiding the sight of my naked eyes, and then tip my head back and let the cheap whisky burn its way down my throat. Something about drinking from a flask smuggled into the bar bathroom makes me feel both pathetic and powerful. Everyone pretends not to look at me, and that's how I like it.

Back at the bar, Robbie throws his heavy arm over my shoulder and starts to give a full bio of the bands that are on the bill, as if I don't already know, wasn't capable of the basic internet search where he got all of his pointless information.

"Aren't you going to ask me about my mother?" I ask. Normally I wouldn't bother, but tonight I'm on a tear.

"Of course," he says, looking admonished. "I just didn't know if you wanted to talk about it."

I slip out from under his arm and hike myself up onto a barstool.

"She gave me an ultimatum."

"No way."

"Yep. I have to take some dumb internship at her hospital or she's kicking me out."

Robbie leans in as a group of people shove up next to us to order drinks. "Do you think she's serious?"

"I don't know. It seems extreme, even for her." I tap my fingers on my chin, remembering the determined look on Mom's face. "But once she says something like that she doesn't usually back down."

"Can you just take it and do the Fox, too?"

I shake my head. "The hours at the Fox are all over the place. It's going to be almost impossible just to keep my job. And the internship is unpaid. I'm screwed."

Drew sidles up to us then and tugs my ponytail, somehow not noticing the seriousness of our conversation.

"Pam's here," he says, referring to his ex-girlfriend—the one he is secretly obsessed with, but pretends to hate. He looks at me, making sure to keep his eyes on my face. Robbie must have talked to him while I was in the bathroom. "You got a cigarette?"

I fish around in my purse.

"Hang in there, man," I say, extending the pack.

"Oh shit," Robbie says when Drew is hulking his way back out of the bar. "I've got it."

"Got what?"

"It's so obvious."

"What's obvious?"

"You can move in with me and Drew! Teddy's out at the end of the month and you and I can share his room. I bet if you do some cooking and cleaning, he won't even charge you much rent."

I swirl this idea around in my mouth for a moment—living with Robbie, living with Drew, cleaning up after two dude-bros who probably piss all over the toilet seat. The taste of it is not good. I frown.

"What?" Robbie says. "It could be romantic. Our first place together."

He leans down and gives me his signature Robbie Sinclair heart eyes, kissing the tip of my nose.

"I'll think about it," I say.

The squawk of feedback and the heavy, wavering sound of the first chord fills the bar, so Robbie takes my small hand in his big one and pulls me through the crowd, all the way to the very front. He tugs me in front of him so that I'm leaning back against his chest, then tucks my hair behind my ear and whispers, "It's all starting, Syd. I can't fucking wait."

7
Caspian

TUESDAY MORNING, MY ALARM WAKES ME up with its tinny arcade music and it's all I can do not to chuck it out the open window. I feel like I didn't sleep at all. Like my dreams had dreams. And all of them were terrifying.

I pull on some cut-off corduroy shorts and a threadbare Keith Haring T-shirt, then throw a thrift-store flannel on top. I scrub my teeth with vengeance. I splash my face with cold water but I still feel troubled and half asleep.

Everything has its place in my life. The unlimited BART pass, the travel amp, the wad of cash I keep hidden in a jumbo box of condoms under my bed. But now Syd knows. She's pinpricked a tiny hole in the wall between worlds and a thread of light is shining through. I'm not sure how to fix it.

I open Instagram again, stare at the picture of the Darlas until I feel almost too pathetic to leave the house. Then I delete the app and shove my phone to the very bottom of my backpack.

My bike ride is extra foggy and I'm half frozen by the time I walk into the hardware store, my glasses fogging as the little bell at the top dings to announce my arrival.

"Morning, Cass," says Josué, my boss, without looking up from his newspaper. He's like Bob the Builder's cantankerous, socialist, queer grandfather—wearing Carhartt overalls every day with a saggy old tool belt. He's Mexican American and he's got shaggy gray stubble on his round face. His voice is booming as he says, "There's a box of gardening gloves in aisle six that needs unloading."

"Got it," I say. I make my way down to the very end of the aisle, discreetly sliding an AirPod into one ear and turning on Metallica, volume all the way up.

There's this powerful, unknowable feeling that's been building in my body ever since Dad mentioned Mom last night. Playing at the BART station only made it worse. This morning it's like a tiger prowling around in my guts.

I was one year and three months old when Mom died, late at night, driving home from a show in Sausalito. She was drunk. Gram told me she went right through the windshield. Death was instantaneous, so I know she wasn't thinking about us or music or anything but *Oh fuck* when it happened. But sometimes I morbidly wonder what she was thinking right before her car crossed into the median.

Dad boxed up every single piece of her and shoved it all into the attic. Except the records. It's like he got exhausted at the very end and gave up. Or maybe he knew he'd never have enough going on in his own life to ever fill those shelves. Maybe he keeps them out just to torture both of us. To remind us of what she did.

The thing is, what happened to my mom isn't death. It's a giant void, a black hole that sucked every part of her inside of it. I don't ever miss her. How can you miss someone you can't remember? But sometimes the void feels like it's going to swallow me up too. Today, I feel like I swallowed it.

The gnashing electric guitars and throbbing bass line settle my stomach and I get to work hanging up the gloves. I sort through the "ladies'" sizes with little purple flowers and the "men's" sizes in striped leather. *What an absurd item to have gendered versions of,* I think. *What a meaningless world this is.*

Sensing my mood, Josué keeps me off the register all morning. I clean out the supply closet, break down boxes in the back parking lot, and organize the long wall of screws, nails, and nuts and bolts. I'm restocking roach traps in the pest aisle when I hear the racket of flip-flops making their way across the linoleum.

"Cass! What's up, stranger?" Jake says. "You're ignoring my texts."

In a world where everything feels like it's falling apart, at least Jake is the same. He's got his favorite MONSTER ENERGY shirt on and looks like he just rolled out of bed, or maybe he's just really stoned.

"Sorry, dude," I say, reaching up to wipe my brow. The fog's burned off and it's hot today; the AC has been broken for about a year and it's sweltering at the back of the store. "Long morning."

"We need to iron out some deets for Yosemite," he says, twirling his car keys around his pointer finger.

"Yeah, sure," I say, not wanting to think about our camping trip right now. "Can't wait."

Jake doesn't react to the obvious note of sarcasm in my voice. "Are you coming to Kaylee's tonight?"

I scratch the back of my neck. "Uh, maybe?"

He turns his baseball cap from forward to backward, trying and failing to smush down his masses of curly hair. "Come on, man," he says. "This is the last summer."

I cross my arms. "Ever? Like Armageddon?"

"Don't be stupid," he says, punching my arm. "I'll pick you up at eight."

I straighten a pile of Catchmasters as I try to make myself want to go. *This is the last summer,* I say to myself. *This is what people do.*

Jake backs down the aisle, pointing at me like he's a football coach and I'm the promising quarterback who just needs a bit of a push. "See you at eight, Forrester."

Jake honks his horn out front at 8:30 and we drive around town for a while in his puke-green Jetta, listening to the radio with the windows down. Then we park up at the top of the road by the Waldorf school and I look at the sky while he smokes a joint.

"I can't believe graduation is Friday," he says.

"Since when did you get so sentimental?"

He laughs. "I know, dude. I can't help it. You and Hannah broke up, we're graduating. It's like the whole world is falling apart."

"I think we'll get through it," I say, but I can't help but feel like he's right, like the ground is crumbling underneath our feet in some kind of slow and deadly earthquake.

He nods. "Let's get to Kaylee's before all the beer is gone."

He opens his car door and stubs out his joint in the dry dirt of the parking lot.

I grab the keys from the ignition and spin them around my fingers. "I'll drive."

The main drag downtown feels extra quiet tonight, like everyone is getting ready for the big day. It's that kind of town, where people can't really focus on more than one thing at once. The Fourth of July is like explosive diarrhea of patriotic colors and fireworks; Christmas is an all-out, red-green-and-Jesus-filled state of emergency.

As we idle at the stoplight in front of Thrift Town, I wonder if I'll ever leave this place. Leave Dad. I couldn't even get up the guts to go away for college. Instead I'll be commuting twenty miles to Hayward.

We pull up in front of Kaylee's house and the party is already raging. Someone is puking in the giant jade plant outside her front door. I drink a beer and then a second, trying to get that glow going like the other night, but I can't shake this feeling that I'm just a ghost, wandering around a life I've never really been a part of.

Around me, everyone seems so light. And loud.

I wander out to the backyard, which feels like it goes on forever, and sink down at the base of a tall oak tree that's outside the reach of the patio lights. My fingers tap a rhythm on the edge of my beer can. I slide my phone out of my pocket.

The Darlas. Sacramento, Saturday, June 15th. 9:00 p.m.

I wonder.

8
Sydney

MY FIRST KISS HAPPENED WHEN I was thirteen years old, on the Fourth of July, at a party at Evelyn Meyer's house. Evelyn was queen of the blond girls, with her beachy waves and lack of acne and uncanny knack for accessorizing any outfit. Cass had dragged me to the party because he had a weird fascination with the normal kids. I'd wanted to go to the fireworks, where we had spent the previous five Fourth of Julys, but we'd had a coin toss and I'd lost. So instead I fumed the whole way to Evelyn's.

"You don't even like America," Cass had said, straightening his glasses. "Or fireworks."

"I like them both better than Evelyn Meyer," I'd replied.

The party was full of Hannahs and Jacksons, beautiful, sharp-edged girls frantically hiding their humanity to impress pimply, indifferent boys with the monstrous proportions of puberty, who popped their collars in this way where I couldn't tell if they were being ironic or not.

We sat for an hour on the sectional in Evelyn's basement, like sardines in a can. We were watching *Wolverine* and trying not to sweat. Cass was squeezed up next to Hannah Westbrook. She kept turning her head to look at him—it made me want to sneak behind the couch with a pair of scissors and cut a chunk out of her thick, straight hair.

The movie ended and Chloe L. said, "Let's play spin the bottle." The idea sent this lightning bolt from my stomach to my neck, even as I was rolling my eyes and pretending it was pathetic. Everyone else made a sort of noncommittal sound, not wanting to admit that they were either very excited or very terrified. That was the way all our worst decisions were made.

Evelyn went first, of course, and the bottle landed on Jackson S., who was the cutest guy there, by the standards of all Basics. His cheeks turned pink, right at the spot where his thick black hair brushed across them. After a moment, he and Evelyn both sort of crawled into the center of the circle and sat up like prairie dogs, hands on their laps. Next to me, Caspian's knee was jumping up and down.

It felt weirdly gross to sit there watching the moment as it happened in slow motion. Evelyn and Jackson leaned in bit by bit until their lips met, and then everyone counted to ten in a weird chant as they just sat there, stuck together, eyes closed, not moving a muscle. I joined in halfway through, unable to help myself. When we finished counting they broke apart. Jackson wiped his hand across his mouth to get the lip gloss off and smiled victoriously.

Hazel was next and she got Paloma, and the two of them kissed in mostly the same way, hands on knees, shaking from the effort of keeping still.

Then it was my turn and I spun the bottle hard and it twirled around and around. It slowed at Cass and for one second I tried to imagine what it would be like to press my lips to his and my whole body got very hot, but the bottle didn't stop until it got to Liam W. He looked me over, suspicious. My hair was still very, very black, just like my ripped-knee jeans and Joy Division T-shirt, and there was a

Sharpie tattoo of a skull on the back of my hand. The sky blue of his button-down shirt was blinding. We both crawled in, eyeing each other like enemies.

Liam swallowed his spit, loud enough for everyone to hear, clearly nervous under the facade of artfully spiked hair and his dad's cologne. I don't know what came over me then, but I found myself reaching out, and I put my hands on either side of his downy cheeks. Maybe because his skin looked really soft or maybe because I could tell how his heart was racing and I wanted to calm him somehow.

Then we were leaning and our lips were touching, soft and dry and warm, and a little voice in my head told me to open my mouth, just a little bit, so our lips could fit together. And then we were kissing for real, our lips were moving, and just before the crowd got to ten, his tongue slid into my mouth and everyone started whooping and then we broke apart, laughing.

My first kiss. It was at once exhilarating and a little uneasy in my stomach.

Then it was Cass's turn and he looked at me and hesitated, hand on the bottle. His color looked off and I could see a little tremor in his thumb. He sat back on his heels and shook his head.

"Nah, I'm good," he said.

I swear I could hear the wind leaving Hannah's sails as he passed the bottle to Layla and scooted out of the circle, heading to the counter to fill up his Sprite.

Later, when we were flying through town on our bikes, the night air cold on our faces, I yelled out a *whoop* over the rush of air. Caspian laughed and shook his head.

We slowed our bikes in front of our houses and stood in the street for a while. I wasn't ready to go inside.

"What happened in there?" I asked.

He looked at the ground. "That game was stupid," he said. The words were layered, words upon words upon words.

"Huh." I grabbed my handlebars and leaned back to look at the night sky, at the tiny, faint stars poking through the layer of smog and light.

He got off his bike and kicked at my front tire. "Something about having your first kiss inside a chanting circle of kids seems grotesque to me."

It felt like an accusation. My whole face flushed with a feeling that was somewhere between indignance and humiliation, and maybe a little bit of pleasure that I had experienced something Cass didn't know about yet. "I think it was kind of awesome," I said.

Cass scowled and I scowled and we stood there for a minute, like the feral cats that roam our neighborhood, wondering if we were actually going to fight over this. And then his face softened and mine softened too. I could never stay mad at Cass back then.

"Hey," he said. "Want to stay over?"

I looked at his forever serious face and then back up at the winking stars one more time. I could still feel the sparkle of that kiss on my lips.

"Nah," I said. "I'm pretty tired tonight. Maybe tomorrow."

Kaylee Henderson's house is beautiful. Or it was beautiful until carloads of teenagers descended on the place like a bunch of land slugs, leaving a slime trail of beer cans and vape cartridges in their wake. Wild roses climb all over the front fence, towering palm trees loom at the edges of the yard, and a winding, seashell path leads to an intricately carved wooden front door with a heavy brass knocker in the shape of a western honeybee.

I stand in front of it, wondering why the hell I'm here.

Why the hell would you want to go there? Robbie had texted me an hour ago.

I'd thought: *So I don't have to spend the night watching you paint clowns in your basement.*

Instead I texted back, **I'm bored.** Because I was bored. Bored to my bones.

But now, as I stand here and try to pluck up the courage to open the front door, I wonder if bored is really what I am.

This morning I got the call from school: I'm going to graduate. I didn't fuck up this one, secretly most precious thing in my life. And even though I might be the only person in the whole world who thinks that scraping into graduation at the very last second by the skin of their teeth is something to celebrate, tonight I feel like celebrating.

I twist the cold brass knob and the door creaks open and I'm hit with a wall of sound. The music is not exactly my taste, but the beat of it thrums back behind my heart. I slip into the house, through the dark foyer and into the living room. I stick to the edges, drifting from corner to corner. Just because I'm here doesn't mean I actually want to talk to anyone.

People flutter around the high-ceilinged room like birds and butterflies, buzzing, dancing, and drinking in colorful, summery, celebratory outfits, and I watch them like an ornithologist, taking data with care, surprised by my own feelings of affectionate interest. I didn't know that Brandyn Lovinger and Isaiah Wilder were hanging out. I never realized the way that Evelyn Meyer watched her little sister's every move. I have avoided these people like poison oak for the past four years of high school, but suddenly I feel a sense of camaraderie, knowing that we've all made it through.

I'm almost at the kitchen when I feel someone tug my arm.

The thick, sweaty fingers belong to Ryan Waters, the goalie of the soccer team.

"Greenfield," he says, because he is physically incapable of calling anyone by their first name.

I step away from him, wiggling my bicep out of his grip, but his eyes don't get the message because they are crawling all over my body like processionary caterpillars.

"You look like a hot vampire," he says, looking at my lips, which are red tonight instead of the usual purple or black I apply depending on how dark my mood is.

Something about his eyes makes the horizon sink at the edge of my vision, but I smile and try to stay steady on my feet.

"I never really noticed how good-looking you are," he says, and I realize how drunk he is, how sloppy. He's white and big, easily over six feet tall. "Because you're such a . . . uh. You know."

Freak is the word he is searching for. Weirdo. Loser.

He studies my face like he is still actually trying to think of the word, like he hasn't insulted me, like he thinks he has a chance. The ground under my shoes starts moving like the ocean.

"Wow. You're a douchebag," I say, and then I turn on my heel and try to walk straight into the kitchen, even though the walls are tilting. I grab a beer from a big, expensive-looking cooler, avoiding eye contact with everyone, no longer interested in any of them. Then I push my way through the pulsing crowd and onto the empty back porch.

Two in, four out. Four in, eight out.

Why did you even come to this party, Syd? Robbie was right.

I light a cigarette, coughing on the exhale.

"You sound like you're dying," a voice says from out in the darkness of a backyard that somehow feels very wild, despite being landscaped within an inch of its life.

"Everyone is dying," I say.

"Also, you're talking to yourself," the voice says.

And then Caspian Forrester emerges from the darkness like an apparition, each part of his body rendered visible by the warm light of the back windows at a slightly different time.

He stands there for a second, right at the edge of the circle of light, blinking at me as though he's bringing me into focus with an invisible camera.

"Hey," I say, forgetting for a moment my oldest grudge, the one that I treasure and wear like a lock of hair in an invisible locket around my neck. "I—"

I saw you at the 24th Street BART is what I'm about to say, but before I can get the words out Cass is gone, leaving the side gate swinging.

"You shouldn't smoke," he yells on his way out to the street. "It's not good for your—"

Heart

Lungs

Teeth

Self-image

Life expectancy

But his voice disintegrates before he can get to the end of the sentence.

The next morning my report card comes in the mail. C- in Spanish, D in American Literature, A- in Environmental Science, D in Consumer Math, B in Music Theory. It's the first A I've ever gotten and even the Ds feel like a win. Because they mean I'm going to graduate.

In a stupid, ridiculous, childish, and impulsive move, I leave the report card out on the table and decide to make breakfast and wait for Mom to get home from work.

She walks in the door at 11:00 a.m., looking exhausted but somehow still sharp in her lilac scrubs and bouncy blond ponytail.

"Oh, wow, that smells good," she says, hanging up her messenger bag by the door. She sits down on a stool at the counter, resting her chin in her hands.

"I made you breakfast," I say.

She takes a deep breath and then sits up suddenly, narrowing her eyes. "Sydney, I meant what I said last night. And Dad agrees. If you want to stay here, you've got to take the internship."

Ouch. I laugh, but it feels forced. "Can we not this morning? I just felt like doing something nice."

I scoop Mom's eggs out of the skillet and tip them gently onto toast. They are perfect, crispy at the edges and soft in the middle, practically floating on top of an even, artfully arranged layer of avocado slices. But when I look over at my mother, something about her face makes me turn around and drop the spatula, accidentally-on-purpose puncturing one of the yolks.

"Oh well," she says when I slide the plate over. "Still looks delicious."

We eat, and Mom tells me about her surgery this morning, and for a while, things feel normal. I love to hear about a rotten carotid artery getting replaced with a thick vein from someone's leg or an entire defective heart getting carefully carved out of someone's chest. Mom finishes her eggs exactly at the part where she left the intern to do the suture, and her eyes start to droop midsentence.

"I'll do the dishes," I say, grabbing her plate. She smiles a rare smile, the one that isn't complicated at all.

"Thanks," she says.

"Hey, Mom, before you go up, I wanted to show you." I gesture over to the table where my report card is laid out like a Christmas ham.

"Oh! Your report card," she says, something tricky diluting her expression. She hops down off her stool and wipes her greasy fingers on a dish towel before picking up the piece of paper.

She looks at it for a while without saying anything, just looking tired. Then she says, "Okay," and sets it back down. "Not too bad." She scrubs both hands down the front of her face. "I'm really tired, Syd. I'm gonna go take a nap."

"Yeah, sure, Mom," I say, turning to the sink and pushing my hands down into the warm soapy water.

9

Caspian

THE NEXT TWO DAYS ARE A blur—downloading Instagram, searching #TheDarlas, deleting Instagram, working at the hardware store, downloading Instagram again, looking at pictures of Hannah smiling with other people, staring at Syd's front porch, deleting Instagram, not packing for a weeklong camping trip, not going to parties, stilted conversations with Dad, riding the train to and from the 24th Street BART.

Graduation inches closer, but for me it feels like life is just dragging on. *Same as it ever was*, say the Talking Heads. Except I'm not some guy in his midforties having a nervous breakdown. I'm an eighteen-year-old kid who is stuck at the starting line. Feet in concrete. Sinking to the bottom of the void.

In the 24th Street BART station, I plug into my amp, anxious for the release of my guitar, wanting to melt the next two hours down into one long fever dream. I listen to the hum of people coming up from the tracks and going down to the tracks, heading into the station and out of the station, all against a backdrop of beeping ticket machines and crackling speakers. This is where I find my first note—out of the noise. And then nothing exists except sound. My sound. One note bleeding into the next, or tripping and falling or sinking and rising, maybe even dying. I don't need to look at the crowd gathering at the bottom of the escalators or the cash piling up in my guitar case to know that this is my best night ever.

I'm sweaty and exhausted as I pack up my stuff with exactly enough time to catch the last BART train back to the East Bay. I'm meticulous about where everything goes: tuner, shoulder strap, picks, ZVEX Fuzz Factory pedal, Loop Station, Memory Man. I transformed Dad's old Makita drill case into a pedal board and all the parts fit inside. The perfect disguise.

I'm about to close my guitar case when a small white rectangle of a business card floats in, Frisbee style.

"Hey," a gravelly voice says. "Wow. That was awesome."

I look up to see a strangely familiar woman in her fifties with snakeskin Beatle boots and vintage Levi's and long, wild, half-black, half-gray hair.

"Thanks," I say, snapping the case locks shut.

"I was supposed to be somewhere an hour ago," she laughs. "But I couldn't tear myself away."

I give her the smile I reserve for strangers, for everyone—the one that leaves a little distance between them and me. I can feel the pull of turnstile but I don't want to be rude. I eye the clock on the wall. Three minutes till the last train.

"I'm really sorry," I say. "But I need to . . ."

"Kit Molina," she says, holding out her hand. "I work out of Soft Landing Studios in Oakland and I have a record label called Mourning Light. I've seen you playing here a few times."

The train screeches into the station. A full two minutes early. I couldn't make it now even if I ran. But the thought of a thirty-dollar

Lyft ride home can't really penetrate the cloud of awe that's settled over my brain. Mourning Light Records. I'm frozen in place, still crouching next to my amp as Kit's hand hangs in the air. I hear the doors of the train open, then close as I struggle to make my arm work. Kit looks toward the ticket machines.

"Shit. Did I just make you miss the last train home?"

"It's all good," I shrug, wanting to say more but struggling to move my heavy tongue around my mouth.

"I can give you a ride if you need it. I don't think I'm going to make this show anyway. My car is parked at Twentieth Street."

Kit starts fumbling around in her purse and at this angle I suddenly recognize her face from an indie-label review I read a few months ago in the (motherfucking) *FADER* magazine. I will myself to say something intelligent.

"You okay?" Kit says.

I shake my head, trying to snap myself out of it. "Yeah, sorry. Just— are you sure? I'm parked in the East Bay, all the way at El Cerrito station."

She just shrugs and motions toward the escalators with her head. "Nice pedal case," she says.

On the way to the car, Kit talks my ear off about this band from Australia she saw last night, about nineties shoegaze, about the difference between deadstock and used vintage delay pedals.

We're halfway over the Bay Bridge before she turns to me and says, "So I think you should come play in the studio. I'd like everyone at the label to hear you."

The statement kicks up a cloud of butterflies in my gut, even as it slithers around my stomach like a snake. Somewhere in the back of my mind, I can feel Syd's pinprick getting bigger, my secret leaking out of the hole and dripping across the floor. I need to get everything back in the box.

"I'm heading out of town this weekend," I say, and instead of sunrise on the face Half Dome, I think of my mother's friends, playing in a bar in Sacramento.

Kit hits the turn signal and switches lanes to pass a chicken truck.

"No worries," she says. "We're starting a big project tomorrow anyway. Come when you get back."

"Hmm," I say, twisting the hem of my shirt between my fingers. I try to push everything back in the box, but *everything* is big.

"Seriously," she says. "I think you should."

"I'll think about it," I say. I know it can't happen, but just for tonight I let myself imagine something different.

When I finally pull up at home, I see Syd smoking on her front porch in the light of the full moon. She watches me with her dark-matter eyes as I climb out, circle around to the back, and cover up my guitar and amp with one of Gram's old quilts. I watch her back. I've seen Syd's face hundreds of thousands of times, have read and reread every one of her million expressions, but for the first time, I find myself thinking, *Sydney Greenfield is pretty.*

"You've gotten bold with those things," I call across the long gravel drive that stretches like a river between our houses.

She shrugs. "My mom's at work and I can hear my dad snoring from here."

I take two steps toward her side of the property line, the rocks crunching under my feet. "Any news about the end of the world?"

"Coming soon," she says. Then she stubs out her cigarette, drops it into the outdoor garbage can next to the garage, and disappears behind the house.

The next morning, I'm standing in a sea of students in blue and white gowns, gendered like garden gloves, waiting for the signal to get in line.

Jake gives my back a hearty slap with his giant, golden-retriever-paw hands.

"We did it, man."

"Hell, yeah!" Connor chimes in.

"Party at Kelso's tonight," someone says.

"I'm going to get so fucking wasted."

All around me everyone seems so buoyant, like colorful helium balloons straining against their strings. Even Dad—dressed in his good shirt, the navy one with white buttons—seemed cheerful this morning at breakfast. But me, I feel neither light nor heavy, just a little tired.

Mr. Landman gives the signal and we all disperse to our spots in line, alphabetical like we rehearsed yesterday afternoon. I look around for Syd, who should be just a few spots behind me, but I don't see her anywhere. Just like her to save it till the last second.

The line starts moving and I can hear the prerecorded graduation march oozing out the side doors, and I can't help but feel like I'm in some kind of funeral procession.

I spot Dad in the audience, Gram sitting beside him, dressed in a hot pink polar fleece. She catches my eye and winks. Gram is pretty much my only living relative, besides Dad. Mom disowned her family when she turned eighteen, never looking back. Sometimes I wonder about them but not enough to actually ask Dad for information.

When my name is called, I trudge up the stairs to the stage, shake the principal's sweaty hand, and take the leather bifold that I know doesn't even hold our real diplomas yet. I'm following the line again, like I'm a cow at an industrial meat processing plant, and I'm almost back to my seat when I hear Mr. Rojas say, "Sydney Greenfield!" and then, "Sydney Greenfield?" and I turn around to see nobody walking across the stage.

10
Sydney

I MEANT TO GO TO GRADUATION. I really did. I put on a dress with fucking flowers on it. I braided my hair. I carried the cheap polyester gown down the front stairs and got into the car with Mom and Dad and Anna and Grace and listened to their endless chatter over the low hum of KQED the whole drive over. And then we got out of the car and walked across the lawn to where the students were starting to gather, and Mom turned to me with this look on her face that was sort of sad and worried, trying to give proper weight to the momentousness of the occasion while still struggling to come to terms with the utter lack of achievement reflected in my graduation—*Accept what is,* her prerecorded meditation is always telling her, *See the beauty of even the hardest moments*—and she grabbed my shoulders and said, "I'm proud of you, Sydney," in this way that tried not to reveal the fact that she's not really proud of me at all, just perplexed, and when my family turned the corner to enter the auditorium, I just stood there looking at the students lined up like a super colony of ants, Jake and Chloe K. and Hannah W., and I tried to imagine myself in that line. I tried. And then I walked away. I left the auditorium and the flock of students in white and navy blue gowns. I crossed the street, walked down one block and then another until I found myself at the hot dog shop on San Pablo Dam Road, the one where Cass and I used to blow our weekly allowance on root beer floats. I ordered one, and the lady behind the counter gave me this look that said, *Really, at 10:00 a.m.?* And I just smiled wide as I felt the invisible corset around my chest loosening, realizing that the whole disaster of high school was suddenly behind me.

Never again will I stare at a test paper and watch the numbers on it swarm around like starlings until the time runs out. Never again will I shove an assignment with a shitty grade down to the bottom of my backpack. Never again will I pretend not to notice the invisible aura that follows me everywhere, the mark of being different, puzzling, weird. The world is mine. And I never have to go back to De Anza High School again.

11
Caspian

AFTER THE CEREMONY, DAD AND I say goodbye to Gram, who has to get back to Martinez for a city council meeting, and then we drive down to Berkeley to eat lunch at Izakaya, the Japanese place where we go for special occasions. Dad did the build-out of this restaurant when I was four or five, and some of my earliest memories are of playing in the giant, half-built booths and driving my race cars over long beams of reclaimed redwood. The restaurant is long finished now, a true thing of beauty, with little wooden alcoves, mud walls, stone floors, and a knobby slab bar at the front. When I'm in this room, I can hear my dad speaking to me in the language of perfect craftsmanship—immaculate physical detail, balance, space, squares of sunlight on the ground—way more than he ever does with words.

Yumi, the owner, is one of Dad's best friends, and when we walk in she is waiting behind the bar of the near-empty restaurant. She has shoulder-length black hair and wears a chic flowy blue linen dress. She claps Dad on the back and gives me a big hug, actually lifting me off of my feet.

"You did it," she grins at me, as though I have done something truly profound, rather than just slinking through the past four years of my life, mindlessly checking off boxes.

"Thanks," I say, shoving my hands in my pockets, feeling exposed but also loved.

"Your mom would be proud," she whispers to me, just as Dad ducks his head inside one of the booths, eyeing the joinery where the beams meet.

She winks and disappears into the back, leaving me alone in the aisle with the awkwardness of her statement. There's no reality I can check it against, no context. A proud mom would require the existence of a mom. Experiences, memories, stories, mementos, inherited genetics or mannerisms. Someone would have to have said to me, *You have your mother's eyes.* Or, *Your mother used to hold the guitar just like that.* Someone would have had to say something.

I slide into the booth across from Dad and pull my phone out of my pocket. Under the table, I download Instagram again.

Yumi comes back, bringing us a little carafe of sparkling water and telling us to order whatever we want. We get several different kinds of small plates, sashimi and dumplings and skewers. I haven't felt real hunger in a while, just a bored, empty-stomached feeling, but Izakaya always has a way of breaking my stubborn streaks.

"You know," Dad says around a mouthful of yellowtail, "I didn't even know what sushi was until I was almost thirty."

"Seriously?"

Dad laughs. "Cass. You've got it so good. I grew up on tuna casserole and landlines."

"Gross," I shudder. "Although sometimes I wouldn't mind not having my phone."

I say it as my fingers caress my mother's picture under the table, so careful not to double tap and accidentally like it.

"Huh," he says. "Guess I'm rubbing off on you."

Dad is the one person I know, Gram included, who doesn't have a smartphone. He wears an ancient Nokia flip phone in a leather holster on his belt. Sometimes he randomly texts in all caps like a meme of a senior citizen.

We eat for a while without talking, which is how we usually do it. A quiet dance of passing plates, refilling water, thinking our own thoughts. Eating in comfortable silence is the soundtrack of our father-son relationship.

"You know," he says after a while, "I'm proud of you."

I try not to cringe. "I know, Dad. Thanks."

He looks thoughtful. And then he tugs at the collar of his shirt and says, "I didn't really have much of a relationship with my dad. He was kind of"—he pauses, setting down his chopsticks—"unreachable."

And then he says, "I just want you to know how much I love you." He says it quickly and then shoves a piece of yakitori into his mouth.

Something about this stirs me up inside.

"Of course, Dad. I know," is what I say. But what I'm thinking is much more muddled than that. *Unreachable*. Most days, Dad is a tiny little piece of space dust orbiting the earth, or maybe fleeing from it on a straight and steady trajectory toward oblivion. Most days, I'm just standing on the ground looking up and wishing I had a telescope.

Rescuing us both from the discomfort of any real, dangerous emotion, Dad says, "You excited for school to start?"

"Yeah," I say, trying to dredge up some enthusiasm. Even with the scholarship and student loans, I know that Dad has sacrificed a lot to get me here.

"You've given some more thought to your class schedule? I know that engineering will take up a lot of your course load, but you should take something fun too."

"Like what?" I ask, mildly surprised. Dad isn't usually a fan of extras.

He smiles, like he's remembering something long forgotten. I remember the little crumpled-up poems Syd and I used to find in the couch cushions and under Dad's bed.

"I don't know. I took a pottery class once that was pretty great."

"I thought you didn't go to college," I say.

"I didn't, but I've dabbled in community college classes a few times." He smiles faintly at the windows behind my head.

"Huh, I didn't picture you as such a Renaissance man."

My dad laughs, a rare belly laugh, and the ringing sound of it makes me feel so momentarily light that words bubble up and I blurt out, "Well, actually, I've been thinking about taking some music classes."

Dad quietly sets down his chopsticks, the laugh swallowed back up into his enigmatic eyes. "What?"

I roll Kit's business card in my pocket, scratch the surface with my nail.

CSEB has an incredible music program, is what I wish I could say.

I think I might be good.

Really, really good.

"Actually," I say, "never mind. Pottery sounds great."

That's the end of our conversation because Yumi comes over and slides into the booth next to me. She immediately begins to regale us with tales of my childhood and of Dad when he was a young builder in the Bay Area. She fills up the silence that stretches between us with more and more words. But even as I try to get lost in the comfort of familiar memories, my heartbeat is still erratic from a near miss with the truth.

On the ride home, my fingers worry the edges of Kit Molina's business card. Bit by bit, the corners bend, unbend, tear apart. By the time we get home, I've torn it to shreds. But it's too late; her number is already in my phone, next to a text that says: Thanks for the ride. And one from Kit that says: Let me know when you're back and we'll set something up.

We pull into the driveway at 4:00. Three hours until we leave for Yosemite. Four hours until the doors open at the very first show of the Darlas reunion tour.

"I've got to go check on a site up in Novato," Dad says. "If I don't see you before you go, have a great time, okay?"

He gives me an awkward pat on the shoulder.

"Be safe," he says, his voice heavy. "Don't forget your headlamp."

I nod. "It's already in the back of the car."

Dad nods goodbye as he heads over to his truck, starting the shuddering engine and backing out of the drive. I sit behind the wheel for a few minutes, unable to drag myself inside.

I should be packing right now. Digging up my Smartwool socks and long underwear. Instead, I restart the engine and start driving. I drive down into town, along the main drag, past De Anza High, Thrift Town, Walgreens, Thai Village. I drive out to Hannah's house and sit in my car at the end of her street like a creep. Then I drive to the reservoir where my dad and I used to take the wooden canoe that he built by hand, and I walk down the trail to the edge of the water. I sit for a while, squinting against the bright sun.

It all just feels kind of surreal. I wish I was having some kind of emotional goodbye, that I was heading off to Juilliard or the University of Chicago or the Royal Academy of Music in London, but instead I'm just stuck here, driving these same roads, going to the same grocery store, living with Dad, spinning my wheels forever.

I skip rocks for a while, watching them slice over the top of the water. Watching them move. My dad can send a rock ten skips out into the reservoir. I remember being a kid, thinking that if I could grow up to be just like him, it would be enough.

As I'm heading back down the hill that leads to our cul-de-sac, I see someone walking down the side of the street, a big white swath of fabric billowing behind them like a cloud. It's Sydney Greenfield, in a dress that's covered in daisies. She's not wearing any shoes and her graduation gown looks like it's about to fly away.

I pull up next to her.

"Need a ride?"

She shakes her head. "I'm almost home."

I study her face, which looks wild and tired at the same time. Her bangs are a sharp black line across her forehead, her eyeliner smudged at the edges of her dark, sleepy eyes. A pair of chunky platform shoes dangles from her fingers.

"Where were you today?" I ask.

She looks away. "Don't worry about it."

I reach across and open the passenger door.

"Come on. Hop in."

She steps back, crosses her arms, kicks at the gravel with a dirty toe. I try not to stare at her legs, which look somehow both soft and angular. Then a sly look blooms across her face. It's familiar in a way that makes my heart twist suddenly inside my chest.

"I'll get in if you tell me about the 24th Street BART," she says.

I balk. "You want something in return? For driving you a quarter mile to your house?"

She nods, flopping her arm over the top of the passenger door.

"Okay, fine," I say.

She grins and gets in, dropping her shoes into the back. "These are awful," she says. Then she leans her head back against the headrest, closing her eyes.

I put the car in gear and swing it back around, away from our neighborhood, away from Syd's house and the unpacked forty-pound frame pack at the back of my closet.

"I'll tell you," I say. "But I don't want go home yet."

12
Sydney

THE LAST DAY OF MY FRIENDSHIP with Caspian started out like this: I woke up in his bed, melted by a hundred sunbeams. I was hopelessly snarled in his gangly limbs, enveloped in the smell of birch-bark soap and sleeping teen boy sweat, and something about the combination was so good that for a moment I thought I could stay like that forever: wrapped up in Cass, huffing him like airplane glue.

The thought was jarring enough to vault me into full wakefulness. "Cass," I hissed. "Get off!"

"Shhhhh," he mumbled, sliding a hand across my mouth. "Sleeping."

I kicked my way out from under his leg, which was hooked across mine like the number four. I was trying to strangle the weird new part of me that wanted to turn my body sideways, to press against Cass from collarbone to knee. I'd woken up in this bed on a thousand other mornings; it had never felt like this.

"I gotta go," I said, trying not to panic. "It's almost seven."

Under Caspian's hot palm it sounded like "Gahagamo. Miahaman."

I stuck my tongue out to lick Cass's hand, my usual trick for this situation, and Cass released me immediately, laughing.

"Shit," he said, rubbing his eyes, oblivious to my lust meltdown and squinting at the grandpa-style wristwatch he always wore, as if he could see the face of it without his glasses or he'd actually understood what I'd said about the time. "You're right."

I sat up, watching him fumble around for his glasses, trying to catch my breath. It felt like slow motion, Cass's shoulder-length hair, dark and thick, falling across his eyes. His chest looked strong and brown from working outside with his dad; I noticed a line of freckles on his left shoulder that looked like Orion's Belt.

Cass's hand stopped and his eyes met mine, sliding down to my chest for a millisecond before flying back up again and sort of looking at the wall, color staining his cheeks. My own face warmed and I felt my mouth fall halfway open.

For a second my heart actually ached.

Oh, shit.

I propelled myself out of bed, pulling on my ratty black hoodie.

"See you out front in twenty?" I mumbled.

He peered at me, head tilted to the side.

"You okay?" he asked.

"Yeah," I said, turning toward the door. "I just don't want to get in trouble."

He laughed, and something about the laugh was so musical and sweet that I accidentally tripped and fell over as I was hopping around, trying to put on my sock. "I don't believe that for a second," he said.

I've got to get out of here. I smoothed down my hair, shoving all the weird feelings down down down. Then I gave Cass my best devil grin and slipped down the stairs, out the back door, and across the backyard like a neighborhood cat.

•••

Now Cass drives us up I-80 and into Pinole, to the trail next to the train tracks and the water treatment plant, the marsh where we used to race our bikes as kids. I climb out of the car and cross the tracks, stepping gingerly in my bare feet to avoid broken glass, walking toward the sand. It's low tide and the air smells like sulphur as we thread the needle between tall reeds and squawking sea birds. I can sense Cass behind me without even turning around, like I used to when we were kids and he'd trail after me everywhere with his shoelaces untied.

There's a lot more garbage out here than there used to be, plastic bags and press-on nails, disintegrating fiberglass chunks of an old boat, an extra-large Jack in the Box drink cup. But it still feels peaceful.

We walk down the beach for a while without really talking and I tightrope my way out over the sticky marsh on a long, weathered piece of driftwood. I'm thinking about all this plastic floating out of the bay, out to sea, out to the Great Pacific Garbage Patch—1.6 million square kilometers of trash-filled ocean—clogging up pelicans and seagulls until their bodies burst. Thinking about plastic always makes me think about death.

Caspian steps out onto the driftwood and the whole thing sinks and rises under his weight.

"Where were you today?" he asks again, and when he looks at me with his serious brown eyes, thoughts of death scatter like dandelion seeds.

"I'm pretty sure it's your turn to share," I say without turning around. I'm still not even sure why I'm here, except for the fact that every step toward my house had felt like an act of infinite divisibility, smaller and smaller by half, slower and slower. Maybe I'd never have made it home, creeping down Loma Vista Road forever, in one long loop of my favorite panic symptom: impending doom.

This morning, before graduation, Mom sat me down, with Dad this time, for another talk just to let me know that they are serious. Dad didn't say a word, dressed in his button-down and Salesforce fleece, itching as usual to get out the door, but I could tell she'd won him over; it's internship or bust.

"You first," Caspian says, ever the enigma.

I turn around to face him and we're standing on the log like Baby and Johnny in *Dirty Dancing*—Mom's second favorite movie—except the tension between us isn't sexual. It's two years of neglect, a yawning canyon of disuse and distance and growing apart.

"You promised you'd tell me if I came with you," I say, crossing my arms.

He shrugs. "I changed my mind. But it's okay, we don't have to talk."

He stares at me and I stare at him and all that space between us seems to creak and groan like the driftwood. Then he turns around and jumps back onto the beach.

"Caspian Forrester, you've changed," I say.

He laughs, and it sounds dry and hollow and lost.

When my feet hit the damp, muddy sand, I say, "I don't know why I didn't go. It just sort of happened."

"It just sort of happened that you missed your high school graduation?"

I shrug, picking up a flat rock and pressing the corners into my fingers.

"I hated that place anyway."

Mountainous hills and hilly mountains ring the bay, softly jagged, green on gray on blue on blue, water, clouds, hills, sky. I remember my dad naming them for me as a child, Mount Tamalpais, Mount Diablo, other mountains I can't quite remember.

"So that's it?" Caspian says.

"That's it," I say.

"Huh."

He pushes his hair out of his face, then turns and starts walking back down the beach.

I call after him, "Your turn!" and it sounds weirdly shrill and I'm feeling childish now that I'm the one trailing behind, owed. I promised myself to never want anything from Cass ever again.

I have to walk fast to keep up with him, and the tiny shells in the sand poke the soles of my feet. I look down, falling into the muscle memory of searching for treasure on the beach: bones, sea glass, clams, nautiluses. The nautilus was always Cass's favorite. I'd find one and press it into the squishy palm of his hand and he would smile at me, revealing the gap between his teeth that I almost never saw.

After a few minutes, I start to fall behind, back into the feeling of not caring. I start to remember why I stay away. A mourning dove calls out long and low through the thick air, singing about death, and right in the middle of the sound Caspian stops, turns around, speaks.

"The Darlas are getting back together," he says.

I stop walking.

He looks out onto the mud flat, which seems to stretch endlessly out into the bay. In a few hours, this place will be covered with gently lapping water, but for now it's just sucking mud for what seems like miles.

"They're having a reunion tour." He pulls his phone out of his pocket, looks at the time. "It starts in two and a half hours."

"The Darlas," I whisper to myself, and a rush of remembered imaginings rises like colored smoke. Ever since Cass led me up to his attic and showed me the old photographs and photocopied show posters of the rough-looking group of girls holding guitars and making rude gestures and tough faces, the Darlas have lived in a cherished corner of my heart. The Darlas: a secret seed that germinated, rooted, and bloomed into a possibility I had never even thought of.

For a while, Cass and I tried to find them. We both pretended that it was just a fun detective game. But I saw the tension in Caspian's shoulders as he hunched over the keyboard of his dad's desktop, googling phrases again and again. Back in my room, I'd pretend for hours to be one of them, playing air guitar and drums to the wildest music I could find.

Caspian looks back toward the parking lot, sighs in this way he does when he's deciding whether or not to give up on something.

"We should go," I say. "You've wanted to see them your entire life."

"Can't," he says. He shoves his hands deep down into his pockets.

"Where is it?" I say.

"Sacramento."

"Then let's go to Sacramento."

"I—"

He looks utterly lost. Bewildered. Like his life is passing in front of his eyes and he can't move his fingers to grab it.

"Do you have anywhere better to be?" I ask.

He opens and closes his mouth.

"Big plans to get wasted at Kelso's house?" I say, twisting the screws, hitting all the soft spots I catalogued when we were kids. "Maybe trying to rekindle with your perfect girlfriend?"

"Fuck you, Syd," Cass says, his face hard in a way I don't remember.

He turns around, and we walk all the way back to the car without saying a word. But when we get to the freeway, he takes the ramp for I-80 east, toward Sacramento.

13

Caspian

I MET SYD THE SUMMER AFTER second grade. Dad and I had just moved from our tiny apartment in Oakland to a tiny house in El Sobrante, where I didn't know a soul. I'd spent the afternoon watching Dad and his friend Chip haul boxes into our bungalow, until I noticed that a girl was staring at me from the porch next door, her eyes narrowed, hair in two long braids that fell over her shoulders.

On that first day, I crossed the driveway between our houses wearing a T-shirt covered in mustard stains, and when I did some stupid trick I'd thought up to impress her, she'd said, "Okay. We can be friends."

Then she'd dared herself to cross the street with her eyes closed. "Hearing is the most powerful sense," she'd said. "Totally overlooked by modern science." Syd was always saying things like that, ridiculous things, with this authority that sounded so certain that I believed her against my better judgment.

When she stepped off the curb and into the street I tried not to think of my mother, of her crumpled car on the side of the highway and her body somewhere in the middle of the lane.

"It's not the same," I'd whispered to myself, twisting the bottom edge of my T-shirt between my fingers.

Syd had made it about halfway across when I heard the distant humming of a car turning onto our street, going fast.

"Hey," I yelled. "Car! Stop! I mean, go! I mean, open your eyes."

Syd didn't open her eyes.

She kept walking, slow and steady, as the top of the car emerged over the rise.

I ran toward her and pushed her out of the street, tackling her to the ground as the car whizzed by, blaring its horn.

For a moment, we were a tangle on the grass, Syd underneath me, breathing hard, looking like she was about to punch me in the face.

"Jesus. What the fucking hell?"

Even though I was shaking with rage and fear, the words *fucking hell* echoed through my mind, exciting and forbidden. But then I looked down at her small freckled face and thought of my mother, covered in blood.

"What is wrong with you?" I asked as I pulled myself up off her, pretending to inspect a grass-stained knee so she wouldn't see the tears prickling in my eyes. "Do you have a death wish?"

"Maybe," she wheezed, trying to catch her breath.

"You're an idiot," I said.

She just rolled her eyes, smoothed the grassy tangle of her hair, and walked back across the street. She didn't look back at me, still sitting in the grass, trying not to cry.

In normal traffic, Sacramento is a little over an hour from El Sobrante, which is lodged halfway between the capital and San Francisco, caught in a tug-of-war between the land and the sea. We drive down the highway, windows down, wind in our hair, Mammatus blasting space rock on the stereo. We float east, like grass seeds in the wind.

I watch Syd in the seat next to me. It's strange having her close like this, captive. I've only seen her from afar the past few years. I'd almost forgotten about the chicken pox scar on her left cheek, or the way she grinds her teeth when she's thinking. There's a whole world of Syd that I don't really remember, that I'd forgotten how much I missed.

And then, twenty minutes in, we hit a wall of Armageddon-style traffic. And we begin to crawl.

"Shit," I say. "I hope we make it."

Syd leans her head back against the seat. "Don't worry. Shows always start way later than advertised."

It's hot in the Jeep and I can feel sweat trickling down the back of my neck, into the collar of my best shirt. Syd blows her wilted hair out of her eyes, cheeks now red in the heat that is coming off the pavement in waves.

We should roll up the windows and turn on the AC, but neither one of us does. Even though we haven't really spoken in forever, Syd and I are accomplices now. We are in adventure mode. That means windows down.

We inch along the highway as the sun sets fire to the horizon, the sky an outrageous neon orange-pink. Syd's normally pale skin glows iridescent, shifting between the colors of the sunset. She's quiet next to me. Even though all the other details are fuzzy, I know for sure that quiet is not how I remember her.

The Syd of my childhood was wild and untethered, slam dancing to music videos in her parents' basement and saying, Louder, Cass, louder, gesturing to my imaginary drums with the top of her air guitar. This Syd is completely contained, barely a sign of life beyond the slow blinking of her long, inky eyelashes as she stares out the front windshield, into the middle distance.

"What are you thinking about?" I say.

She rubs her cheek with the back of her hand.

"Nothing."

We drive through In-N-Out when we're halfway there. An hour and a half till show time. I text Jake: **I'm not coming. Don't tell my dad.** And he says, **Are you kidding?** And I say, **No.** And then he sends me about thirty more texts that I don't have the energy to read. Dad texts: **Have fun. Don't drink and drive.** And I write: **I won't. I promise.** And despite the anxious thought looping through my mind, *We're going to miss the show,* by the time we are back on the highway, the sun only a suggestion, a smudge of purple at the edge of the sky, traffic starts moving again. We arrive at the bar a half hour early.

"Take off your shirt," Syd says, when we are safely parallel parked along a narrow side street.

My mouth drops open but no words come out.

She rolls her eyes, tugging at the button-down that I've been wearing since the ceremony this morning. "I've never been there but I'm pretty sure the Watering Hole is a bar," she says. "As it stands, there is a very slim possibility of you getting through the door. That shirt is going to take your chances down at least twenty-five percent."

It dawns on me that in all my weeks of obsessing, I never really gave much thought to how I'd get myself inside any of these shows. I suddenly feel like such an idiot. Like I'm thirteen years old again, having forgotten a lighter to light the clove cigarettes Syd procured from her cousin Danny.

My undershirt is sweaty and gross, but it's cooler now, so I unbutton my dress shirt, shrug it off, and grab a hoodie from the back seat. Syd looks out the window, tapping on the glass with a chipped black fingernail.

"Don't worry," she says. "I have a fake ID and we'll figure out a way to get you in."

"You have a fake ID?"

She shrugs. "I stole it from Isabel."

I look at the side of Syd's impenetrable face. "Do you use it?"

"Yeah." She looks at me like I'm a child. "For shows."

I think about her in some dark bar in Oakland, lost in the music, leaning her head back and closing her eyes like she used to when we were kids. A lens in my brain that's been trained on the past zooms in, changes focus. I've been drinking warm beer and making out in people's basements for the past two years and she's been off doing something so much cooler, something I'll probably never understand.

I take my keys out of the ignition and start to open the door.

"Leave your wallet in the glove box," Syd says.

I look at her like, *You've got to be kidding.* But Syd just opens the compartment and looks at me with black eyes.

"You're such a Boy Scout," she says. "Just do it."

I listen, then follow. Follow, follow, follow. That's the way with me and Syd. She's the leader. I'm the wimp.

She leads me down the street, around the corner, up to the bored-looking bouncer who is perched out in front of the club and I try, I really try, to look cool. Even though I feel like I'm hooked up to a lie detector and any moment a giant light-up sign that says UNDERAGE is going to flash on above my head.

"IDs," the bouncer says, barely looking up from the screen of his phone. He's got a tattoo on his forearm that says FUCK IT. A glimmer of hope appears.

Syd digs her ID out of her purse and hands it over. She leans slightly forward, sneaking over the line and into the bouncer's space.

"How's your night going?" she asks as he eyes the 100 percent valid California license in his hands.

The bouncer grumbles, "Fine," then gestures for me to give him mine.

"Someone stole my cousin's wallet yesterday," Syd says, brushing her hair back over her shoulder. "But I can vouch for him."

I shove my hands into my pockets and nod, trying to look down on my luck.

The bouncer peers at me. He's skinny and scruffy, not the kind of guy you'd ever really imagine bouncing anyone.

"Sorry," he says. "I can't let you in without ID." He looks Syd up and down, like he's trying to make sense of the odd combination of messy black hair and fresh black lipstick, floral sundress, and gas station flip-flops we picked up in Vacaville. Then he says to the region of her chest, "You, Wednesday Addams, are good to go."

"I can't go in without my cousin," Syd says, crossing her arms, trying to look nice despite the obvious anger rising up to flush her skin, turning her neck a blotchy pink, just like it always used to when she didn't get her way. "Please."

"Sorry," he says. "Nothing I can do."

Syd grinds her teeth next to me. "Asshole," she says.

He hands back her ID and laughs.

We retreat halfway down the street, my heart sinking like a boot full of concrete. Heat is still radiating off the sidewalk, making the orange streetlight waver.

"Are you okay?" Syd asks. She pulls a cigarette out of her purse and tucks it between her lips, then crosses her arms, making no effort to locate a lighter. Then she puts the cigarette back, digs out her inhaler, and puffs it into her mouth.

"Yeah," I say. "This is my fault." A whole week of stalking and obsessing and secretly considering, and I didn't even think of a decent plan.

Syd looks at me and I see a kind of pity in her night-colored eyes that makes me feel pathetic. I look at the ground, trying to make my face neutral, but I'm still trying to stomach the fact that this isn't happening. I drove all the way to Sacramento with Sydney Greenfield, the Darlas are here, right inside that building, and I'm still not going to get to see them.

I look back at Syd in her wrinkled dress and smudgy eyeliner, and I'm hit by a wave of homesickness that nearly knocks me off my feet. The thought of turning back now, of going back to our separate lives on either side of the driveway, suddenly feels so disappointing that I almost can't stand it. "Do you want to try to catch a movie?" I ask. "I'm sure Sacramento has a—"

"Excuse me," a voice cuts in. I look up to see a very tall white woman with long wavy blond hair and red lipstick, dressed all in black. "Any chance you could help me unload my amp? Just my luck I threw out my shoulder the day before I go on tour. I'm getting fucking old."

I look at her again, under the flickering streetlight, and she looks like she's being illuminated by God or angels or a UFO. There's a halo of holy light in the flyaway hairs around her head. Like she's been sent down to Earth to offer me a chance.

"Yeah," I say, adjusting my glasses. "Of course. Definitely."

"Cool," she says. "My car's just right over here."

We turn to follow her as she strides out to the curb and pops open the trunk of an ancient VW Beetle. "My wife said she'd help me but she's running late tonight, of course. Bedtime was a nightmare."

"Really," I say, trying to suppress my shit-eating grin. "It's no problem."

"Hey," Syd says, giving me a meaningful look. "If you don't need me, I'll just meet you in there." Then she slips off down the street. I watch her for a second before turning back to the car.

The woman smiles. "I'm Julia. You're here for the show?"

"Yeah," I say, hefting the giant amp out of the trunk and swaying a little on my feet.

"Nice," she says. "We need all the fans we can get."

I follow her around to the back entrance, through a narrow hallway and up onto the stage. Through a slit in the curtains, I can see that the room is already packed with people milling around, waiting for the show to start. The crowd is mostly older, people in their thirties with beanies and elaborately patterned button-down shirts. I set down the amp just as I spot Syd, sticking out like a sore thumb, sliding onto a bar stool at the back.

"Looks like I missed sound check," Julia sighs. She turns to me. "Thanks so much for your help."

Julia reaches into her pocket and pulls out a string of carnival tickets. "Here," she says. "Take my drink tickets. I really only drink bubble water these days and there's plenty of that backstage."

"That's okay," I say, thrusting my still-tingling hand into my pocket. "I'm driving."

"Got it," she says. "Well. Enjoy the show."

I make my way off the stage and down another long hallway, past what must be the greenroom, where the door hangs open. I nonchalantly peer in as I stride by, never stopping my forward motion, and the people inside pass like a view from a train. They're sitting on shabby velvet couches. Laughing. The whiteboard posted next to the door says *The Darlas*.

An hour later, Syd and I stand in the darkness, in the lull after the opening act, waiting for the show to begin. I watch her out of the corner of my eye while I pretend to stare at the empty stage. I can't make out much but the shape of her, the slow rise and fall of her shoulders, the wildness of her hair. It feels so surreal, standing in this darkness next to Sydney Greenfield.

The Darlas, all in black, float onto the stage like ghosts. They pick up their instruments, fuss with pedals, and adjust the mics, and something inside me hums with recognition. When the house music fades and the stage lights come up, a fluttering motion catches the corner of my eye: Syd, brushing her long bangs out of her eyes. Her face is open and awed, pale and round like the moon.

Then the first chord rings out loud and thick, washing over everything. Julia stands in front of the microphone at the center of the stage, a blond wood Telecaster slung over her shoulder, waiting as the intro begins. The drums kick in at exactly the moment I knew they would. Even though I've never heard this song. I've never heard the Darlas at all, but somehow the sound feels exactly like I imagined.

On the left side of the stage, a guitarist hunches over their Strat, fingers a blur, notes melting one after the other, running over and under and into one another. I try to picture my mom up there, lurking over at the edge of the stage, fingers working the strings, but the Darlas are all vibrating, pulsing, and alive, and I've only ever seen Mom in photographs, dead, and quiet, and still.

The music is somehow dreamy and driving at the same time. Julia's voice is like warm water and she tips her head back and sings with her eyes all the way closed. Next to me, Syd moves slowly back and forth, her eyes closed too, soaking in music like the sun.

The show passes in a fog of euphoria that's so heavy and deep that I barely remember who I am. "This is our last song of the night," Julia finally says, breaking through the trance of the past hour. "It was written by Iris, who should have been here tonight. It's called 'Caspian.'"

My heart seizes up at the sound of my name. My mother's. I can feel Syd turn to look at me, the back of her hand brushing mine, but I keep staring up at the stage, afraid that if I look back at her she'll see everything. That she'll use it against me somehow.

The drummer counts off and then the band is sliding into the song. Four bars of intro, bright and joyful. Completely unlike the mother I've always imagined, careening into the center of the highway.

When you were born all the trees were in bloom.
Life was humming like a morning in June.

The words drift through the club and I'm glued to the spot,

completely still in the middle of a crowd that is swaying like tall grass.
I can't move my body.

> You dragged me under a great big wave
> Pulled me down into a deep, deep cave
> Looked me in the eye and you saved me.

I feel a weird mixture of empty and dizzy. Julia opens her eyes just
for the briefest half second, and it feels like she's looking right at me.
And then they are closed again and I wonder if I imagined it.

> My youth is now yours
> Fields full of flowers
> Time
> Turn on the music
> Just dance through it

The words repeat again and again, the whole band singing it in a
round until I feel like a human blur just listening. The sound builds
and builds, and then begins to pull back like a wave, bringing the
room slowly back down to earth. When the last chord dissipates,
the room erupts into applause and Julia steps forward to say, "We're
the Darlas. Thank you for coming out." She gives a tiny half smile
and then says, "We're heading to Reno tomorrow, maybe we'll see
you there." And then the band disappears.

Eventually, the lights turn on. The sweaty people around me slowly
trickle out, leaving more and more room until it's just me and Syd in
the middle of the floor.

"Are you okay?" she says. She looks concerned.

I nod, not able to speak or move.

"You sure?"

I shake my head, hard, finally snapping myself out of the daze.

"Yeah," I say. "I think so."

We follow the last of the crowd out of the bar, making our way down the sidewalk in the darkness. When we get to the car, I turn to Syd. Sweat has glued a few strands of hair to her cheeks, and her bangs are pasted to her forehead. Her dark eyes look wild in the moonlight.

For a moment, my body sways toward hers, drawn in like a magnet. She takes a step back, a sharpness in the set of her lips.

Then she looks at me and says, "Reno?"

And I nod, willing to follow this band anywhere.

14
Sydney

IT'S ONE HUNDRED AND THIRTY-FIVE MILES from Sacramento to Reno. Cass and I are both fully caffeinated from drinking soda all night, so we leave right after the show. We drive along the dark, long, lonely stretch of I-80 and I wonder if the Darlas are doing the same thing right now, in a caravan of cars or maybe a van packed full of gear. I wonder what kind of pedals they have, what they've done to their guitars, how everything fits together to make a sound like that.

There's hardly any moon tonight and the highway feels lonely. Cass doesn't look at me but instead keeps his eyes trained to the circles of the world that are illuminated by the front headlights. He's distant as ever. Just like that Simon and Garfunkel song: a rock, an island. The loneliest boy in the world.

He puts on Nick Drake and taps the steering wheel along to the runs of the piano. His fingers are longer than I remember, nails cut into neat rectangles, callouses everywhere from the strings of his guitar.

We don't talk at all. I can't think of a single thing to say. I wonder how that made Cass feel, standing in the middle of a crowded room and listening to a song his mother wrote about him. But I know Cass, and I know he'd never tell me.

Instead, I open my phone, which has thirteen missed calls, from Mom, Dad, and various siblings.

I text my mother: **sleeping at sheila's**

And she writes me back: **where on earth have you been all day?**

I wonder what she would say if she knew that I was about to cross the state line.

My eyes are threatening to close by the time we get to the desolate outskirts of Reno, and the ringing in my ears from the show has finally begun to fade. We drive around the strip and decide on a motel that looks like the right combination of inexpensive and nonhazardous with an expansive parking lot, half empty, half full. Cass parks the Jeep and unearths his amp and guitar from a well-disguised hiding place in the back.

"I'll bring these in just in case," he says. As if I care.

All I have is my favorite purse, a thrifted black leather crossover with long tassels, and those stupid shoes that I would throw into the nearest garbage can if it weren't for landfill overflow. Cass lends me a sweatshirt from the back of the car and we wander inside. I feel sleepy and suddenly very far from home.

We walk into the motel office, which is cramped with a grumpy-looking clerk sitting behind a large plexiglass window and two video slot machines tucked in the corner next to a small vinyl loveseat.

When the clerk asks for a credit card, Cass looks at her with wide, helpless eyes. For a moment he looks like he might cry. And it's just like Cass, isn't it? To have no real plan. No skills for this.

I have a credit card. I applied for it the day after my eighteenth birthday but have never used it for anything because Isabel had credit card trouble her freshman year of college, buying six pairs of shoes on Zappos and then never making a payment. The experience was so humiliating, the cringe so deep, and so many pathetic, mascara-black tears were shed at the thought of being bailed out by our simultaneously disappointed and doting parents, that I swore I'd never use mine.

Since my talk with Mom, I've been contemplating it: how far I could get on an eighteen-hundred-dollar limit. If I could somehow avoid living with Robbie and Drew. If I could float myself until I figured something out. I'd have to be so careful with every dollar. I definitely could not afford a last-minute road trip or a motel room in Reno. Especially when I'm supposed to be at the record store tomorrow afternoon. But here we are. No way to back out now. So I dig around my purse for my wallet, slide my credit card onto the counter.

"Where did you get that?" Caspian says, staring as if I've just unsheathed a light saber.

"I applied for it," I say, shrugging casually, like I'm not watching my future go up in flames.

"I'll pay you back for everything," Cass says, his face guilty and tired.

"Half," I say.

The walk up to the second floor is quiet, except for the metallic thunking of our feet on the concrete and metal steps. Maybe it's hitting both of us at once that we're about to share a room for the first time since that day in the tenth grade, the one when, suddenly, we didn't anymore.

Luckily, there are two beds. The carpet is maroon and gold, the bedspreads and curtains are forest green, and the television looks like it actually works. It's cozy enough, even though everything smells a little bit like poison-strength cleaner.

I carry my purse into the bathroom. I brush my teeth with the spare toothbrush I keep in the side pocket and wash off my eyeliner. I take off my bra under my dress because even though the bathroom door is closed I feel weirdly exposed knowing that Cass is out there with his sad eyes and floppy hair. Then I zip his sweatshirt up again, pull up the hood and breathe deep, just once, smelling Cass's chamomile shampoo.

When I walk out of the bathroom, Cass is asleep on top of the covers of his bed, his body sideways with his feet on the floor, arms stretched out to the sides. His T-shirt has ridden up and half of his stomach is bare.

In another lifetime I would take off his glasses, place them gently on the nightstand, untie his shoes, brush his hair back from his eyes. I might sneak under the covers and curl up next to him. But we are in this lifetime and so I leave him there, turn off the lights, pull my own covers back, stare at the ceiling, and try to figure out why I'm here.

15
Caspian

IN THE MORNING, I WAKE WITH a start. Somehow in the high of last night everything had seemed so simple. Syd and me, rushing head-long into an ill-advised adventure, just like old times. Now my mind is a whirlpool of guilt and anxiety. I've lied to my dad. I've ditched my friends. I'm in Reno, Nevada, with Sydney Greenfield and the Darlas.

Aside from the music and the box of cash under my bed, I try not to lie to Dad. It seems like a stupid line to draw, but still, it means something. I've created a carefully constructed ethical code for myself over time, with a strict set of rules for each piece of my life, everything in its place, none of the parts overlapping. Now it seems like all the lines are blurring—me and Dad, me and music, me and Syd.

"Shhh," she whispers from her bed, voice raspy with sleep. "I can hear you thinking."

I flop over onto my side, put on my glasses, and look at her sleepy, frowning face. I remember the one thousand mornings we've woken up together, Syd hurrying back to her yard before her mom came home from an overnight shift. I try not to notice the pink of her lips or the brown of her eyes or any of the small details that I haven't gotten to see all these years, watching Syd from across the driveway. Instead I ask, "What are you going to tell your mom about this?"

"Hmmm," she says, closing her eyes again. "It depends. What's the plan here?"

"I didn't really make a plan," I say, running a hand over my jaw. "If you can't tell."

"Really?" Syd makes a face of pretend shock and before I can remember that we aren't really friends anymore, I grab a pillow from my bed and launch it at her face.

"Mistake," she says, just before leaping across the three feet between our beds and landing on my back like a spider monkey, sharp fingers tickling my sides. I'm immediately overcome with helpless waves of laughter, sucking down stale motel air and the scent of Syd, thick waves of black hair falling down around my face.

"Okay, okay, I give up!" I gasp, trying to shake her off me before I have to think about how much I like it.

"Say it," she says, half out of breath, hands still poised an inch away from my skin.

I roll my eyes and turn to face her. It's funny how quickly the forgotten line resurfaces in my memory: "Sydney Greenfield is the supreme ruler of all things."

"And . . . " she says, raising her eyebrows.

"And I am but a lowly worm."

"Thank you." She retreats back to her bed and for a few seconds the room is awkwardly quiet as we come back to the reality of present-day Syd and Cass and the strange mess we are in. Suddenly, her face looks a little sad. "We should probably head back after tonight," she says.

"Probably," I agree. Even though I know it's the right thing to do, I feel my buoyant mood begin to deflate.

"Unless . . ." she says, a sly smile sliding onto her lips. It's a transition I've seen a million times, a curtain drawn back from across a window to let in the light.

"Unless what?"

"Cass," Syd says, giving me a meaningful look. The sheet has left an impression on one cheek and her hair is rising in a black cloud behind her. It makes her look of disapproval a little less potent.

"What?" I say, trying to ignore my growling stomach.

She sits up straighter, crosses her arms. "Don't be a chicken."

And here we are, right back to our elaborate game of truth or dare, like it hasn't been two years since someone made the last move.

I feel the back of my head, my own rats-nest hair; my mouth is dry and sour from sleep. I don't have any more clothes. I don't have a toothbrush or socks or a cell phone charger. I don't have the cash I keep under my bed. But I look over at Syd, barefaced and cross-legged on her side of the room, a glint in her geode eyes. A challenge.

"Fine," I say. "Let's keep going."

While we wait for our half-off motel breakfast—bacon and eggs for me, vegan scramble for Syd—she calls the record store where she works and leaves a message explaining that her grandfather has died and she'll need the next week off to fly to Minneapolis for the funeral. Both sets of Syd's grandparents died before she was born, and her entire family is from California. But she is a really good liar and even I feel convinced by her story.

Then we attempt to make a plan. Neither of us has more than the clothes on our backs, plus Syd's credit card with its eighteen-hundred-dollar limit and forty-seven dollars cash in my wallet.

There are eight shows between Reno and New York: Salt Lake City, Moab, Santa Fe, Austin, New Orleans, Athens, Charlotte, and DC. If we budget carefully and turn back after Santa Fe, we'll both make it home in time. My dad will think I've been in Yosemite, Syd's boss will think she's been in Minneapolis, and everything will go back to the way it was.

During our money discussion, Syd's face is tense and she tears her napkin into a little pile of scraps on the table. I don't remember her being this mysterious; usually every thought rides on the surface of her skin, comes tumbling right out of her mouth.

"I can pay you back," I say again, feeling guilty. "For all of it." I think of the nearly four thousand dollars under my bed and kick myself for not bringing any of it with me.

She just shakes her head, frowning. "Don't be stupid," she says.

I flick a tater tot crumb at her, trying to get her to crack a smile. I'm still not sure how to do this, how to be here with Syd, who is so different from who she used to be. She seems not to notice me at all, attention drawn to where her phone vibrates with a notification on the surface of the table.

"We should probably avoid social media while we're out here," I say. "So our parents don't find out."

If Syd is offended, she doesn't show it. She just shrugs. "Social media is capitalistic anathema anyway."

I shovel in a large mouthful of eggs, rolling my eyes. She watches me as I chew, swallow, and wipe my mouth with a napkin. "I've been worried, but there you are. Same old Syd."

She takes a sip of her black coffee and looks out the window, into the parking lot, which is now almost empty. "Hardly," she says, tucking a long black strand behind her ear.

I eye the gluey fake cheese pooling on her plate. "What happened to you? Cheeseburgers used to be your favorite."

She shrugs. "Appropriate anxiety about the end of the world."

"Ah." I clear my throat and set my fork down. I look at Syd's fingers on the table, noticing the chipped polish, the nails bitten down. As a child she was always vacillating between anxiety and hubris. Now, almost two years since the last time we really talked, it's easy to tell which side is winning.

"Did you text your mom back?" I ask, gesturing to where her phone is buzzing again and again next to her plate.

"Nah. I'll give her a little more time to build up steam." She looks down. "That's Robbie."

"How's that going?" I ask, not sure if I even want to know, and then suddenly positive that I don't.

She shrugs, "Fine. For now."

Her face is so expressionless that for a moment I almost feel sorry for Robbie.

"Brutal!" I laugh.

"What?" She's laughing too, almost silently, under half a smile. "We both know it's doomed," she says.

"Yeah, but that's your general outlook on everything, isn't it?" On the table, my own phone starts buzzing with an incoming call: Kit Molina. The bacon in my stomach turns to cement.

Syd looks at me, one eyebrow raised, as I fumble with the phone, trying to silence it. I've been trying to forget about Kit and the record label and all the things that I don't know how to tell myself I can't have. I think about my dad, sitting quietly on the couch, my mom careening across the interstate. Another buzz erupts a moment later: one new voicemail.

Syd watches me like she can see the whole melodrama unfold on my face, but she doesn't say anything. She just finishes her coffee, balls up her napkin, and sets it carefully onto her plate with her silverware. "What do you want to do today?" she asks. "Doors are at eight."

I shrug, swallowing down the last of my panic. "I'm open."

"Well," Syd says, "you need a toothbrush. Let's start there."

We walk the shabby yet glittering strip of downtown and then find a Walgreens, where we get a phone charger, underwear, toothbrushes, and coconut water. Then we hit up a few thrift stores, for which Reno is apparently famous. I buy a couple pairs of shorts and some funny T-shirts so I have something to wear besides my day-old graduation clothes. Syd buys black high-top Converse, a blue faux-fur coat, red cowboy boots, and a short black sequined dress.

"What?" she says, adding a few T-shirts and cutoffs into her cart.

"Nothing." I smile and turn the shopping cart toward the checkout.

We spend the afternoon in the laundromat, watching the clothes spin around and around. We don't really talk. I text Dad: **Doing great.** And he writes back: **Don't forget to take pictures.** I cringe a little at the lie implied in my lack of response.

Syd's phone keeps buzzing but she almost never even looks to see who it is. Instead, she reads a beat-up copy of *Beloved* that she found at the Salvation Army and I follow the outline of the side of her face, trying to figure out what, exactly, is different.

I keep looking at my own phone and the voicemail notification from Kit. When the silence in the laundromat gets to be too heavy and I can no longer pretend I'm not even a little bit curious, I slip out the front door and make myself listen.

It's both underwhelming and somehow completely ensnares my imagination.

"Hi, Cass, it's Kit. Something's come up. Call me when you can."

All the boxes inside me start to rattle, their various inhabitants awakening and demanding to be let loose. I try to tamp them down, but it's no use. It's already begun; I should at least find out what she wants. I press the call back icon.

Kit picks up on the third ring.

"Cass!" She says. "I'm so glad you called."

"Yeah!" I say, which seems like a weird response, but it's the only word that I can seem to get out.

"How's your trip?" she asks.

"It's good," I say, looking back through the window at Syd, slouched over on the bench seat. She twists a strand of hair around one long finger and I'm hit with a sudden pang of affection.

"Awesome," she says. "Look, I'm calling because we have this band—Spectral Mountain—they're sort of psychedelic pop. Have you heard of them?"

There's a beat of stunned silence because, yes, of course I have, but I'm not sure if I'm supposed to say that or not. Kit keeps going.

"Anyway, they're scheduled to go on tour in Europe starting in August, but one of the guitarists just left the band. It's going to fall apart if we can't find someone else, which will be a huge disaster for everyone." Pause. "Normally I'd ask one of the people on our roster, but I just felt like you'd be perfect for this. Any chance you'd be up for filling in?"

More stunned silence. A whole eternity of it. My brain is broken.

"Cass, are you there? I think you might be cutting out."

I clear my throat. "No, yeah, I'm here. I mean that sounds amazing but—"

Cal State, engineering, Dad, life. Fuck.

I lean my head back against the building, looking up at the too-bright afternoon sky.

"You don't have to answer right this second, but maybe you could think about it in the next day or so and give me a call? I'll text you the dates."

I don't really need time to think about it. I know it's impossible. But one of the boxes flies apart and this voice inside of it says, *If you say no, this will be the greatest regret of your life.* And so instead I say, "Okay. I'll let you know as soon as I figure it out."

"Great." She says, like it's already done. I can almost see her smiling on the other side of the line. "Talk to you soon."

And then she's gone. Through the laundromat window, Syd looks up and meets my eyes, like she knows what a colossal mess I'm making.

When we head out for the show, Syd's wearing the sparkly black dress with a T-shirt over it that says FML. Her knees are knobby and scarred. Looking at them, I get a sudden a vision of Syd at ten years old, flying off the seat of her bicycle, and I think *I was there for that.* For a second I have the overpowering urge to kneel down and trace one of the white half-moons with my pointer finger.

Instead I give her an awkward thumbs-up. "I like it."

She looks down. "I figured it's okay because the sequins are black."

"Wouldn't want to spread joy or anything."

Syd gives me the middle finger and turns to look at my clothes. "You look normal."

Normal. A loaded word where Syd is concerned.

"Thanks," I say, pocketing the room key. When we walk toward the stairs, she's just a little bit ahead, like she's trying to leave me behind.

16
Sydney

THE SHOW TONIGHT IS IN A casino lounge—which is eighteen and over—but I use my fake ID so I can buy two-dollar well drinks. I can't tell if I even feel like drinking tonight, but I down one anyway, to muffle the swirl of thoughts that are swarming my mind. I've just taken a week off work that I can't afford. My internship starts in mid-July and I need to find a place to live. Robbie is texting me every five minutes in a nauseating mix of **Where are you babe** and **I talked to Drew and he's down!** I should be home, figuring all of this out. But instead I'm here, egging Cass on like we're still little kids.

I order a second drink and down it fast, letting the edges blur. I pull out my phone and see a text from Mom: **Where are you?** I hover my thumb over the keypad, trying to figure out what to say. I'm so far beyond the point of no return. Might as well really go for it. I write back: **You wanted me to move out. So I did.** Then I turn my phone off and shove it down to the bottom of my purse.

By the time the show starts, I am three drinks in, and Cass is eyeing me warily from his bar stool. I hate when he gets like this, all high and mighty. I think of myself back in the hotel room, standing there while he ogled my legs. I liked it, the way his mouth dropped partially open. But it also makes me want to pour sugar into the gas tank of his stupid car.

I shoot him my best eye daggers, trying not to notice his brown eyes, trying not to imagine grabbing a fistful of his long dark hair. Instead, I let the questions repeat in my mind: Why am I here? Why am I holding Cass's hand again, forcing him to live? I know better than to think that this will turn out well.

But then the Darlas come on, in a hypnotizing blur of sound. The lead singer, who we met last night, has feathery blond hair like Stevie Nicks and a long white dress that swishes around as she moves to the music. There's a new guitarist where Cass's mom would have been, all in black, head bowed. The drummer and bassist move in a mesmerizing, perfectly synchronized rhythm, and I think that you'd be able to know the beat of the song, even if you couldn't hear it, just by watching their bodies. The Darlas play different songs from the last show and then some of the same ones in different ways, and I try to imagine the Iris of Cass's attic up there with them, swaying like poppies in a field and then thrashing around like wildfire.

Oh. I think. This is why I'm here.

The alcohol has weakened my resolve and as the songs go by I find myself drifting to where Cass is perched on his barstool, just as awestruck as me.

"Wow," I whisper into his ear and he swallows and nods, eyes never leaving the stage.

After the show, when the Darlas have transformed back to mortal humans, we head to the back table where Julia and the bass player are selling CDs and T-shirts. Now that the glow of the stage is gone and the house lights are back on, they look almost like a couple of artsy white

Bay Area moms, like maybe once they change their clothes they'll head over to pick up their kids at Berkeley High. I wonder what they look like to Caspian, who is trailing behind me, shoulders slouched, as though he's trying to disappear.

"Nice skirt," Julia says to me as she counts a stack of singles. Then she looks up from the little cash box on the table and smiles. "Hey, it's you two again. Are you following me?"

Cass's face turns bright red.

"Just fucking with you." She laughs, reaching out for a handshake. "I don't think I got your names last night."

I take her hand, trying not to look as starstruck as my eleven-year-old self wants me to be. "It's actually a dress," I say, lifting my shirt a little to show the bodice. "Great show. I'm Sydney and this is—"

"Calvin," Cass says behind me, clearing his throat.

I turn to Cass as if to telepathically communicate, *What the hell?* but he pointedly ignores me, cheeks still flaming red.

"Cool," Julia says, not seeming to notice our silent exchange. "This is Sunny."

"Hey," Sunny says, grinning and spinning a Sharpie on the table-top. She has a messy topknot of mousy brown hair and a black T-shirt, with several gold necklaces layered on top, and a tattoo of California poppies that stretches all the way up her arm. Sunny plays bass and I know way too much about her from the intense amount of Instagram stalking I've done in the past twenty-four hours. For example: she's a home birth midwife, lives in Petaluma, and is a single mother to one tall and bony ten-year-old son.

I clear my throat. "Can we get a CD?"

"Of course," Julia says. "On the house, since you made the trek twice and are officially our favorite fans. It's from the original lineup, recorded in 2004." I watch Cass eye the cover, which has a photo of the Darlas, Iris included, sitting on an orange couch in a messy old apartment.

Sunny slides a CD across the table. Her fingers are covered in chunky rings, with chipped red polish on her short, square nails. "We don't have any vinyl or cassettes like the cool kids. Still slinging CDs like it's the early 2000s."

"Don't worry," Cass laughs. "We are not the cool kids."

"Except that time you sold out in the tenth grade," I retort sarcastically. Cass blanches. I grin and say, "What? I'm just fucking with you, Calvin."

"You wouldn't be heading to Salt Lake tomorrow, would you?" Julia cuts in, stifling a yawn. "Fuck," she says to Sunny, "I am not used to staying up past ten."

I laugh. "We might," I say. Even though Cass and I agreed to keep going, part of me still feels like it's a mistake.

Julia's face lights up. "Any chance you'd be into coming early and helping us unload again? My toddlers have destroyed my back. Tonight was a nightmare."

Cass nods, hands still shoved down deep into his pockets. "Yeah. No problem."

The other two Darlas come up to the table, still sweating from the show.

"This is my wife, Jasmyn," Julia says, motioning to a tall woman with long curly black hair, ancient Doc Martens, and a long flowery dress. She's the lead guitarist. The internet told me that she moved to California from Venezuela when she was twenty-five after falling in love with Julia through a ridiculously romantic letter-writing affair, that she owns a comic store in Oakland, and that she and Julia are the mothers of two perpetually blurred-by-motion children, names unknown. "She's the newest member of the band," Julia says, not knowing of course that I already know this. "And this is Charlie. Charlie, Jasmyn, meet our new roadies."

"Roadies!" says Charlie, the drummer, who is white, small, and wiry, with close-cropped blond hair and vintage Levi's. I know that Charlie is nonbinary, works as a marine biologist studying vulnerable whale populations, is married to a carpenter named Jasper, and has a two-year-old daughter named Valentine. "Yes!" Charlie says. "We've finally made it. After all these years."

Even though I prefer to look mildly scary to new people, I find myself grinning.

"Fifty bucks a show? You can do the merch too," Sunny says.

"You don't need to pay—" Cass starts to say, but I think of my credit card and blurt out, "It's a deal."

Charlie nods. "You're hired."

17
Caspian

WE SPEND THE NEXT TWENTY MINUTES lugging amps and drums out to a big eighteen-passenger van with FLOWERLAND painted on the side. Then we linger in the parking lot with the Darlas as they rehash the show. Syd and I stand on the outer edge of the circle, right on the line between streetlight and darkness. She's close to me, close enough to smell her familiar, unfamiliar smell: honeysuckle, Froot Loops, three vodka sodas.

I study the faces of the Darlas, the beads of sweat, the laugh lines. I try again to picture my mom here, with all the subtle wrinkles that never got a chance to settle into her skin, all the softness that never got a chance to round out the sharp edges of her limbs. Would she still be off to the side in every picture? Would she be as mysterious as she seems?

The Darlas head to their hotel and Syd and I walk for a while along the strip. We walk under a giant archway of lights that says *Reno: The biggest little city in the world*, Syd's face glowing with blue light. We pass casinos, pawn shops, and all-night diners. Syd stops in front of a sign for a casino called the Mother Lode. She looks at me with mischief in her eyes and says, "Have you ever gambled?"

I shake my head.

"Me either," she says. She holds up the rolled-up cash from our first night as roadies and waggles her eyebrows. "Should we give it a try?"

It's almost midnight but I feel wired. Plus, drinking has loosened Syd up and I don't want to waste this rare good mood.

I glance toward the doorway, which is surrounded by flashing gold and green light bulbs. "You only live once," I say.

We follow chintzy clinking sounds into the casino, a giant room where the carpet is paisley, the lighting is low, and a moldy liquor smell wafts through the air.

"Blackjack?" Syd asks.

I raise an eyebrow. "Do you even know how to play?"

She shrugs. "Fake it till you make it."

"I don't think that's the right saying for a casino."

Syd laughs and I do too, a relaxed energy ping-ponging between us like the flashing lights on the rows and rows of gaming machines.

"Fine," she says, shaking her head. "I'm guessing you want to start at the slots."

I head over to the bill changer. "Yep."

"You are like an eighty-year-old in an eighteen-year-old's body."

I shrug, straightening my glasses. "I take that as a compliment."

I change a ten and Syd gets two beers and we meet at the back row of slots by the side wall. We stop at a dusty machine at the very end. Lucky number seven, it says at the top.

"How do you feel about the number seven?" I say to Syd.

"I feel good about it," she says, inspecting the faux gold detailing. "Uneven numbers signify change."

"Really?" I watch her as she hangs her purse on a little hook at the side of the machine and gestures for me to sit. She doesn't look drunk at all, except for her wide, unguarded smile.

"I don't know," she says, shrugging. "I heard it once on a podcast and it sounded right."

Next to us, an old lady with wraparound sunglasses and a plastic bucket of quarters is posted up at a machine that is covered in shabby good luck charms she must have brought from home. A line of troll dolls perches on the top like they're about to start a musical number.

"That one was Zelda's favorite," she says to us, gesturing to our machine.

"Who's Zelda?" Syd asks, her face warm and friendly.

"She used to be my best friend," the lady says.

Syd looks like she's got a million questions on the tip of her tongue. "What was she like?" she says.

"A total asshole," the lady replies, and Syd nods, like she's just said something terribly wise.

I try to hold back my laughter, and say, "Well, thanks." And the lady nods and turns back to her machine, plunking another quarter in. I turn to Syd. "Do you want to do the honors?"

"No way," she says, leaning against the side of the machine. In her T-shirt, her glittering black dress, and heavy eyeliner, she looks like an off-duty villain at Disneyland. "I'm trying to manifest bad luck these days."

"That doesn't even make sense," I say, laughing. "But okay."

I pull down the handle and the all-analog machine chugs into motion in the most satisfying way. We watch as cherries and lemons and dollar signs spin by. There's a rhythmic clicking and dinging and shifting of gears. Something rushes through me like a gust of wind. Then the machine slows, stops, and the number seven lines up perfectly in all three windows. A siren goes off and a cop car light at the top of the machine starts flashing. Quarters spill out of the tray and onto the floor.

"Holy fuck," Syd says.

"You two just won three hundred bucks," sunglasses lady says, handing us an empty plastic bucket from her stack. "That Zelda always was a lucky bitch."

"She blessed us!" Syd whispers, pressing both palms to the front of the machine.

"Wow," I say, taking the bucket. "Thanks."

I bend down and start scooping quarters into the bucket. Syd crawls after a few that have run into the aisle. When she stands back up she's flushed and starry eyed.

"Should we play blackjack now?" I ask.

Syd gets back up to her feet and looks around the casino. It's more than half-empty, and the low lighting gives everything a kind of creepy zombie apocalypse vibe.

"Nah," she says, holding up her half-empty bottle. "I think I've hit my limit. Let's get out of here."

We wander for a while, but downtown Reno looks exponentially more chintzy and depressing at one in the morning than it did earlier in the night. The sidewalk is desolate and everything smells like a hangover.

"What are we going to do with that three hundred bucks?" Syd says.

I shrug. "Gas money?"

Syd jabs me with a sharp elbow, right below my ribs. "No way. It's a gift from Zelda. We have to do something special."

"Like what?"

"Like tattoos or something."

I smile, an old, familiar feeling nipping at my heels. Drunken, wild abandon with a little bit of dread mixed in. "Huh. What would you get?"

Syd closes her eyes. "A tiger with ZELDA written across its teeth."

"Wow."

"What? She's obviously our good luck charm."

I turn to look at where Syd's stopped on the sidewalk. There is something magical about the fall of her disheveled hair, the wildness of her limbs as she waves them about, gesturing in a slightly drunken manner. I imagine a tiger curving right under her collarbone and I have to blink a few times to get back to the thread of conversation. "I thought you were manifesting bad luck," I finally say.

Syd starts walking again. "Zelda changed my mind. Just think about it."

"Okay," I shrug, knowing that I've probably already lost this one. If anyone can convince me to get a tattoo, it will be Syd. "I will."

She opens her purse and pulls out a cigarette, walks for a while without lighting it, just holding the end between her lips. She looks at once so grown-up, so different, and also exactly like the girl I used to know with the dusty socks.

"When did you start smoking?" I ask.

"A long, long time ago," she says.

She lights it, inhales deeply, and stifles a little cough as the smoke comes out again.

Are you okay? I want to ask. But instead I say, "Ready to head back?" and we turn around and walk along the abandoned strip, all the way to our motel.

"Hey," Syd says as we walk down the outdoor hallway on the second floor, the yellow light suddenly making her eyes look heavy and tired. "I love hijinks as much as the next guy, but why didn't you just tell Julia who you are?"

I fumble in my pocket for the room key, swiping it over the lock pad, remembering how exposed I felt when Julia said my name onstage, right before she sang my song.

I shake my head. "I don't know."

Syd pushes past me, traipsing into the room without turning on the lights, and flops onto my bed. "Isn't that kind of why we're here though? For you to get to know the Darlas and find out about your mom?"

"Yeah." I take my shoes off and lie down next to her, looking up at the dark outline of the ceiling fan. "I guess? It's not like I really thought any of this through."

I stretch my arms over my head, needing more physical space for this conversation. My legs still want to walk, but there's nowhere to go.

"Huh," Syd yawns, shimmying her dress down in that magical way girls have of taking off clothes that are under other clothes. Her shirt is long but her legs are still mostly bare and it's hard not to stare at them, glowing white in the darkness. Then she scoots up the mattress and climbs under my sheet. She must be drunker than I thought.

"Get in here," she says. "You don't want to sleep on top of the bedspread. It's where all of the bacteria congregate."

Part of me could be awake forever, could walk around this hotel room for hours, crumpling up Syd's cigarettes one by one and doing pushups against the wall. Or I could scroll through my phone, all the way back to the origin of the internet. But instead I make my way up and under the covers until I can feel Syd next to me, a radiating heat source in the air-conditioned room.

"Cass?" she says.

"Yeah?" I say.

"It's okay."

"What's okay?"

There's a pause so long that I wonder if the conversation is over. And then she says, "Not knowing."

"Okay." I nod, but somehow not knowing now feels worse than it did when I started.

There's more that I could say, words fluttering around just out of reach, but Syd is already breathing slowly with sleep. I watch her for a while, her ribs rising and falling, hair sweeping across the perfect expanse of her forehead. I feel a compulsion to reach out my finger, run it along the curve of her cheekbone, to see if the skin there is as soft as it looks.

Instead I get up and head to the bathroom, brush my teeth, wash my face, climb into the empty bed, and let my thoughts race until dawn.

The next day Syd looks at me from the passenger seat and says, "Are you ready?" Then she slides the Darlas' self-titled CD into the stereo. We are somewhere between Reno and Salt Lake City, in a mountainous wasteland of gray rock. Syd's phone is plugged into the aux cable and the GPS lady chimes in with directions from time to time to punctuate the monotony.

Syd woke up this morning grumpy and hungover, distant and quiet again. It was almost like last night never even happened. I tried not to be disappointed as I climbed into the car and drove us farther away from home.

Now, after easing our way through two Velvet Underground albums, she tugs nervously at the end of her braid, as though this CD means something to her too.

The first strains of track one slip into the quiet car. Even after only two shows, I know this one; the sound of Julia singing like Tina Weymouth and Charlie banging hypnotically on the drums, but on top of that, folded in, snaking around, threading through the music is my sound, the sound of the BART station: my mother's mint green, 1957 Telecaster guitar.

For three songs, I listen to my mother play. She's as good as any of the greats, Eric Clapton, Robert Johnson, Bonnie Raitt. She plays like lace curtains, knowing exactly which pieces of light to let in.

"It's sort of like the Roches on acid," Syd muses into the quiet between songs, and I'm startled, not having even remembered where we are.

I don't know how to respond; despite my love of music, my actual lexicon of musical knowledge is so much smaller than Syd's. So I just wait, listening to the hissing white noise between tracks.

The first few chords of the next song strum out, quieter than the one before, a song I haven't heard. And then a voice starts singing and

I don't recognize that either. My brain scrambles around, trying to place it, coming up completely blank.

Syd gasps. "It's her."

I listen to the disembodied voice on the speakers, trying to make the word make sense. Her. The voice from my first year on Earth, from before that, from the body I used to live inside. "The Circle Game" came on in Gram's kitchen once and she said to me, *Your mom used to sing that song when you were in her belly.* But now, all these years later, there is nothing familiar about her at all, not in the way I'd hoped it would be. Still, it pulls at something inside the void. Somewhere, another thread begins to unravel.

18
Sydney

IT'S ALMOST SEVEN HOURS FROM RENO to Salt Lake City, and Cass and I listen to the CD eight times. We drive through thick forests and up into giant mountains and listen to the songs again and again, until the sound of them becomes a part of the landscape rushing by my windows. For a while rain falls, and then it stops. Heavy cartoon clouds come and go. We stop for drive-through fast food, tossing the crumpled-up paper bag into the back seat. Every time the album finishes, Cass says, "Play it again," in a voice that is serious and guarded. By the time we pull up outside of the bar where the Darlas are playing tonight, I've memorized almost all the lyrics.

The Darlas must not be here yet because their giant white van is not parked outside. Cass and I just sit in the car staring at the distant mountains, with a heavy quiet settling between us.

The sky here is cloudless, the blue of it somehow light and deep at the same time, diffuse at the edges and concentrated in the middle. It's a color that could be manufactured into water bottle labels or plastic dishware. It doesn't feel real.

"That was intense," I say.

"Yeah."

"You okay?"

"Yeah."

Sometimes talking to Cass is like talking to a brick wall.

He's sitting in the driver's seat looking sweaty and rumpled, his dark hair hanging down around his face, the big brown orbs of his eyes glowing behind his glasses. I want to reach out and touch him, tuck a strand of hair behind his ear.

"I see where you get it from," I say instead, thinking about the past four hours submerged in Cass's mother's music.

"What?"

"You know what."

Cass keeps staring straight ahead, out the front window, all the way to the jagged, purple ring of mountains on edge of the horizon.

"How come you never told me?" I ask. I remember this game, and if I push enough, I know I'll get something.

I look at Cass's fingers, gripping the steering wheel as if the car is still moving. I think of those fingers, lighting fast on the neck of his guitar.

The music feels like a bigger betrayal than anything else that happened between us. The past resurfaces and amplifies all the old feelings: me pushing, Cass hiding. Both of us pretending to never need anything from the other. Back then I wanted to capture him, to open him up and read his secrets. But trying to understand Caspian is like trying to grab at smoke. It always has been.

He shrugs. "I just wanted to keep something for myself, I guess."

The words hurt exactly as much as I thought they would.

With Cass I never kept anything for myself. A mistake I will never make again. I chip at the jagged black square of polish on my thumbnail.

I want to just be quiet, to hide everything like Cass does, but I can't. I dig my fingers into the edge of my seat and say, "I keep looking back at everything and feeling like I didn't really know you at all."

He turns and looks at me, his eyes moving across my face. "You know me better than anyone else ever has."

The moment is broken by the loud screeching of brakes as the van pulls up behind us and the Darlas spill out of it, looking almost as rumpled as we do.

"Fuck," Julia yells. "I'm going to piss my pants."

She runs inside the bar as Sunny comes around the back of the van, stretching her arms, a soft-looking giant blue cardigan bunching up at her elbows. "I guess that's our cue," Cass says, opening his door. I can't tell if I'm disappointed or relieved. Somehow, it feels like he's won again. Like he's always, always winning.

When we get to the van, Jasmyn unceremoniously shoves a kick drum into Cass's arms. She's wearing red sparkly cat-eye sunglasses and white platform Birkenstocks, a wrinkly linen dress bunching up around her knees.

"Hey, people," Charlie says, handing me a guitar case. Their bleached-blond hair sparkles in the sun and I catch the words SLOW DOWN tattooed across their knuckles in black ink.

"I can carry more than that," I frown.

"Fair enough," they say, winking and stacking a few more things on top. "I'll stay with the van."

Jasmyn gestures for us to follow her around and through the side door to the club. Inside, it's a lot like the venue in Sacramento— painted-black hallway, rickety stage, stale beer smell. It feels like

Benders or the Make Out Room or any other bar in San Francisco.

We make a few trips to and from the van until everything is up on the stage and everyone is busy setting up instruments.

"You guys can hang out in the greenroom if you want," Julia says. "There's beer in the cooler and we're gonna order pizza in a little while."

I wonder fleetingly if she knows how young we are. If she cares.

Cass heads back down the hallway but I find an abandoned barstool over near the wall at the back of the bar. I just want to be alone for a while. I want to sit in this familiar place and watch the sound check. I want to see how the music of the Darlas comes to be.

In sixth grade, Dad was out of work for almost a year, and on afternoons when he was too tired to search the internet for jobs that didn't exist, he taught me everything there was to know about electronic music. For once, he wasn't out of the house before it got light and back after dinner, or coaching Levi's basketball games on the weekends. For a while there, he was mine.

"The engineer on this album is a genius," he'd say, sliding a record out of its sleeve and telling me about tightly mic'd drums and gated reverb. He made me realize that music is a time and a place, that the people behind the soundboard can be magicians if they want to. Then he got a job at Salesforce and everything went back to the way it had always been.

The sound person tonight has long blue hair with black roots, a septum ring, and a lot of eyeliner. I watch them uncoiling cables and nestling microphones into cradles, next to amps, and inside drums.

It's intricate work; everything has to be precise. Bad sound can ruin a show.

I've spent the last few years running the mixing board for house shows of really bad bands from De Anza High. It's the one thing people at school talk to me for. I am a wizard with limited electrical supply, and I can make the shittiest Guitar Center equipment sound all right. But I've never gotten to run sound inside a real club.

When everything is in its place, I watch the sound check. Each instrument is played in isolation and the sound is adjusted back in the booth, then everyone plays together and the levels are adjusted again. It's almost my favorite part of any show, witnessing the way it all comes into focus.

The Darlas joke with each other as they go through the check. Sunny and Charlie keep busting into the bass and drum combinations of random television shows like *Law and Order* and *Curb Your Enthusiasm*. The sound person has to remind them that the opener is coming soon and ask them to please stay on track.

"How does it sound, Syd?" Julia asks in the middle of a song.

I'd almost forgotten I was here.

"Perfect," I smile. "The reverb here is really nice."

Julia looks at me and grins. "I see you, Syd," she says.

Later, in the greenroom, I'm halfway through a slice of olive and mushroom pizza when my phone blows up with another text from Robbie. Cass raises an eyebrow. My phone has been buzzing all day with texts from Mom, Dad, Isabel, Anna, Grace, and even Levi. The entire Greenfield crew has been recruited to this cause. I've been texting them all back, except for Mom: **I'm safe. I'm fine. I just need a little space. I'll call you tomorrow. I promise.**

I've convinced my friend Gen from work to cover for me, so my family thinks I'm staying at her apartment near the Berkeley campus. **Just for a day or two,** I said to Dad. **Just to clear my head.** I envision him scrubbing a hand down his face. He hates being pulled into the middle of things.

"What's going on in there?" Cass says, gesturing to my scrunched-up face.

"Just my life exploding," I say to Cass.

He looks thoughtful and takes a giant bite of pizza. I look down at the text stream; Cass leans in to read over my shoulder. Robbie and I are halfway through an arduous conversation. I wasn't sure how to tell him about the past two days, so I did it in my usual fashion, blunt and without too much finessing.

I don't understand, he says. **You're on a road trip with your next door neighbor?**

I sigh. Boys are so clueless. **Yup.**

The dorky guy with the glasses?

Yup.

Should I be worried?

Yes, I think. But not like that. He should be worried because I don't really miss him. Or because the thought of moving in with him and his cousin makes me feel sick.

You should always be worried, I text back, with an upside-down smiley face. That should give him something to freak out over for a while.

I press the little moon symbol, silencing my phone. Then I take another bite of pizza.

"You are so cold," Cass says.

I think about my life with Caspian, how he's always been one step beyond where I could reach him. "Takes one to know one," I say.

19
Caspian

AFTER THE SHOW, WHEN SYD AND I have lugged all five hundred pounds of gear back to the van, we sit with the band around a giant booth in the bar, our motley crew a loud contrast to the healthy-looking, outdoorsy people chattering all around us. The Darlas are loud and Syd is quiet and I am listening, tapping my straw against the side of my water glass.

We are three days in, seven hundred miles from home, and still, I haven't even figured out what I'm supposed to be doing. I want to turn to these people and say, *Tell me everything.* And at the same time I want to torch the table, burn the whole bar to the ground. I want to say, *How can you be here when she's gone? How did you let her get into that fucking car?*

That's the thing that doesn't square. The Darlas are cool, they are some of the best musicians I have ever seen, and most of them are also moms. They have young kids who are all stuck at home with partners and grandparents, and they talk about them constantly, with annoyance and also with deep, raw affection. In my ten years of imagining, I pictured a lot of things—tattoos, drug problems, narcissistic aging rock stars—but I did not imagine this.

I'm staring at the menu, silently reading each item—gin and tonic,

Bloody Mary, tequila sunrise—wondering what exactly my mom had to drink before she died, when Sunny turns to me, rings tapping the side of her glass. Her hair is down tonight, a long thick sheet that flows down her back. On the inside of her wrist she has a tattoo that says WALT, the name of her ten-year-old son.

"So," she says, "what on earth made the two of you want to follow a bunch of old folks like us across the country?"

I drop the straw back into my glass and straighten my coaster, anger scattering and nerves making my heart race. I'm so unprepared and not any good at subterfuge, a rabbit rustling in the bushes, about to be discovered. I clear my throat. "Would you believe me if I told you I didn't know?"

She tilts her head to the side, scrutinizing my features. I try to shrink back without moving, to hide behind an errant strand of hair. "Maybe?" she says, and I feel the full force of her mom-ness aimed at me. It's terrifying. "I just don't think we've ever had such devoted fans before. Especially any that are your age."

I try to laugh but it never really gets off the ground. "Not even back in the day?"

"Well." She smiles. "That's different, I guess."

"My mom was a fan." I let the half-truth slip out, some part of me wanting to bring her here.

"No shit!" Charlie says, smiling wide from across the table. They run a hand through their short blond hair. "I wonder if I know her. Our world was pretty small back then."

"She's not alive anymore." I can feel it in my stomach, saying those words which I hardly ever have to say because we've erased her so well. Suddenly everyone at the table is looking at me. I take off my glasses and clean the lenses on my shirt, allowing the world to blur for a second.

Charlie's face falls. "Shit. I'm so sorry."

I lift my shoulder in a shrug, to minimize, to hurry through this part of the exchange. "It's okay. She died when I was a baby, so . . ." I look down at the table. "Her name was Alex," I lie. "Alex Henderson."

Syd kicks me under the table, hard enough to hurt. She's been hunched over her phone, texting with her boyfriend; I didn't even realize she was listening.

"Alex Henderson." Julia stirs her drink, looking into my eyes. There's something about Julia that feels so wise, like she was born hundreds of years ago. "It doesn't sound familiar."

I suddenly feel hot all over, like the lie is written across my face. I wish everyone would stop looking at me.

Syd clears her throat, finally looking up from her spot where she's been skulking in the corner. "Tell us about the Darlas back in the day," she says, a perfectly timed rescue. She doesn't look at me, but I somehow know that she will collect the favor at a convenient moment down the line.

"The Darlas back in the day . . ." Charlie says, spinning a coaster on the table. "Huh."

"We were a handful," Sunny says, blowing her bangs off her face.

"A straight-up laundry bag full of mountain lions," Julia says.

Jasmyn looks up from where she's been typing on her phone. "I wasn't a part of it," she laughs. "I'm just here for the tour."

"It's sad about Iris," Syd says, and for a second the whole table stops moving. And there it is, classic Syd, taking things a step too far. My cheeks burn. The only sound at the table is Julia furiously stabbing her straw into the ice cubes at the bottom of her drink. Jasmyn gives me a long look and then reaches up to tuck a piece of Julia's hair behind her ear. Suddenly I realize that most of the bar has emptied out and it's just our table left. The bartender and waitress are laughing in the corner, leaning in over a cell phone.

"We should get going," Sunny says, clearing her throat.

"Calvin and I need to get going too," Syd says, watching my face as I awkwardly wait for everyone else to slide out of the booth.

In that moment, I'm ten years old again, watching Syd do one of her stupid tricks, embarrassment burning my cheeks. A small voice inside my head says, *Why are you here?* And I'm not sure if it's talking about Syd or me.

20
Caspian

WHEN WE WERE YOUNG, SYD AND I spent most of our summers at the town pool. We'd ride our bikes up out of our cul-de-sac and down the winding hill into town. We'd lie down on towels in the shade of a moldy old umbrella, read comics until we were slick with sweat, float in the cold water until our lips turned blue, and then race back to our towels again to wrap up and lie down in the warmth of the sun.

The pool was a popular hangout for kids from our school, and I always felt this pull when we were there; I wanted to be with Syd, to protect her from the weird looks and giggling packs of middle schoolers, but I also hated being on the outside. I wanted to belong with the group of boys roughhousing in the deep end and doing backflips off the diving board. I wanted to hold hands with one of the girls reading magazines on the loungers, the ones who had soft skin and long hair and smelled like coconuts.

The last time I ever went to the pool with Syd, we were thirteen years old. It was the day after Syd's first kiss, and I was still a little thrown by the whole thing. I didn't understand how she could waste an important rite of passage on a guy like Liam W. And I didn't like the feeling I'd gotten in my stomach while I'd watched her do it.

We were sitting on loungers and eating Bomb Pops from the ice cream truck, blood red dripping down our chins. Liam and Jackson were sitting nearby. They kept looking at us and then whispering and bursting into laughter. I was embarrassed and annoyed but Syd pretended not to even notice.

When they got up to walk to the snack bar, Jackson turned around and started wiggling his tongue at Syd in some kind of bizarre, lewd gesture. Beside me, I could feel her body harden, ready for a fight.

"You look like you have rabies," she said, wrapping her Little Mermaid towel tighter around her chest.

"Liam is probably the one with rabies," Jackson retorted. "After you slobbered all over him last night."

Liam snorted, holding in a laugh, and shook his head, turning to look at the pool instead of at our faces.

Syd's cheeks turned red, a flush like an instant sunburn spreading across her face. Despite her effort to look unbreakable, I could see the memory of her first kiss spoiling like cake in the rain.

"You're a pig," I said, clenching my fists at my sides. The last nub of my popsicle slid off the stick and hit the ground.

"Your mom's a pig," Liam said, and Jackson said, "Oooooh!" and bumped his fist. I flinched. For a moment I felt like I was outside of my body, like I was watching everything happening from a few feet away. I pulled back my fist as if to throw a punch, and then I just stood there for a second, coiled and ready to strike, but also stuck, unable to move to the next step.

Then, next to me, Syd ground out, "Caspian's mom is dead. Asshole."

It took a moment of stunned group silence before her words

registered. Around us, the sounds of splashing and shouting stretched and warped, echoing at the edge of our circle of shock. I saw a wave of shame wash over Syd once she realized she'd revealed my secret. I waited to feel it, anger or embarrassment, consuming rage. But I felt completely numb.

Eventually, Jackson and Liam slunk away. I waited for the numbness to subside, unable to look at Syd hanging her head in regret at my side. But it didn't.

Finally, I said, "I gotta go," lobbing my stick at the garbage can and missing. I grabbed my towel and walked to the pool entrance, trying my best to disappear into the wobbly heat of the afternoon.

I wake in the dark to a sharp poke in my side.

Ouch.

"Cass," whispers Syd, "Get up."

I don't really know where I am, except that I'm too hot and my phone is poking into the side of my face and I want to keep sleeping, maybe forever. "No," I grumble.

"Come on," she says, tugging at my blankets, a move which I have somehow predicted because I'm already gripping them tightly, which jerks her body toward me. She seems to give up for a moment, then leans down even closer and whispers, "Caaaaaaaspian," her warm breath close to my cheek.

Wow, my body seems to say as it is jolted to life by the smell and shape of her, hovering just out of reach.

"We have to get going," she whispers, right next to my ear.

Wow wow wow.

I open one eye to look at the alarm clock on the nightstand, which

I now realize is in the middle of the Super 8 motel room where we slept last night. Without my glasses, I can just barely make out the shapes; I think it's 6:30 a.m. I groan and sit up, gently pushing Syd out of my space, using every one of my tricks to try to calm my body down. I put on my glasses and the world comes into sharp focus, the dim motel room, Syd's long, wild hair. "Christ, Sydney, what is wrong with you?"

"It's a surprise," she says, her eyes round and innocent. "Come on, Cass. I dare you."

She walks over and flings open the blackout drapes to reveal a freshly risen sun that tries to burn through my retinas.

"Unghhhh," I grumble, and consider pulling the blankets back over my head, even though they smell a little musty.

I look up to see that Syd's dressed already, in black denim shorts, a T-shirt, and her new red cowboy boots, arms full of goose bumps from the aggressive motel AC. My arms get matching goose bumps looking at her skin. Mirror neurons, although to other parts of me that are still stunned by sleep, it almost feels like lust.

Syd drives and we stop for gas, sticky buns, and weak coffee before heading South on I-15 toward Moab, where the Darlas are playing tonight. I put on my sunglasses and wake up slowly.

This morning Syd seems different. More talkative, almost bubbly. The way she always is after going too far. This is one of our many dances. One of the ones I wish I could forget. But still, looking at the wide line of her lips, curled into a thoughtful half smile, the numbness feels like it recedes an inch or two.

We hit Spanish Fork and Syd misses the turnoff for 198 without flinching. I watch the sign for Moab float past the half-open window. "Aren't we supposed to be going the other way?" I ask, as the lady on my navigation scolds us to turn around and take the next ramp, rerouting and rerouting over the Shins on the stereo.

Syd grabs the phone from my hands and swipes the map app closed. "Road trips are all about detours, Cass."

Then she tosses the phone into my lap and rolls down the window.

Two and a half hours later we are in the absolute middle of nowhere. Long brown grass, little stands of trees, and a vast rolling land of crisscrossing telephone wires. Wherever this is, it is not Moab, Utah, which is where we are expected in just under four hours.

"Syd, where are we?" I ask, still feeling tired and wary after last night. I'm frustrated that once again Syd is in control and I'm flying blind, that she can't ever seem to let me move at a reasonable pace.

I think of my friends, of Hannah with her perfect, heart-shaped mouth and hands that were always warm and never, ever pushed too hard. I desperately want to miss her. She deserves that, but no matter how hard I try, I just don't. She's probably hiking Half Dome at this very minute. And I'm in the middle of Utah with Sydney Greenfield. Everything is upside down.

A couple minutes later, Syd pulls over and turns off the car. I look up from my phone—which is open to a text from Kit Molina: **any updates?**—to see that we are deep inside a grove of aspens. I can't see anything except for trees around us, stark white trunks with dark slashes across their faces. A million silvery green leaves are all shivering in the wind.

"Pando," Syd whispers, reverently.

"What?" I say. I feel my frustration receding, even as I try to keep hold of it.

Syd opens her door and the rush of air smells clean and earthy.

"Pando. *Populus tremuloides*. There are forty-seven thousand aspen trees here and they're all connected by the roots. It's the largest single living organism in the entire world."

We walk away from the car out into the trees, and the aspens begin to transform around me into a single being, the flutter of its leaves parsing out sunshine to the forest floor. Lace curtains. Mom's guitar.

And now I feel like I'm eleven years old again, but not in a bad way, just following Syd, slightly in awe as she shows me something I'd never even thought to notice.

"Scientists think it's around eighty thousand years old," she whispers.

The thought of that many years makes me tired, makes me feel every hour of sleep I didn't get last night. Time expands outward as I try to imagine it. My own lifetime, a giant heap of insignificant experiences, shrinks down to fit inside.

We walk until we can't see the car anymore and then I sit down, leaning my back against one of the tree trunks. Syd keeps walking until her long black braid and jangling bracelets are out of sight. I try to make myself perfectly still, to disappear. I listen to the relentless soft rustling-leaf sound, which I realize is its own kind of music, not unlike the Darlas' or mine.

A car passes on the road. I feel utterly alone, and also not. I think about the void of Mom that's always there, even when I try to forget. I wonder, if I stayed out here long enough, if just being in the presence of so much time and space would make it begin to feel small.

I think I fall asleep, because when Syd kicks my shoe, I'm suddenly jolted back to the present.

"Time to hit the road," she says, holding out a long, spidery-fingered hand. I hold onto it and it's cold as ice pops, colder than the bottom of the ocean.

We're halfway between Pando and Moab, in the middle of a desolate land of white rock and scrubby pines, before the calm of the forest breaks like an eggshell and the numbing hum of the real world returns. Maybe it's another missed call from Kit Molina, which makes me think about my secret, impossible dream of traveling the world with my guitar. Already this feeling of being on the road, of lugging amps and staying up late and music, is better than anything. Or maybe it's the text from my Dad: **I know you probably don't have any service but wow I really miss you.** Which reminds me that none of this can ever really be.

After a while the space between Syd and me starts to feel too big. We haven't talked in a hundred miles. We've been behaving like acquaintances, quiet, quiet acquaintances, for most of this trip. We've settled into an easy groove, taking turns driving and choosing the music, compromising on car snacks. But I know, at some point, the past is coming for us.

"What are you doing next year?" I send some flimsy small talk out into the vast expanse of seemingly uncrossable quiet between us.

"Honestly?" she says, looking out the window at the salt-colored rocks. "It's kind of a mess. I got a sound apprenticeship at the Fox, but my mom wants me to do this medical internship at her work."

A sound apprenticeship at the Fox. Another new piece of Syd clicks into place. Something incredible and unexpected that I didn't even realize people our age could do. I suddenly remember being a kid, watching Syd adjust all the knobs on her dad's fancy stereo, trying to get the levels just right as a song blasted from the speakers.

"Wow," I say. "That's incredible."

She reaches up to the window and touches the glass, her hand actually shaking a little. It's unsettling to see Syd unsure about anything, but here she is, visibly balking. She shrugs. "I don't know. Could fall through."

I poke her bony shoulder, wanting her to lighten back up. "Probably won't though. You always were a music genius and you were born under a lucky star."

She rolls her eyes. "You mean the sun?" She gives a pointed look to where my left arm is resting on the edge of the window. "It's probably giving us cancer right this very minute."

I laugh out loud at this. "And yet you've got a purse full of cigarettes in the back seat. What gives?"

She sighs. "I'll probably quit soon. But you've got to try things you, you know?"

"I guess?"

Syd taps her fingers on the door. "What about you, what's your plan for next year?"

"CSEB for engineering."

"Engineering? Huh."

I shrug. "Turns out I'm really good at math. Plus, my dad loves it."

"But not you?"

I try to ignore the twinge of unease that comes at this. "I like it all right."

Syd's quiet for a while, watching the place where the lines of rock seem to undulate as the car rolls past them.

"I'll quit smoking," she finally says. "If you tell me what's eating you."

"Really?" I say, frowning in disbelief.

Syd, never one for attachments, reaches into her purse and pulls out a cigarette, snaps it in half. She raises her eyebrows.

"Yeah, really."

She lays her seat back like a lounger, and suddenly I feel like I'm in an old-fashioned psychoanalyst's office and Syd is about to spill her guts. Except Syd is Freud here, and I'm the one who has to share my feelings. But it's either this or back to loaded silence, so I squeeze the wheel and do it.

I could tell her about Kit or Dad or the BART station, but instead I cut to the heart of everything. "I can't really feel anything," I say. The weird truth lingers for a while in the air of the car with the dust motes.

"Huh," Syd finally says, her voice searching. "What do you mean?"

"I mean," I say, scanning the horizon, looking for words, "I graduated. I was dumped by Hannah, who was the girl of my dreams. I found the Darlas and have traveled hundreds of miles away from home and I don't feel anything."

Syd is clearly getting into therapist mode, tenting her fingers and carefully scanning my face. She's playing a part, but I can tell that underneath she's a little worried. "When did it start?"

I search back through memories and memories and memories, finding nothing.

"I don't know," I shrug. "The beginning of time."

Syd doesn't say anything for a long while. Like she's searching her memory too. Or maybe she just knows that there isn't much else to say about it. But, as the miles pass, I start to feel a little lighter. The last song of Bill Withers fades into Joan Jett.

Then she says, "Talk to me about blow jobs," and I nearly drive the car off the road.

"Jesus, Syd." I run a hand down my face. "You've got to give a person some warning. Especially when I'm driving."

She laughs, and her laugh is scratchy and careless, real. "Sorry. I'm just always looking for tips to improve my game."

"Jesus. Fuck." I laugh, trying to rein in the giant erection that is suddenly brewing under the steering wheel. I take a deep breath. Think about electronics. "Let's just say that at this point most people with dicks are just really lucky to have a mouth anywhere near the vicinity. I wouldn't sweat the technique."

"Huh," Syd says, grinning deviously. "Good to know."

"What about you?" I say, the words leaping from my mouth without checking in with my brain at all.

Syd is thoughtful, biting her bottom lip, and suddenly I have to stuff down a bunch of dirty thoughts that are all competing for space in my imagination.

I roll down the windows and a big gust of wind comes in, whipping the ends of Syd's wild black hair up across my shoulder. I scan the road for an exit sign—I need to get out of this car.

Syd sinks down even lower in her seat and says, "Sometimes he does this thing with his tongue where he just kind of presses—"

An image of Syd's boyfriend's cigarette-filmed mouth flickers into my mind and I get the sudden urge to bash my head into the steering wheel.

"Nope," I say. "I can't do this."

Syd breaks into laughter, holding her stomach and half spitting out a mouthful of bubbly water she's been trying to drink while lying down. It takes her a few seconds to get herself back together, which is okay because I am busy trying to scrub the images of Syd, and then Robbie and Syd, out of my brain.

"I'll just say," she says, "pressure is the magic concept here."

"Pressure." I repeat. Out of the corner of my eye I see Syd's freckled cheeks go almost as red as mine.

Utah is a wasteland of ecru rock and tiny towns and hillsides dotted with one-story houses with vinyl siding, until suddenly it's not. Suddenly the rocks turn rusty orange and begin to tower in perplexing shapes against the sky, making the startling blue of it even bluer.

"I feel like, at any moment, a dinosaur is going to stomp right across the fucking road," Syd says. She is craning her neck behind the steering wheel, as though somehow she'll be able to take it all in. The windows are down and my arm is hanging out of the car, fingers combing through the air. Neil Young is crooning and it feels as much like a perfect moment as anything ever will.

Until Syd says, "I love Neil Young and all, but this is some misogynistic bullshit."

And I laugh, hard.

We stop at a viewing station and Syd pulls out the peanut butter and bread we picked up at Target this morning when we bought our camping stuff from the Fourth of July section at the back corner of the store—a bright red dome tent with an American flag across the backside (on sale for thirty bucks), a red cooler, two camping chairs, and two American flag towels. Luckily my dad has this weird thing about keeping sleeping bags in the trunk—*In case of adventure*, he said once, although I don't think this is what he had in mind.

Dad. Something about all of this feels so wrong when I think about him at home on the couch, drinking his Lagunitas and watching the ball game. I need to end this sooner than later. I need to call Kit Molina. But I don't want to think about it right now.

We sit side by side at a concrete picnic table and I stack the bread four slices high on Syd's knee, taking a slice and spreading the peanut butter. We eat our sandwiches, watching a hawk coast high above the red desert.

"This is probably the most exquisite and deadly place I've ever seen," Syd says.

I frown, flicking a crumb from my shirt. "Deadly?"

"Yeah. Rattlesnakes, black widows, hobo spiders, scorpions. Not to mention dehydration, hypothermia, poison sumac, sunstroke."

"Wow, Syd," I say. "You really know how to kill the vibe."

She laughs, "Kill the vibe!"

I roll my eyes, but inside I'm amazed at how much I am *feeling*. Everything is suddenly turned up to ten. Hot sun, brilliant red rock, Syd. I say, "Remember when you went through that phase where you wanted everyone to call you Black Widow?"

"Oh god," she shakes her head. "I was such a nerd."

"We both were," I say, thinking of my Star Trek glasses case and STEM RULES lunch box.

"Yep," she says. Then something in her face tightens and an awkward silence returns.

She says, "Did you know that Hannah and I used to be best friends?"

I try to picture it and fail completely. That's how it's been these past few days: I keep scrabbling at the past but I can't always seem to remember it right.

"I know," Syd says, flicking a crumb from the top of her thigh. "It's kind of hard to believe. I actually used to be a Normal. I mean, as normal as one can be in second grade. Or as normal as I could have been."

"I'm so mad that I missed it!" I laugh, even though the thought of Syd being normal makes me inexplicably sad. "So what happened?"

Syd's face is serious under her big dark sunglasses. "Well," she says. "We were having this career day discussion and I said I wanted to be a pet mortician."

"Of course you did."

"Right?" She laughs. "What other job is there? Anyway, then Hannah said, 'That's weird.' And Gwendolyn agreed. And I never spoke to either of them again."

It feels like there's more to the story, but I don't push. Instead I just say, "Why didn't you ever tell me? I mean, when everything happened with us." It seems like such a weird way to try to describe the slow implosion of our friendship, but I'm too much of a wimp to say it any other way.

She just shrugs and says, "It was ancient history." As though dead and ancient things aren't her very favorite.

Under the table, I scrape my shoes across the dusty red earth. I feel a sudden desperate need to get us back to the carefree feeling from before. A car pulls up beside ours, a mother and three blond kids spilling out of it. I get an idea. "I dare you to make yourself a peanut butter mustache and then go up and ask them for directions," I say.

Syd grins, already unscrewing the lid from the peanut butter jar. "You're on."

21
Sydney

TONIGHT'S SHOW IS AT A BREWERY in Moab that is full of ruddy-faced outdoor types who are mostly there to drink and talk, not to see a band of witchy geniuses playing music. The Darlas battle the crowd while Cass and I stand in our tiny bit of floor space, next to a large group of loud guys that erupts into a chorus of "Dude!" every few minutes, despite my near-constant death glaring. As we are packing up the van afterward, when Sunny and I are struggling with her bass amp, she shrugs and says, "You can't win 'em all."

In the parking lot, Julia lights a cigarette and my fingers itch for one, but Cass gives me a sharp look from where he is standing at the edge of the desert, talking on his phone.

"The sound tonight was garbage," Julia says.

"Way too much gain," I agree. "It's like he thought you guys were KISS or something."

Julia looks thoughtful, takes a long drag.

"Would you quit already?" Jasmyn yells from around the front of the van.

"I'm on vacation!" Julia yells back. Still, she stubs it out. Then she turns to me. "You should sit in the booth tomorrow night."

I almost drop Cass's bottle opener keychain on the pavement.

"Really?"

Julia smiles and nods. "I've seen you skulking around the sound check the past few days. You look like you know what you're doing."

I shrug, trying not to look as excited as I feel. "I'm good at skulking, I guess."

"Good," Julia says.

Charlie joins us, making a group of three. They lean against the side of the van and look up at the night sky.

"Don't you just feel like you could do this forever?" they say.

And yes, I absolutely do. I imagine this life, where I never stop. And I wonder what it would take to make it real.

22
Caspian

THAT NIGHT AFTER THE SHOW, WE camp with the Darlas a few miles down some dark and winding canyon road, the ancient rocks towering above us. Syd and I struggle in the dark for a laughably long time, trying to set up the sale-aisle tent.

"I thought you knew how to do this," she says, as I try and fail to get both sections of tent poles to stand upright at the same time. "Aren't you supposed to be camping in Yosemite this entire week?"

"This tent is garbage," I grumble in reply, not wanting to think about the alternate timeline where I'm still in California.

"Come on, Cass," Syd chides, then she catches herself. "Calvin. Come on, Calvin. This tent is amazing and you know it."

It's surprisingly big once we've got it set up. It's roomy enough that it won't be awkward to sleep in it side by side, and it has a mesh-covered opening at the top for star gazing. Syd lies down on top of her sleeping bag for a moment and sighs deeply. "See?" she says. "Told you so."

We stay up late, sitting in our $10.99 American flag camp chairs beside the fire, listening to the Darlas as they reminisce about the old days and talk about my mother without really talking about her. Images start to form in my mind, and I can see them: young and wild and staggering around the Mission after a night out, filling a booth at Taqueria Cancun and eating burritos at three in the morning. I can't help wondering where I fit in, me and my dad.

Across the campfire, Julia and Jasmyn huddle together on a woven blanket. They are wearing matching polar fleece and baseball caps, and I can almost see their kids here, climbing in and out of their laps. Charlie has on a MARINE MAMMAL CENTER beanie and a Day-Glo orange puffy jacket and they're tipping back in their camp chair, playing air drums and looking up at all the stars, passing a bottle of red wine back and forth with Syd and Sunny, whose lips are ringed in purple.

Syd is quiet tonight. Like me, she seems overwhelmed by the vastness of this place. I look across the campfire at her dark wide eyes, and I wonder if she has a void like mine. I wonder where it would even come from. It's weird that I wouldn't know, that there are so many big blank spots in Syd's life that I know nothing about.

But for the second time today, my own void starts to shrink in the presence of so many ancient rocks, so many millions of winking stars. The light from these stars is from a time before my mother was even born. Something about that is comforting.

Julia walks to the van and pulls out a beat-up acoustic guitar with sunflowers painted all over the face of it.

"You really were children of the nineties," Syd muses, eyeing the chipping yellow paint.

"Yeah," says Charlie, "we had sunflower everything."

Everyone's quiet for a while as Julia strums a sad melody and hums along. Charlie closes their eyes and Jasmyn lies all the way back, look-

ing up at the night sky. I study Julia's face. She gets this look sometimes that's so haunted and lost. Just like my dad.

There's a break in the music and just as Julia's about to set the guitar down onto the soft red dirt, Syd says, "Calvin plays guitar." I give
her a sharp look, dread pooling in my gut, but she just looks back at
me and shrugs, a smug smile on her face.

Everyone is looking at me, so I immediately shove down all the
anger and embarrassment that's rising in my chest like heartburn; I
try to smile, but I probably look like an axe murderer. For a moment
I consider getting back into my car and leaving Syd, all of them, right
there in the campground. I could drive down one of those roads that
winds into the heart of the desert and never come back.

But I have to play my part. So I just take the guitar that Julia is holding out to me and say, "I'm not that good."

Syd, may she burn in hell, grins and says, "He's lying. He's a musical genius."

I shake my head ruefully, cradling the guitar awkwardly in my
hands, as Jasmyn says, "Play something, Cal!" The sound of her
encouragement is so mom-like that I almost lose my nerve. Then the
rest of the Darlas start chiming in, whooping and laughing, and then
the sound dies down and everyone is just waiting.

I close my eyes for a few seconds. I can do this. I can play something simple, something that won't reveal too much. But it's been
days since I've touched a guitar; even I know it's a lost cause. I lose
myself as soon as I begin, my fingers pulling and bending the strings,
the song of the past few days coming so easily it's like breathing. It's
like the void doesn't even exist, like I do know how to talk to people,
to think, to feel. It's almost like I'm not empty at all.

When I'm done, when I finally open my eyes again, everyone is staring at me silently, mouths open. I'm immediately full of something uneasy that feels like regret. I've never played for people I know before and I don't think I actually like it. It's like my skin is crawling all over my body.

Julia is the first to break the silence. "Holy fuck," she says, taking a long sip of her sparkling water.

Charlie lets out a low whistle. Syd's lips pull into a smile that is somehow not a smile at all.

I just shrug and hand the guitar back across the fire. "I think I'm about ready to turn in," I say. Then I walk back to our tent, without looking at anyone, especially not Syd.

23
Sydney

SOMETIME AFTER MIDNIGHT I HEAD BACK to the tent, slipping off my shoes and crawling quietly through the flap door. Cass is lying on top of his sleeping bag. I close my eyes and try to fall asleep, but he's restless and loud, turning one way and then the next, letting out these deep sighs, rattling his legs.

I feel restless too. Twisted and tangled like a fly in a spiderweb.

My mother called this morning, once. Then she texted: **Just talk to me Syd.** I almost convinced myself to pick up the phone and tell her everything. But then I let the scene play out in my mind: that disappointed face on the other end of the line, the tired, disturbed frown.

Instead, I texted Dad: **Good morning, I'm fine.**

He said, **Call your mother.**

I said, **Not a chance.**

Next to me, Cass shifts again, turning to face the tent wall and the vast desert beyond it. We are back to back, and the four inches between us feel like they are full of fire ants.

I almost feel bad for telling his secret tonight. But I'm too frustrated with him for being so clueless and childish and scared. I'm so annoyed that I could pull my own hair right out of my head.

Actually, I'm not annoyed, I'm panicked. End-of-the-world-style panic. We've been on the road for only three days and we've already spent more than five hundred dollars on gas and hotel rooms. Each gallon of gas that we buy with my credit card is one step closer to the end of this whole charade, to the end of every possibility of a solution for my life. Tonight in the parking lot with Julia I caught a glimpse of a life for myself, one where I was completely free. That idea—*What if I never stopped?*—worms its way through my mind and all of my restless limbs, making me think of the places I could go if I just didn't look back. But letting myself do that is idiotic. Because the truth is, I'm going to have to move in with Robbie. Either that or give it all up, leave my internship, come crawling back to my mother, dye my hair blond and turn into an Evelyn.

I'm totally and completely fucked.

What I didn't tell Cass as I skulked through Pando today, watching his folded-up legs and gangly brown arms curled up against the tree, is that the whole thing, the entire forest, is dying. Mysteriously, the grove has stopped making offspring. The old growth is getting older and nothing new is coming up. They think it might be cattle or insects or global warming. So typical: every good thing in nature ruined by humankind.

When the world starts to lurch like it's about to actually fall apart, I turn to Cass, taking in a sharp breath.

"Hey," I whisper. "Are you up?"

He lets out a frustrated sigh and turns over to face me.

"Yeah."

"Me too."

"Duh."

"Duh."

The tension breaks and I can see him trying not to smile, can just make out the gap between his two front teeth in the darkness. I know he's mad at me for before; I'm mad at him too, but somehow it's easier than it should be to get back into this rolling rhythm with him, this easy, easy laughter.

"Remember how you asked me what was wrong with me and I told you?" he says.

I wonder how hard it was do it, to tell me something that—on the surface of it—meant nothing and yet I somehow understood: *I can't feel anything.*

"Yeah . . ." I say. "Sort of."

"Your turn." He grins.

I balk. "No way. I quit smoking for that. You have to give me something first."

He's quiet for a few minutes; I listen to the steady in and out of his breath. "Do I even have anything you want?"

I twist a strand of my hair, tight. *Your thoughts. Your freckles. Your secrets.*

"Your firstborn child? For witchcraft purposes."

Cass shifts on his sleeping bag. "Creepy, but okay."

A soft burst of laughter floats into the dark tent from somewhere outside. "Actually," I say, "I want you to tell the Darlas."

There's a long pause, and then a deep breath. "Okay," he says. "Just let me do it when I'm ready."

I nod. "Okay, just don't take forever."

I tuck my hands under my head and look through the tiny square of mesh at the top of the tent, at the hundreds of stars crammed into one patch of sky, trying to figure out where to begin.

"Well, remember the internship my mom got me at the hospital?"

Cass clears his throat. "Yeah."

"She says I have to do it or she's kicking me out."

"Seriously?" Cass's smile disappears, and the outrage in his voice triggers something strange inside. The protectiveness there is so familiar. I suddenly feel like I might cry.

"Yeah," I say, furiously trying to blink back the tears. Crying in front of Caspian Forrester would be a fatal mistake.

I can feel him scanning my face in the dark and I suddenly wish he would pull me into his chest, underneath his heavy arm, like he always used to in sleep. I inch back to my side of the tent, into safer territory.

"So what are you going to do?" he asks.

I close my eyes. "I have no idea. Robbie wants me to move in with him and his cousin, but that sounds like a nightmare. I don't even think I want to date him anymore."

I think, *Why did I just say that?* I'm letting my guard down. Revealing things I haven't even told myself. Making mistakes.

Caspian says, "You don't?"

I try to read his expression but it's hard in the dark.

"I'm not sure."

He swallows. And then an awkward quiet settles on the tent. I listen to the desert sounds. A hundred years pass.

Finally, Caspian clears his throat. "What does your mom think about the Fox?"

I sigh. "She doesn't know about the Fox."

He pauses. "Why don't you tell her?"

Just like Cass, to ask a stupid question like that.

The crying threatens again, and the tear that snakes its way down my cheek makes me feel murderous. I wipe it quickly before Cass can see.

"Are you really asking me that question?" I deflect.

He laughs quietly. "I guess that's fair."

I turn onto my back again, trying to calm the feeling of a hundred bull wasps crawling over my skin. Cass's feet slide noisily against the nylon of his sleeping bag, still restless. Outside something skitters across the ground.

"Can I ask you a question?" he says.

"Sure," I say, eager for a distraction.

"What happened to us?"

The words are unexpected, and they sour the fragile camaraderie of the past few minutes. Suddenly anger flares back up so hot and overwhelming that I can't even speak. I'm so angry at him for not knowing, for even having to ask at all.

"Was it my fault?" he asks, quietly.

I'm watching the silhouette of his profile, which is barely visible, the rise of his lips and nose a sharp, mountainous horizon in the darkness. I can see his mouth part to let his breath out, and it's coming fast, like asking these questions is costing him something. But of course he would never say what it is. The bull wasps become murder hornets. I want to reach out and wrap my hands around his neck, to sting, to swarm, to hurt, to squeeze.

I want to say, *Why do you even care?*

He turns his face toward me, and I can just make out the sweep of his eyelashes blinking in the darkness.

"Are you angry?" he says, ignoring the fact that I still haven't answered anything at all. What I am is so far beyond mad. It's a different emotion altogether.

"Sometimes," I say, finally putting him out of his misery. A small dose of the truth.

In my mind, I try to time travel. I try to think back to all those times of being left behind. All the half-hearted invitations, all the embarrassed looks. I can't let myself forget how much it hurt.

"I'm sorry," he says, dark eyes glittering.

"For what?" I say, then I turn away before he can even answer.

24
Caspian

THE NEXT DAY, AS WE DRIVE through the tiny bottom left corner of Colorado between Moab and Santa Fe, we are caught in a thunderstorm. For a long time the weather seems separate, a glob of purple moving along the horizon, the rain an abstract, slanted line across the deep green plain.

I watch Syd watching the sky, a serious look on her face. Last night, when she told me she was angry, I felt something, sharp and uncomfortable, piercing the cloud of nothingness that always surrounds me. And when I woke up to the muffled light of the sunrise seeping into our tent and looked over at the soft shape of her, chest rising and falling with the easy rhythm of sleep, I felt an almost irresistible impulse to reach out and pull her into me.

We drive southeast, the Cure on the stereo. It is our last drive away from home; tomorrow we will turn around and all of this will end— the cheap, bad convenience-store food and the bickering over the cell phone charger and Syd's growly voice singing to the Clash, the way she winces every time the gas light turns on. My heart feels heavy, like it's not ready to go.

Somewhere far away thunder rolls, steady and contained. Syd's eyes stay glued to the horizon, where the road seems to get swallowed up by the violet-gray color of the storm. Again, I feel that compulsion to reach out and touch her.

She's been quiet this morning, after last night's awkward conversation. Like she was at the beginning of the trip. With everyone else I like the quiet, but with Syd I don't; it frustrates me.

Syd reaches over to turn down the music. Then, suddenly, the storm is right here. We are pushed by the wind and pelted with rain. It glazes the windshield so fast that the worn-out wipers struggle to catch up. I put them on as high as they'll go, but water piles up before the blades can make the return sweep. A truck streaks by us on the two-lane road, the force of it pushing the Jeep toward the shoulder. Syd gasps and I pull the car over to side of the road, turning off the engine and hitting the emergency flashers.

We sit for a moment, safely parked on the wide shoulder, listening to the pounding rain. I fleetingly wonder about the Darlas in their giant van. I try not to panic as I imagine them lurching down the highway.

The thunder arrives then, cracking the sky all the way open. Lightning flashes. The hair on my arms floats up into the air. Electricity from outside seems to fill up the car; the tiny space that's now full of wrappers and coffee cups and discarded layers of clothing is buzzing with this weird energy. It makes me want to turn to Syd and shake her. To say, *Talk to me. Tell me what I did.* But her head is turned away from me, looking out the window as though she can actually see the landscape through the water rushing down the sides of the car.

I look down to where her long fingers curl on the door handle like a threat. It doesn't feel safe, even inside the car, and I try to think of a way to keep her here, out of the rain and lightning. But that's the thing about Syd: you can't make her stay anywhere.

As soon as the thunder begins to recede, she does it, and my heart leaps into my mouth. She flings open the door and jumps out of the car, into the battering rain. I sit there for a few seconds, feeling the way all the energy is drained out of the small space when she leaves it. And then, before I know what I'm doing, I open the door and leap out after her.

The rain is violent. Stinging. It's like standing inside of a car wash. I'm drenched in a second.

Syd starts spinning around with her palms up to the sky, like she's in that Blind Melon music video her dad showed us once, and she looks completely beautiful with her mouth open and hair plastered to her forehead.

She yells out, "FUUUUUUUUUUUUUUCK."

It reminds me of being kids, the easy way curse words would fall right out of her mouth.

The storm ends almost as abruptly as it began, the block of rain moving on to another part of the highway. We stand there for a few minutes, shivering and watching the sky change color.

Then Syd turns to me with a crooked grin and walks back to the car.

We get back in and I crank the heat. Syd starts stripping off her clothing. She's down to her bra before I can react and she's yanking down her jeans when she says, "What are you doing, creep?" And I realize that I am staring, gazing, leering at Syd, at her soft stomach and sharp collarbone and wild limbs, with my mouth wide open.

I can feel my face turning red as I look away, at my rain-covered window. My heart is galloping inside my chest. All I can think is *soft* and *freckles* and *Syd*.

"Shit, sorry."

I close my eyes and start to yank my own shirt off, trying to come back down to earth, but Syd is twisting around in her seat to grab clothes from the back and I end up jamming my elbow right into the flesh below her hip.

"Ouch!" she yelps. And then I try to jerk back and realize that I am somehow truly stuck inside my own shirt. I fumble around, banging my limbs into various parts of the car, until she says, "Here, let me help," and her hands grab the fabric and tug it up over my head in one smooth gesture. She's sort of leaning over me then, almost naked, her smooth, wet, hot skin close to mine. The car is warm and foggy and her hands are on my shoulders and she's looking down into my eyes, all the way down to the dangerous depths. She's almost at the void.

And then I'm possessed by some other version of myself, one who reaches up to tuck my finger under the strap of her bra, sliding up and down her impossibly perfect skin from her collarbone to the end of the flat plane above her breast. A drop of rain falls from her nose onto my forehead. Her breath smells like satsuma mandarins. My mouth waters.

And then, despite all odds, regular me wrests back my consciousness and I grab my hand back, horrified, like I've touched a hot stove, and sort of prop Syd against her seat. *What the fuck are you doing, Cass?* says the voice of reason inside my head.

"I'll get the shirts," I say.

I feel like I might never recover from this, but then Syd laughs and says, "You'd better." And for the first time all day, it feels like she doesn't hate me.

25
Sydney

WHEN WE GET TO SANTA FE it's still raining, although the biblical downpour has slowed to a drizzle. The sky is kind of purple and the buildings are all a bright orange red, even in the flat light of the heavy clouds.

Cass and I haven't talked in almost two hours. We haven't listened to music. The soundtrack of our ride into town is just the rain and the awkward noises our bodies make as we shift around the car, which has shrunken to about half its size since our surprise roadside encounter. In my head is an unspoken loop: *mistake mistake mistake mistake.* In the past twenty-four hours I have made so many mistakes I can't even count.

Like this morning, when I broke up with Robbie via text while Cass was inside the gas station. He called me six times after that, but I didn't pick up.

Or yesterday, when I texted my boss at Amoeba that I wouldn't be back for three more days and he told me that it's fine—I'm off the schedule for the rest of July.

Cass pulls into the lot of a motel called the Shooting Star, stopping in a parking spot right next to the office. He turns off the engine and sits there, staring through the front windshield like he's trying to think of something to say.

"Maybe we should camp tonight," I say half-heartedly, even though I don't really feel like spending the night sleeping on the wet ground. The continual dwindling of funds is grating on me, especially since I now have nowhere to go once all of this is over.

Somehow, in that thought, *nowhere to go*, I find a tiny seed of hope. I look up at the motel. It's a little out of place, a dirty stucco building in a sea of smooth, clean adobe, but it looks safe and warm, with flowery curtains and a hand-painted vacancy sign in the office window. It's our last show with the Darlas, but what if it wasn't? Tonight, I'm in the booth. If I do a good job, maybe they'll take me with them. I think of the stops left on the tour: Austin, New Orleans, Philadelphia, New York. I could find a job. I could find a life. But whatever happens, I'm going to have to figure this out on my own, and a maxed-out credit card is not a good place to begin.

"Are you sure?" Cass says, still not looking at me, watching the rain patter gently on the windshield.

"Let's just wait awhile," I say. "Maybe it'll let up."

Cass nods and swallows, reaching for the door handle, even though he's obviously got nowhere to go. He's right: the air in this car is suffocating.

"I'm gonna take a walk," I say. And then I slip out into the rain.

For some reason, I find myself calling Isabel, the oldest of the Greenfield brood and the one who seems to get me the least.

"You are in deep shit," she says to me when she picks up the phone.

"What else is new?" I say.

"Seriously, though, Mom is beside herself."

I feel a little guilty at that. But not guilty enough to do anything. "She'll get over it," I say. Then I remember that it's a Wednesday afternoon in LA. "Are you at work?"

Isabel is an assistant to a stylist who works her to the bone. She never, ever takes calls during the day.

She sighs. "Yes. I'm hiding inside a bathroom stall right now." She pauses. "I was worried about you."

I feel comforted but also frustrated. They always expect the worst from me. They're not always wrong. I look down at my damp clothing; I am crouching in a doorway to hide from the rain. Six hundred dollars in credit card debt. Feeling completely lost. "I'm fine," I say. "Better than fine."

Even as I say it, tears start welling up.

"Yeah, sure," she says. But I don't think she believes me. Once a fuckup, always a fuckup. The Greenfield motto for failures like me. "Listen, I gotta get back to the fitting. Is there anything I can do?"

"No," I say, swallowing my emotion down. "I really am good. Can you just tell Mom to stop worrying about me?"

"Ha!" Isabel says. "Good one." I hear the sound of a door opening, and then she whispers, "Shit," and hangs up. And I'm all alone on the street.

Later, at a small club on the outskirts of town, I help the Darlas set up their amps and pedal boards. Then I help the sound person mic the drums and check the board. For a while I feel like I'm back in the basement with Dad and he's showing me the inside of his fuzz pedal, the way all the wires come together. *It's about balance*, he'd said. *Input and output. Volume and gain. Clarity and softness.* I forget everything that's wrong in my life as I adjust the knobs and levers until the perfect combination of crackle and melt is achieved.

But I'm not in the basement; for the first time I'm standing at a real mixing board, in a real venue. In a few weeks I could be working at the Fox Theater, where the board changes almost every night and there are two full crews, one for the stage sound and one for the house. Yoko Ono has performed there, and Primus and Metallica. I want the Fox so badly it hurts, even though it's starting to feel impossible.

I'm about to slink off the stage and find a place to hide until the show when Jasmyn says, "Are you okay?"

I look at her kind eyes, her black Stratocaster, and her long purple vintage dress, and for a second I think I could unload everything right here. Could just come out and say, *I'm so, so lost.* But I don't even know where I'd begin.

26
Caspian

WHEN I WAS A KID I was obsessed with other people's mothers. I would stand at the side of the playground and stare like a creep at the mothers on the benches as they fumbled through their bags for a Band-Aid or a tissue, or chatted on their phones. On rare occasions when I was invited to someone's house for a playdate, I would skulk around by the kitchen, waiting for a mother to ask if I wanted a snack, and then I would watch as she'd arrange things on a plate in a way that felt so careful and kind. At night, I would lie in my bed and wrap the word around myself like a blanket: *mother, mother, mother.*

The past few days I've been thinking that word a lot. Because suddenly an image of my mother has started forming in my mind. I can almost picture her here, with the rest of the Darlas, tall and dark, together with everyone else but a little bit separate, like me. She'd sit next to Charlie and they'd both FaceTime home every night, Mom calling me and Dad, telling us jokes, telling us to be good and not get too lonely.

When you were born all the trees were in bloom.

At night, when I think of the words of that song, it almost sounds like she loved me.

• • •

Tonight, when we are all sitting backstage at the club, waiting for our last show with the Darlas to begin, Julia looks at me and says, "Go get your guitar."

I'm sitting on a musty purple couch, obsessively reading through my very short text stream with Kit Molina, trying to find a way to tell her no while also telling her yes. Maybe Calvin could go on this tour, while Cass stays home and does what's expected. Maybe Calvin could have kissed Syd in the car today, while Cass held all the lines firmly in place. If only double lives really worked like that.

I look up, Julia's words having finally trickled down through my consciousness. "My guitar?" I ask, clearing my throat. I slide my phone into my back pocket and adjust my glasses, looking up into Julia's warm blue eyes.

After four days with the Darlas I've learned that Julia is the mom of the moms, the kind who kisses you all over your face and makes you cookies and smooths your hair while you cry. But she's not a pushover.

She crosses her arms, nudging my foot with the toe of her black boot. "The one I know you're hiding in the trunk of your car. Play with us tonight."

I frown. There's only one way she could know that I've got a guitar out there.

I haven't seen Syd since she left me in the parking lot of that motel, with no plan and three hours to kill. I was still, am still, completely wrecked by the feeling of her skin under my pointer finger. Only now, in the face of yet another spilled secret, do I remember how angry with her I was last night when she told everyone I could play.

The problem is, once Julia, Charlie, and Sunny see my mother's guitar, they'll know. Another box will come falling open and I'll have to admit that I've been lying this whole time. I might have to make good on my promise to Syd, to tell them who I am and talk about my mom. I might have to actually start to know her. She might not be safe and loving, like the mom I've begun to hope she was. Or maybe she would be, and that would be worse.

But this is part of the game, Syd and me, tit for tat, and I can't back down from another dare, so I look at Julia and say, "Okay." And then I go out to the parking lot and get it.

When Jasmyn sees me in the hallway, tuning up and trying to hide, she says, "Sick, hand it over."

I give her the guitar, knowing that she's the one person that won't recognize it and hoping no one else finds me back here.

She plays a few quick and quiet riffs—you can barely hear them without the amplification—but her smooth style is unmistakable.

"How did you get so good?" I ask.

"I should be asking you that," she says, raising one eyebrow. She's got intricate eyeliner on tonight; I saw Syd wrangling her onto a stool in the dressing room during the opening act.

"I asked you first," I evade.

She shrugs. "I just never stop. I play all the time. Jules and the kids get pretty annoyed, but"—she shrugs—"you gotta do what you gotta do."

The sound person peeks their head around the corner. "Two minutes," they say.

Jasmyn hands me the guitar back. "This is a really nice guitar, Calvin," she says. I'm probably imagining the gleam in her eye as she turns back down the hallway.

Onstage, waiting for the lights to come up, my heart beats much too fast and I feel lightheaded, like I might fall right over. My hands are shaking on the neck of my guitar. I'm not ready.

In the sound booth, Syd avoids looking at me. Traitor. She didn't talk to me once as she mic'd my guitar amp, except to say, "Could you move over a little?" and, "Okay, play something."

From the front of the stage, Julia looks back at me, down at my guitar, and winks. And then the first song starts, with a G minor from Jasmyn. That's all it takes. My foot starts thumping and my fingers flex against the fretboard and it feels like breathing underwater, like I'm doing this thing that should be impossible but is also as involuntary as the beating of my heart.

I've never played with anyone else before, except for the recordings inside my headphones. This is nothing like that.

I close my eyes and trace the lines of my mother's solos, memorized from hours of listening in the car, every note burning at my fingertips. It's like the first time I ever played, and the first time I ever busked, and the first time I tackled Syd to the grass on the neighbor's front yard and felt her bony eight-year-old body heaving breaths underneath me, making my face burn.

Halfway through our set, I look up through the churning crowd of bodies and catch sight of Syd at the soundboard. I always knew she loved music and that she understood technical aspects of records that were well beyond my grasp. But seeing her there, so intensely focused, so seriously *good* at what she's doing, is a strange surprise. I wonder if this is how she felt when she saw me at the BART station.

She looks up for a second and catches my eye, staring at me with palpable intensity, and she looks so much like her younger self that I almost forgive her. I'm almost glad she's blurted out my secrets. After all, this is our last show. There's not really any more damage to be done.

By the time the music ends I'm high as a kite. I barely notice what everyone is saying to me as they clap me on the back while we put away our instruments. I can barely get myself off of the stage without floating away, right through the ceiling of the club. All I can think of is texting Kit Molina and telling her: I'm in.

But just as I'm fishing my phone out of my backpack, stumbling down the hallway that leads to the back parking lot, past the sound of the next band starting up, it starts to ring in my hands: Dad.

Of course I don't answer, because it does not sound like Yosemite here in the back of this club in Santa Fe, New Mexico. I just stand there, looking at his name on my screen while the phone vibrates in my hand.

For a second I imagine telling him everything. Sitting him down on our shabby couch, the records watching us from the corner of the room. What would he do? What would he say? If I went on this tour, I would have to postpone my entire first semester. Maybe even the whole year.

I open up the voicemail and bring the phone to my ear. The tenderness in his voice is almost startling:

"Hey, guy. I miss you so much. Call your old man when you get a chance, would ya? You know I worry."

Those last words knot in my throat, the reedy tone in his voice, the loneliness. I turn off my phone, tour forgotten, and slide it back into my pocket.

THAT NIGHT, AFTER THE SHOW, THE Darlas invite us back to their Airbnb on the outskirts of town. The mood is festive. It feels like a going away party, for our last night all together. We sit in a giant living room that is decorated with fancy southwestern decor: white couch, crystals, giant circular mirror, the skull of a horned sheep. Charlie plays DJ, going deep into nineties Seattle grunge. Sunny mixes cocktails and mock-tails. Jasmyn and Julia slow dance around the living room.

Cass and I sit on the couch, a little apart, our heads leaned back on the giant pillows. His hand is three inches from mine, which feels both too close and too far away. I can't tell whether he's mad at me for telling Jasmyn and Julia about the guitar in the back of the Jeep, but tonight I'm not that inclined to care.

Sunny takes over as DJ and Charlie plops down on the other side of me. They're wearing black jeans and a crisp white button-down with a silver bolo tie. "Creep" by TLC comes on. "God, I love this song," they say.

I nod. "Me too. I remember my aunt Kelly showing me the music video. I begged my mom to buy me silk pajamas."

Charlie laughs. "Actually, me too. But probably at least twenty years before you did." They lay their head back on the cushions, mirroring

Cass and me. "Hey," they say. "You were good tonight."

I feel my cheeks grow warm from the compliment. "Thanks."

Charlie rolls their head to the side to face me. "Where did you learn to do sound?"

"Lots and lots of bad house shows. And douchey Guitar Hero guys who insist they know what they're doing when they don't."

Charlie nods. "Oh yeah. I've dealt with plenty of those guys."

"They're everywhere."

Charlie clears their throat. "I know you've got your internship and everything, but if you're ever looking for a job, let me know. I know people."

I know it's the kind of thing people say all the time, but for some reason when Charlie says it, I feel a little less adrift. "Thanks," I say.

After a while, Cass gets up and heads for the kitchen and Sunny sits down in his place.

"We were just talking about how amazing Syd is at the sound-board," Charlie says.

I can't tell if it's Charlie or the Tom Collins I've been sipping, but my face feels like it's on fire.

"Well, shit," Sunny says. "I could talk about that all night."

"No thank you." I giggle.

I close my eyes and listen to the song and try to absorb the feeling of these two kind, wise people on either side of me. I don't know when I'll ever feel this good again.

28
Caspian

THE RAIN HAS STOPPED AND THE puddles are black under the midnight sky. Everyone is half-drunk—or completely sober, in the case of Julia and me—and laughing and the kitchen is so full of noise and it's one of those moments where I feel the void even more because my brain is working hard to figure out what it would be like if she were here instead of me. I played her guitar tonight, played her music, note by note. I wonder what she would say if she'd heard me.

I slip out the sliding glass door, onto a weird little half patio that's covered in potted cactuses and painted tile, and I lean my head back on the side of the wall to look at the stars.

"You okay?" says someone out in the darkness, and I realize that the disembodied voice is Julia, across the patio, her face barely visible in the neon orange glow of a cigarette tip.

"I think so," I say. "You?"

"Yeah," she says. Then, "Sometimes all this"—she motions to the warm light of the kitchen, the perfect scene inside it—"is really hard."

I nod, running my hands along the bumpy stucco at my back.

"Do you miss your mom?" Julia says.

"I was really young," I say, giving the easy answer, the one I give to everyone.

"I know," she says. There's a double meaning to the words because now she knows. And I know she knows. And she knows I know. But neither one of us has come out and said it.

"I guess," I say, reconsidering. "It's weird. I don't know if I do or not."

She waits, seeing if I'll say more, or gathering her thoughts, and the kitchen noise floats out into the air around us. "Losing Iris was really hard," she finally says. "I know it's not the same for me. But, fuck, sometimes I don't think I'll ever get over it, and it happened over fifteen years ago."

"What was she like?" I ask, relieved that I'm somewhat hidden in this shadowy corner and Julia can't see my face, can't see how pathetically eager I am for any scrap of the person who made me.

"She was like . . ." Julia pauses, and I can feel the enormity of what she's going to say before she finishes. "The sun. Or maybe the moon. She was always changing, but the feeling of her full glow was unlike anything in this world."

A lump rises in my throat, holding back all my words. This is the moment I've been waiting for. And I don't even know what to ask or say.

"That's all just poetry though," Julia says, crushing out her cigarette, fading back into the darkness. "I don't know. She was beautiful. Quiet and reserved but funny as fuck. She was my best friend."

Again, I try to think of what to say. *This is your chance*, I think. *This is your chance to know her.* But I just stand there for seconds and seconds, my breath coming fast, fear snaking up my legs. I want to ask about the rest of it. About the darkness that swallowed her up, that I sometimes feel is pressing in on me too. But I can't.

The sliding door opens then and Syd slips outside, timing uncanny as usual, and stands right next to where I'm leaning against the wall. She scans the starlit desert.

"Hey, Calvin," she says. "Julia."

And then, "It's fucking beautiful out here."

And then, "Did you know that there are almost seven hundred different kinds of wildflowers in New Mexico?"

And I can't believe that I ever was stupid enough to lose her.

Julia says, "I didn't." She steps into the square of light from the kitchen and smiles a sad smile. "I'm exhausted. You two can crash on the sectional tonight if you don't feel like setting up your tent."

Right before she slips inside, she turns to me and says, "I'm around tomorrow if you want to talk a little more."

I nod, even though she can't see me. Still unable to say a word.

29
Sydney

CASPIAN AND I STAY OUTSIDE ON the patio, even after the house quiets and the inside lights turn off. We're sitting on the ground, leaning back, looking up at the sky and listening to the night sounds of the high desert. Somewhere, a coyote makes its ridiculous yipping-howling sound and for a second I feel like I'm home again, on the cul-de-sac at the bottom of a long, washed-out road.

Tomorrow we'll be turning around and heading back there, to the quiet street and the pink house where my sisters will melt their faces in the backyard and Dad will never be home, where Mom will always be tired, where we will FaceTime with Isabel and Levi on Sundays and things will never change, where I will stay until I disappear.

Caspian is beside me, quiet as a gray wolf, close enough to touch. Every few minutes he makes a hopeless sighing sound. I wonder if he feels as lost as I do.

"Are you all right?" I ask.

He looks helplessly up at the sky, face momentarily open. For a second I think that he might tell me everything. But then he looks down at the ground, runs a hand through his hair, and says, "I'm fine. Just tired."

"Huh," I say, slightly annoyed at the familiar deflection. I used to be okay with the way that Cass never seemed to reveal his thoughts but now I'm not sure if I am. I decide to push a little. "What was it like tonight?" I ask.

Cass just shrugs. "It was all right," he says, faking a yawn.

This time his avoidance makes me angry. I'm over a thousand miles from home, hundreds of dollars in debt, in the middle of New Mexico, risking all the carefully laid plans I had for my life. And yes, I *wanted* to come here, but also, I did this for Cass. And he's just as scared and closed off as he ever was. He's wasting this whole thing.

I'm still angry about last night, about this afternoon, about losing Caspian in the treacherous waters of De Anza High. I'm angry about how he called Hannah fucking Westbrook the girl of his dreams. All of it seethes under the surface, bubbles right up under my skin, as Caspian just sits and sits and sits, not saying anything. And then, finally, when I can't hold it in any longer, I explode.

"Do you really not understand what happened between us?" I say, my voice too loud, even though I'm not sure I understand it myself, except for the one thousand bee stings I felt, for the way the venom poisoned me.

"I don't know," Cass says, sighing deeply, looking away. "I mean. I guess I drifted away for a while. But wasn't I always doing that?"

"Yeah." I nod, clenching my teeth. "You were."

He turns to look at me, face soft and vulnerable, like the spot between the ribs where you're supposed to sink the knife. "But I always came back."

I turn my face toward the blackness of the desert. "Until you didn't," I say.

"I would have." It feels uncertain, like he's convincing himself.

"Maybe. Maybe not."

That's the trouble with what happened to Cass and me. It was so quiet and confusing. He started drifting away, bit by bit, in small, almost imperceptible increments. He started making other friends. Hannah's friends. Friday and Saturday nights weren't mine anymore. By the time I got mad about it, he almost seemed relieved. He was heading toward a place I would never belong and we both knew it. We stopped talking. We sat on opposite ends of our lunch table. And then he was fully absorbed into the throng. Beautiful girlfriend, AP classes, school dances, all of it. And I was left behind.

He shifts beside me, but I will myself not to look, not to help. "I just"—he lets out a frustrated sound— "don't know how to— Fuck. I am so bad at this."

I dig my nails into my palm. Endlessly frustrated. "You gotta figure it out, Cass."

He looks down at the ground. "I know."

Upstairs, someone turns on a light. It paints Cass's cheekbones and the dark circles under his eyes into sharp relief.

Against my better judgment, I ask the question that's been bothering me all day.

"Is Hannah Westbrook really the girl of your dreams?" I say.

He shakes his head, his eyes deep black pools of sadness. "When I'm sleeping, I'm not sure I even dream at all."

The anger I feel when I think about those days is like a thick yellow snake that wraps around my heart, but something about Caspian's deep sorrow unwinds it a little.

I take his hand in mine, and his fingers squeeze tight, like he's afraid I'll take it back. Long seconds pass. His shoulders sag. He knows he's off the hook for now.

"Seven hundred wildflowers?" he says.

I nod, and then he says, "You are the wildest flower of all."

His eyes look right into mine. The impression of where his finger slid along my chest today feels like it's burning. And then he's coming slowly toward me, breathing hard, his fingers reaching out and brushing my cheek. I look past his shoulder at the desert all around us, dark and dangerous.

"There are also seven different species of rattlesnakes," I say, voice shaking. "So you should be careful."

Cass seems to remember himself then, leaning back into his own space, pushing off the ground and dusting off his pants. When I stand up he reaches for me, like there might be more to say, but I slip back through the sliding doors before he can catch my hand.

30
Caspian

IN THE MORNING, I WAKE UP on the sectional sofa in the Darlas' Airbnb, my head and Syd's almost touching at the corner, my fingers somehow tangled in her hair. It's still dark and I lie there for a few minutes, listening to the sounds of Syd breathing and the house settling around us.

When I can't stand the closeness anymore I slip out of bed and sneak into the kitchen. The light is on over the stove and Charlie's there, measuring tea into a metal strainer, their hair sticking up in all directions.

"Hey," they say, voice quiet and raspy from sleep.

"Hi," I whisper, opening a cupboard to try to locate the coffee grounds.

"Over here," Charlie says, gesturing to the drawer next to the stove. "These rentals always have the weirdest kitchen layouts."

Of all the Darlas, Charlie is the least outgoing. Our mutual quietness has made us confidants somehow, together in our ability to be still in the middle of all the noise.

"You're leaving today," they whisper.

"Yeah," I say, fumbling with the coffee maker, trying to figure out how to put the filter in. "I really wish we weren't, though."

"Then don't," Charlie says. Neither of us are really looking at each other, both absorbed in our tasks. I can't think of anything to say, because I want to agree and know that I can't.

Charlie drums fingers across the countertop. They are always drumming quietly on some surface or another, or tapping their foot or whispering something rhythmic under their breath. It's soothing, and I like knowing that there are other people who always have music in their heads.

The kitchen is big and empty, with an island and stools and a breakfast table, and the light from the stove just illuminates our little area by the oven and sink. It's so early that the sun is barely starting to rise on the edge of the horizon. We both turn to watch it for a while, through the back patio doors.

Then Charlie says, "You probably already know this. But you're really, really good at the guitar." They grab the kettle off the stove just as it starts to whistle. "Just like your mom."

I try to respond, but all my words form a glob in my throat. Charlie pours water onto the tea strainer, then leans against the counter for a couple of minutes while it steeps. Neither of us says anything. Then they pat my shoulder once and leave the kitchen, mug in hand.

When the coffee is ready, I pour a cup, black, and then step out the patio doors. It's cold out here; the warm mug feels good in my hands. I stand for a while, watching the way the sun paints everything orange-gold. And then I pull my phone out of my back pocket and call my dad.

"It's early," he says when he answers. I remember that it's an hour earlier in California, probably still dark.

"I couldn't sleep," I lie, "so I walked over to the visitor center. They have Wi-Fi here."

"Ah," he says, his voice heavy with sleep. "So what do you think? Is it as beautiful as you thought it'd be?"

I look out at the seven hundred kinds of wildflowers, gilded in the morning light.

"Even more," I say. And it doesn't even feel like I'm lying.

And then Dad says, "I love you, Cass," in this most gentle way. His third I love you in just one week, and something about it makes my heart falter. I clear my throat, wanting to say something meaningful, but I can't think of anything. I've seen and done so much, but I can't tell him about any of it.

"I'm coming home in two days, Dad," I joke. "Don't get too mushy on me."

I know then that we really are leaving today, and that even though I've gotten out of bed to tell him everything, I won't.

Syd and I clean and pack the car after breakfast. We don't have that much stuff, but somehow it all seems to have exploded across the back seat, littering my car with socks and hair ties and pizza crumbs.

"I feel disgusting just thinking about having eaten so much garbage," Syd says, holding up the plastic wrappings from three different microwaveable bean and cheese burritos.

I laugh half-heartedly but don't say anything back.

My thoughts are anxious and my body feels wrong. It's way too soon for this to be over. Before this trip, I hadn't felt anything in so long, but here it seems like I feel everything—playing guitar on stage with the Darlas, hearing people speak my mother's name, getting mad at Syd and then forgetting that I'm angry, touching her skin and remembering everything, trying to figure out what went so wrong with me.

As everyone gathers in the driveway to say goodbye, I am desperately trying to think of reasons not to go. I am willing Syd to push me like she always does—just a little more time, one more trick, one more show, one more stop. But she doesn't. She just hugs everyone and climbs into the car and curls up in the passenger seat with her bare feet on the dash.

Standing in the gravel of the driveway, Julia puts both hands on my shoulders and looks deep into my eyes. She's applied a fresh coat of red lipstick and she smells like expensive herbal perfume. "I'm so glad you came," she says, "Caspian."

I laugh. "You figured it out."

"The first day." She shrugs. "Seriously though. Your mom would have fucking loved this."

"Thanks," I say, not knowing exactly how to feel about that.

"Call me," she says. "If you want to talk more. If you want to know—"

"I will," I say, pulling gently out of her grasp.

Before I get to the car, Charlie tackles me into a tight squeeze and Jasmyn and Sunny pile on the outside. "Come on, Syd." Julia calls, "Group hug!"

Syd climbs back out of the car and then we all stand in the driveway in a tight knot with Syd and I at the center, until embarrassingly I start to feel like I'm going to cry.

"Okay, okay," I say, making my way through a blur of lipstick kisses and hair ruffling until I'm safely in the driver's seat with the doors closed, the Darlas waving from the lawn.

I pull out of the driveway and onto the street and Syd puts on Radiohead and the music is calm and melancholy, but as we wind through the neighborhood I feel my fingers gripping the wheel tighter and tighter, my heart beating wildly out of time. I think about Ace Hardware, Hannah's basement, the swimming pool in Jake's backyard, our dusty old coffee table, covered in mugs. It all feels like another person's life.

The car starts to feel smaller and hotter, the light too bright. My chest feels tight. I can't do this.

Just before we get to the highway I pull the car over and turn off the radio, parking crookedly, only halfway off the road.

"What's up?" Syd says, looking up from her phone. She isn't wearing any makeup this morning and her black hair is braided into a wispy crown. She looks like a forest creature, the kind that could trick you into sleeping for a thousand years.

I lean my forehead on the steering wheel, trying to catch my thoughts. But then Syd reaches out and puts a small, warm hand on my shoulder. She leans her face down close to mine.

"It's okay," she says.

I swallow, closing my eyes. "I know."

A car swerves around us, honking loudly. Syd startles upright and I open my eyes.

"Shit," I say, and Syd laughs. I realize in this moment that I always want Syd to be laughing.

"One more show?" I say. "I've always wanted to see Texas."

Syd watches me for a moment, like she's trying to see what's behind my eyes. Then she grins.

"Fiiiiiine. Okay. One more."

Five hours later, the Jeep's AC is struggling. The heat of Texas is overwhelming. We are inside of a giant convection oven and the sun is burning us to a crisp, blazing right through the car windows and the T-shirts we've draped over our window-side arms.

Now that we have left New Mexico and driven the car several hours farther away from home, the euphoria of making a rash decision has faded and my brain has tangled itself into a massive knot of panic. I don't know what I'm going to tell Dad when I'm not home on Friday. It's twenty hours from Marfa to El Sob, and there's no way we can make it in time. Syd is going to lose her record store job. My secret is going to be blown. My perfectly compartmentalized life is going to fall apart and I'm going to be swallowed up by this new part of me that I barely recognize, this person who acts irresponsibly and lusts after his former best friend and plays guitar everywhere, not just in the low light of the BART station. I feel like I've made a huge mistake.

I glance over at Syd on the seat beside me. Her shirt is damp with sweat and I am working extra hard not to ogle her chest or her legs, which are folded up against the dashboard in zigzagging lines. This new person possessing my body is clearly someone who *wants*.

With Hannah, things were always good. Sweet. We never had sex in the old-school, patriarchal sense, and I was fine with that, but we got pretty close to it a million times. I always felt grateful for those minutes when the emptiness inside me was dulled and quieted, my hands wrapped around fistfuls of Hannah's smooth golden hair. But something about watching the stretch of bare skin on Syd's back when she leans forward to rifle through the glove box in search of napkins is suddenly a hundred times more thrilling and intimate than anything Hannah and I ever did.

I'm reminding myself for the third time to keep my eyes on the road when Syd reaches over and grabs my arm, hard.

"What was that?" she says, her voice full of something that is either excitement or fear.

I'm shocked back to the present, to the long, straight road and the blaring sun. Megan Thee Stallion is playing, loud, on the stereo, part of the playlist of musicians from Texas that Syd has been making all day.

"What?" I say, confused.

Syd is gesturing wildly, turning her head to look back through the rear windshield. "Behind us. It looked like a giant fucking swimming pool."

I'm still trying to catch up to what she is saying, to break through the heat and the intensity of my own internal monologue and the feeling of Syd's hot fingers digging into my arm.

"Cass. Turn around."

"A swimming pool?"

"Jesus Christ, just pull over," she shouts.

I turn left at the next side road, then flip a U-turn. When we are back on the main road, I see it sparkling in the distance, what looks like the biggest swimming pool I've ever seen. It looks like heaven.

The Darlas are in Marfa tonight but they don't actually have a show; they're visiting some old friends with a new baby. We can make this stop, because for the first time we don't have anywhere to be at 6:00.

We pull the car through two giant stone pillars that say BALMORHEA STATE PARK. People are lying on towels in the shade and swimming in what signs tell us is the world's largest spring-fed swimming pool. It's L-shaped and must be the size of a football field. Everyone we see looks crisp, reanimated; they are moving around in bodies that are the opposite of the listless, lifeless bodies that Syd and I currently inhabit.

We pay the parking fee and find a spot in the giant lot, Syd rifling through the Target bags for the American flag bathing suits we purchased on clearance in the Fourth of July section back in Salt Lake City.

In the locker room, I peel off my clothes in a sweaty stall and try not to think about Syd doing the same thing just across the concrete walkway. The stress thoughts are still buzzing like bees in my head. Dad. Syd. Kit Molina, whom I haven't heard from since two days ago when she texted, **any updates?** And I'd said, **soon!** feeling like the worst kind of loser. But when I set my eyes on the crystalline water, all other thought leaves my mind. I lope across the dead grass and cannonball right over the edge, my body slicing through the heavy heat and then sinking down into the cold, deep water. I stay under for a long time, watching the sun filter through the dark blue. When my lungs are burning I kick my way back up.

"Holy hell, this is amazing," Syd says as she surfaces beside me. I didn't even realize that she was dressed already but now she's here, her body all wavy and discombobulated under the water, like a cubist portrait of itself. I try to keep my eyes on her face, but then I'm looking into her big, dark eyes and feeling dizzy. A drop of water slides down her nose.

"What?" she says.

"Nothing," I say.

"Okay," she says, rolling her eyes and kicking away gracefully.

"It's just like the good old days," Syd says, not a trace of bitterness in her voice.

"Just like the good old days," I repeat. "Race you to the stairs?"

Syd is gone before I even get a chance to kick off the side, but I gain on her quickly, swerving around a couple of kids playing with a beach ball. I'm about to overtake her when she turns and dunks me, and water rushes up my nose.

When I finally get myself to the finish line Syd is waiting, a smug smile on her face. "I win," she says.

"You cheat," I say, my eyes narrowing.

"Whatever, you're just jealous."

I shake my head and then pretend to swim away. When Syd comes after me, I dunk her back, and her claw-like fingers dig into my sides.

For an hour, we float on our backs in the deep, icy water that's a shocking dark blue and full of tiny little fish. I forget about the Darlas, I forget about my dad, I forget about Kit Molina. I almost forget about Syd, except for when she drifts into me and the planes of our forearms touch.

The sun moves across the highest part of the sky. The afternoon comes and goes. The intensity of everything is brought down by the cool temperature of the water and I know that all I need to do is this.

31
Sydney

A WEEK AFTER MY SIXTEENTH BIRTHDAY, I suspected I might be in love with Cass. He was already dating Hannah and I hadn't said a word to him in weeks. The space in my life that he used to inhabit was like a toothache; there was never a time when I didn't feel it. But I stubbornly ignored his calls and texts, unable to shake my anger and embarrassment.

One morning I was walking out to the car when I spotted Cass, sitting on his front porch, staring into space like usual. But the way he looked at me when my screen door slapped against the frame, it felt like he had been waiting for hours. For me. His eyes looked lost, his long hair disheveled and his mouth slightly open so I could just see the gap between his teeth, which I had longed to touch for eight years. He looked so impossibly sad and I wanted to take it from him, to wrap my arms around his sadness and swallow it up.

His lips moved to form the shape of my name and in that moment, my whole life flashed before my eyes. Swallowtail butterflies swarmed my stomach, my head, my chest, my fingertips. My sister honked the horn but I couldn't move my feet.

The town of Marfa is strangely disappointing. There is no show tonight—the Darlas play again in Austin tomorrow. It's a weekday and almost everything is closed. The streets are empty. It feels like no one actually lives here at all.

Underscoring the desolation is Cass's quiet, which feels somehow even quieter than usual. I close my eyes and try to remember yesterday afternoon: Cass staring up at me with actual desire. But already it feels unreal, like it never even happened. Cass is a hundred miles away.

Time seems to move slower out here in the desert. We drive out of town and peek through a chain-link fence to see some Judd sculptures, large and sharp in a soft green-brown field. We get dinner at a restaurant that is too expensive for us, but it's the only thing that's open.

We walk through the plain, square grid of streets, not talking, our footfalls strangely aligned. And even though I'm still mad at Cass for being such a hopeless, hapless, clueless person, I wish I could find a way back to him.

The sun is just starting to bend at the edge of the sky when we find ourselves on a small street, right on the edge of the high desert. And right there at the end of it, the orange-pink sun illuminating the front window in one perfect beam, is a tattoo parlor with a sign in the window that says: ZELDA'S.

"Cass," I breathe, and his face looks as if I've pulled him out of a daydream so deep that he's surprised to be here walking down this street on planet Earth.

"Yeah?" he says, adjusting his glasses along the bridge of his nose.

"Look," I whisper. I point to the shop window and his eyes follow. "Zelda. Remember?" It's like she created this place in the middle of the desert. Just for us. "It's fate."

"Syd," he says, in a voice that brings me straight back to childhood: he sounds nervous and skeptical, in need of a push.

"Cass," I say.

"No," he says, crossing his arms over his chest. "No way."

"Come on!" I say. "We have to. I dare you."

"I am not coming home with a tattoo. My dad would never recover."
When he says that, my dad, there's a flash of sadness behind his eyes.

"Get it on your ass," I say, poking him in the side, in the ticklish
spot right under his ribcage. "He'll never know."

"I am not getting a tattoo on my ass," Cass says, adjusting his
glasses, but now he's laughing and it's exactly the opening I need. I
grab his hand and tug him toward the shop.

"Fine," I say. "Be a baby if you must. But at least come in and keep
me company while I get mine."

Twenty minutes later, we are curled up on a white velvet sofa in the
front window, flipping through binders. Cass, thoughtful as usual,
stares at a page of wildflowers, frowning. I watch his eyes scan the
images, trying to send him telepathic messages. Do it. You might feel
something. You might feel better.

"I'll get a tattoo," he finally says, looking up and meeting my eyes,
"if you call your mother and tell her about the internship." His hair is
tucked behind both ears, and he has the same look of determination
that he did this morning, when he told me that he wanted to keep
going.

"You're out of your mind," I say, voice flat, turning page after page
of hummingbirds, "if you think I'm doing that."

"Who's the baby now?" Cass says. I can't help but feel like he's getting at some bigger truth. I think about Mom, Robbie, the internship,
all the dangling threads of my life that I'm too scared to acknowledge.

Maybe I really will keep going after this, keep moving east, farther and farther out of reach. Maybe I'll forget about the internship altogether and just follow the Darlas to New York. I could stay there and never see anyone ever again. I bet that New York is a place where any kind of freak can fit in.

In the end, of course, we both get one. It's ingrained in us, this pattern: dare, push, bargain, acquiesce. I promise to call my mom. I even let Cass pick my tattoo: a rabbit's foot (for good luck), under the word Zelda, on the side of my ribs. Cass gets a small field of irises right under his heart. I watch his face as he clenches his jaw against the pain of the needle and it's like I can see something inside of him begin to change.

We walk back to the car in darkness and I can't quite see Cass's face but I almost think he might be smiling.

"What are you thinking about?" I ask, feeling that old rush of trying to decipher what's in his head.

"I'm not," he says.

"Cop-out," I say.

"Speaking of cop-outs," Cass says, his shoulder bumping against mine, "it's time for you to call your mom."

We reach the car then and Cass holds out his palm for the keys.

"I'll call her tomorrow," I say. "I promise."

"No way," Cass says. "I just let someone poke me repeatedly with a needle for an hour. It's time for you to hold up your end of the bargain."

"Fine." I sigh, and dig my phone out of my pocket. Inside, I'm terrified, but I don't let him see it. I open the door and slink down into my seat as far as I can go. Then I turn to Cass, who is watching me with his distant eyes. "A little privacy please?"

"Sure," he says. "I'll walk around the block. But you have to show me your phone when I get back, so I can see that you really did it."

"Whatever," I say, rolling my eyes. My hands shake as I pull up her number.

My mother picks up on the second ring, and the mix of panic and tenderness in her voice is startling and sweet. "Sydney?" she asks.

"Hi, Mom."

The warmth quickly cools and hardens into anger. "Where are you?" she says, voice razor-sharp.

"Nowhere," I say. "I'm fine. But—"

"Sydney, do you know how much you scared us? Not showing up for your graduation and then just disappearing for five days without answering any of our calls? What the hell were you thinking?"

The truth is, I've been planning this conversation for days, imagining exactly what I would say, but the wall of her anger and disappointment makes all my words scatter.

"I—" I stammer. "I—"

"You weren't thinking," she says. "Were you?"

I try again. I take a deep breath.

"Look, Mom, I need to—"

Need to what? Suddenly I don't know how to get from here to what I need to say, how to get through the fact that I've disappointed her again, that I've messed up again, that I'm becoming exactly who she expected me to be.

Through the windshield, the world lurches, the sidewalk tilts; through the open window the sound cuts out.

"I need to go," I finish. Then I hang up the phone.

I try to suck in a breath, but already my chest is crushing in on itself. I can vaguely feel my phone vibrating and vibrating down by my feet. My hands are tingling and my forehead is sweating and it feels like death is so close I could reach out and touch it.

Two in, four out. Four in, eight out.

I lean my forehead down onto my knees, willing the world to stop moving so fast. But wave after wave of panic hits me and all I can do is crouch down as small as I can.

A loud voice loops through my head: *you weren't thinking you weren't thinking you weren't thinking what's wrong with you why are you such a—*

"Syd?" Cass's voice drifts in through the window. I hear his footsteps getting closer, feel my car door opening.

"Are you okay?" he asks, so quietly I almost don't hear it.

I can't really talk. If I talk I might start crying and if I start crying I might never stop. Cass rests his hand on my back, gently, carefully, like he's afraid I might break.

With his other hand, he reaches into my bag and digs around until he finds my inhaler. He hands it to me. I take a puff and feel all of the tiny parts of my lungs start to reopen.

"Can you sit up?" he asks, tugging gently on my shoulder. I suddenly feel like a rag doll, like I'd go in any direction if he just pushed a little.

I lean back against my seat and my breath slows down and Cass is staring at the side of my face with an intensity that feels like a beam of light.

I close my eyes. "Just a panic attack," I say, and Cass nods but he doesn't move, not for a long time.

32
Caspian

AFTER A WHILE, WHEN SYD'S BREATH has slowed all the way down
and the color has returned to her face and her long, thin fingers have
finally stopped shaking, we drive out on Highway 90 to try to see the
Marfa lights.

Syd reads the Wikipedia page out loud: *Otherworldly orbs of light,
floating just above the desert, UFOs, will-o'-the-wisp.* She's always loved a
good ghost story. Especially when it means she doesn't have to explain
what's on her mind.

Even though I'm worried about her, I don't push. I don't want to
explain what's on my mind either. I don't think I could if I tried. All I
know is that in two more days, everything is going to fall apart. One
way or another.

I've been thinking a lot about what happened with Syd. Maybe
it started long before Hannah, before high school. There's always
been this feeling with us, this jolt of electricity. Like the needle of
the tattoo gun as it drew the flowers on my skin, hot and stinging.
Syd made me feel alive. She made me feel loud. But she also made
me feel out of control. Syd would never just let me be still, be quiet,
blend in. She was always poking at my secrets, reading my thoughts
and then blurting them out in front of everyone. It was like she
thought if she didn't push, I would never get anywhere. And maybe

she was right. But something about it made me feel exhausted.

When we get to the exact right abandoned stretch of highway, I pull the Jeep over to the side of the road and we climb up onto the hood. The night is warm and full of stars and for a long time we sit side by side without talking at all. I can feel the flutter of Syd's dress against my leg. I can still feel the way her hands trembled in mine when she took the inhaler from me. I didn't like that—Syd pale and shaking and lost. It's not how she used to be.

"Do you believe in ghosts?" she says.

"I don't think so," I say. Without meaning to I think of my mother, climbing into her car, drunk. I shudder. "What about you?"

"Maybe." She looks out into the desert. Her hair is pulled up into a topknot and her ears look small and delicate. "How can anyone ever really know?"

"I guess."

Then we see a light in the distance—a light that truly looks like a ghostly orb of mist. Out of the corner of my eye, I see Syd still, a gasp catching in her throat. But then the light quickly bends and shifts and turns into the headlights of an approaching car.

Syd shrugs. "They say that almost all sightings can be attributed to human light sources of some kind."

I watch her face, the way the disappointment catches for a moment and then slides away like it was never there. I shake my head. "Still, kind of a bummer."

Syd leans back against the windshield, looking up at the sky. "Do you think she's out there somewhere?"

"Who?" I ask, as though I don't know.

"Your mom," she says. "I mean, what do you think happens when we die?"

The question pokes at something inside me. I want to believe that part of her is still alive somewhere. But I don't think I can.

Syd reaches over and tugs at my shirt. "Whatever it is," she says, "I bet it's fucking amazing."

I lean back so that we are shoulder to shoulder and for a while we both just breathe, lying next to the giant stretch of empty highway.

"Hey, Syd?"

"Yeah?"

I clear my throat. "I want you to know that I heard what you said last night. And I'm figuring it out. Sometimes it just takes me a while."

She nods. "I know." Then she sits up and smooths her shirt. "Come on. Let's go."

ON FRIDAY NIGHTS WHEN WE WERE young, Cass and I used to go to Benders. They had five-dollar cheeseburgers and waitresses who would roller skate around the parking lot in little French-maid-looking out-fits and smoke in clusters by the dumpsters on their breaks. I found it all very misogynistic but there was also something weirdly comforting about the way it never changed.

Sometimes it felt like everything was changing, the texture and weight of every experience, and everyone was just transforming into worse and worse versions of themselves. In high school, the guys got more arrogant and entitled. The girls found more ways to bend them-selves into who everyone thought they should be. And anyone who didn't fit neatly into one of those categories was left for dead.

Cass and I were sitting on the curb one Friday night the sum-mer before junior year, drinking vanilla milkshakes, when Hannah walked by with a gaggle of her automaton friends. Cass and Hannah weren't dating yet but he'd been staring at her awkwardly for years. Hannah and her friends were mostly wearing skirts and I marveled at the shiny orange color of Hannah's perfectly shaped legs. They reminded me of playing with Grace's old Barbies, the weird joints where the hips meet the pelvis, the fascinating, permanent high heel shape of the feet.

The girls kept walking but Hannah stopped, turned, and said, "Hey, Cass."

"Hey." He looked up and smiled, and his voice did this weird fake-deep thing.

"Hey," I said, fake deep, copying him.

"Hey, Sydney," Hannah said, as though she was addressing a pile of old mattresses on the sidewalk. She looked back at Cass, playing with the charm on her tiny silver necklace.

"What are you up to tonight?"

I snorted. "You're looking at it."

Hannah fake-smiled, perfect and plastic. "Cool. Well, we're heading up to Ryan's later if you want to come hang. It's not a party party, but his parents are in Tahoe and they just got a hot tub."

I rolled my eyes. "Obviously we don't want to go hot-tubbing with Ryan Jacobsen. We'd probably get ringworm."

Caspian poked an elbow into my side as Hannah's smile curdled.

"Oh, well. Okay, then. I guess I'll just see you on Monday," she said, flouncing off after her ridiculous friends. "Bye, Cass."

Caspian watched the receding wave of blond, and each second he sat there like a drooling idiot filled my stomach with something dark and sticky. When she was out of sight, he set down his milkshake, turned to me, and frowned. "What did you do that for?"

"What?" I shrugged, poking at the gravel with my toe.

Caspian tapped the top of my knee. "You know what."

I stood up, brushing off the backs of my legs. I'd had enough of this stupid night. "Cass. Who cares? Those are not our people."

But his expression stayed stormy as we unlocked our bikes.

Something sharp poked around my guts. Something new. More

than the usual exhaustion of Cass's quest to be a Normal. Whatever it was, it hurt.

Cass was quiet as we rode our bikes through the darkness of town. When we got back to our street he sped ahead and was almost through his front door by the time I stopped in front of the house. Cass and I had watched movies in his living room almost every Friday night since we were eight years old, but there he was, slithering inside like a silverfish.

"Not going to invite me in?" I joked, trying to hide my hurt. He looked toward me but not at me, like he couldn't make out my face, even though I was right under the streetlight.

"Nah," he said. "I'm tired."

"Really?" I tried to study him but he was already turning away again. In my stomach, the poking turned into the stabbing of a hundred little knives.

"Yeah," he said. "I've got to . . ." And the words trailed off as the screen door slammed behind him.

"'Night, Cass!" I yelled half-heartedly as he disappeared up the dark stairs.

I was still for a minute, listening to the soft, oceanic sound of the highway in the distance, to the neighborhood cats rustling in the bushes, to the ridiculous sound of coyotes yelping beyond the eucalyptus trees.

I felt shocked. Cass had just ditched me. Because I insulted Hannah Westbrook. The mixture of feelings that had been building for months threatened to boil over and I started to feel the kind of anger that made me want to do something awful.

I charged up to the Forresters' front door and barged right through, not bothering to knock. Cass's dad was nowhere in sight; the whole house was dark. I took the stairs to Cass's room two at a time and pushed the door open to find him sitting on his bed, curled over his phone.

"What the hell?" I said, out of breath.

Cass looked up at me with a faraway look, his patented Caspian Forrester *I don't want to talk about it* facial expression.

"You're just going to ditch me?" I said.

He sighed. "I'm not ditching you. I just don't feel like hanging out tonight."

"Because of what I said to Hannah?"

Caspian shook his head. "Just forget about it. We can hang tomorrow."

"No." I set my jaw.

"No, what? You don't want to see me tomorrow?"

"No. I'm not going to forget about it."

Caspian sighed in frustration, tugging on the ends of his long dark hair. Next to him on the bed, his phone lit up.

"Who are you texting?"

"Nobody." He flipped it over. My jaw fell open in disbelief.

"What are you doing?" I asked.

"I'm just trying to be . . ." *Normal.* That was the unspoken word at the end of the sentence.

"God. You are such a fucking sellout."

"Not everyone wants to be like you." The words hit me like a slap. Even worse was what he didn't say. Like you: a freak, a weirdo, *not* normal.

"Got it," I said, spinning on my heel to leave.

"Syd, come on." Caspian tugged at his hair. Next to him on the bed, his phone was jumping up and down like a cricket.

But I was already halfway back down the stairs and out the front door, just in time to see Hannah's dark green pickup truck pulling up outside.

On the way back to the campsite, the desert is so dark. An inky, nothing dark. My favorite kind. Inside my head there's nothing but a pleasant sort of calm buzz, the kind that usually comes after the panic has gone away.

We pass an orange streetlight and see hundreds of bats swarming around it, fluttering in and out, battling for the insects that must be gathered there.

"A slaughter," I say.

And Caspian says, "Tell me about it."

He leans sleepily over onto my shoulder. It has been the longest of days.

When we get back to the spot where we pitched our tent this afternoon—a campsite in a long row of other identical campsites, all square patches of dirt with rusty barbecues and campfire barrels—it's quiet and dark; most people seem to be asleep.

I'm not ready to go to bed yet, so I lay out the towels in front of our tent, and on my back I watch the sky that's riddled with stars and seems to be somehow off-kilter, in a good way, like you can actually feel the world turning on the edge of the horizon.

Something about the otherworldliness of this place is calming. I always feel that way about things that are strange, weird, unusual. I feel that way about the Darlas too. It's nice to have this night off but I'm excited to be in Austin tomorrow, unloading amps and untangling microphone cables.

After a while Cass comes out and thunks down beside me. His Caspian smell washes over the desert smell and for a moment his presence seems to eclipse everything, even the stars.

"I thought you were sleeping," I say.

"Nah," he says. "I was waiting up. But you never came."

There's a pause after he says that, as we both feel the meaning of the words settle in.

Then he's lying back next to me, our hair mixing together on the ground. Our hands are millimeters apart, hotter between our skin than the rest of this desert, which is still an ungodly Texas hot. I can feel Cass holding his breath next to me, can feel the thrum of his blood behind his skin and it's truly perplexing. I don't know what to make of this particular rhythm.

What is happening to us? I think.

"You scared me back there," Cass says after a while.

"My favorite," I say.

Cass doesn't laugh. "Seriously, though. Does that happen a lot?"

"It used to. And then I saw this therapist for a while and it stopped. But it's been happening again lately. I don't know why."

Caspian's face is serious and sweet in the darkness. "Maybe you should start seeing them again."

"Maybe you should too," I say.

He scratches his eyebrow and says, "You're probably right."

That's when we see the first shooting star. I almost can't believe

I'm seeing it, even while I'm seeing it. It's slow moving, covering an inch or more of sky before it disappears.

"Did you see that?" Cass whispers. I look over and his eyes are wide behind his glasses.

"I did." I smile, without even meaning to.

There's another one and another. Stars falling through the universe, slow and bright and silent. And then Cass looks away from the sky, props himself up on his elbow, and looks right down into my eyes. His tongue slides over the gap between his teeth.

I feel like I'm a snake charmer. Like I've been trying my whole life to lure Caspian out into the light and every time I'm almost there he slinks back inside himself. But now here he is, hovering over me, his head floating in some inhuman and beautiful way, his outline awash in starlight. It's too dark to really see his face but I feel the intensity of it as he lowers himself slowly, slowly, slowly down. Until his nose is touching mine, until we are breathing each other's breath, until his eyes double and triple in my blurred vision and I feel my heart beating behind my belly button.

His lips brush against mine, just barely, but it's shocking, like two dry objects making a spark. I remember an experiment in Chem class on electrical charges; there was a glass wand, a balloon, a rabbit pelt. In this moment, he's the pelt and I'm the balloon, or I'm the wand and he's the electricity, or I'm the balloon and he's the experiment. All these combinations are circling and circling as Caspian's lips, hot and full of sparks, press against mine.

And then, just like that, we are kissing. His hand is holding the side of my face and his lips are pressing and moving in this way that is so sure and insistent, so utterly un-Caspian. It is hot and perfect;

I feel it everywhere. And then Cass's body is slanting down, pressing mine into the blanket, his knee between my knees, his hand moving down toward my hip. I am overpowered by this kiss, drugged by it. Suddenly Caspian is the snake charmer and I might never snap out of this spell.

We kiss for what feels like an hour, or maybe only a handful of minutes. Both. Neither. It's hard to tell. Our hands have moved inside of each other's clothing, are roaming over inches and inches of hot skin. His fingers brush against the gauze that's covering my tattoo and the sting reminds me that something about this is permanent. I'm never going to forget.

And then, seemingly out of nowhere, I remember the other thing that I was never supposed to forget. A hundred old hurts tumble out of a closet that's been closed up tight for years, and everything lands like a pile of old shoes in the space between our chests.

Caspian is a deserter, a betrayer. He is not safe.

"I can't do this," I whisper, pushing the words against his lips, forcing them to stop.

"What?" Caspian says, his eyes hazy with lust, sweaty hair matted against his forehead.

I bolt upright, pushing him up with my hand so as not to knock our teeth together.

"I'm going to bed," I say, smoothing my damp and wrinkled shirt.

Cass looks confused and crestfallen as he runs a hand through his hair. Then he turns away, facing the endless expanse of open desert. If Caspian has a feeling about all this, I'm sure to never know it.

"Yeah," he says, his voice composed. "Sure."

• • •

Later, when I'm in the tent, lying on top of my sleeping bag, trying to escape the itching heat of the Texas air, when Caspian starts sleep-breathing in the way I've listened for since I was a child, when I'm satisfied that the moment has been sufficiently ripped apart, I let myself combust. Hundreds and hundreds of tears come, every single doubt and fear. I shake with them, silently, long into the night.

34
Caspian

ON THE DRIVE TO AUSTIN, SYD is like a cartoon version of herself. I thought that after last night she might not be up for talking today, but instead she is talking constantly, about everything: the color of the sky, the heat, every species of animal that inhabits the state of Texas. It's like if she doesn't leave any spaces in the conversation, she won't have to address what happened.

For the first time, maybe in my whole life, I actually want to address it. I want to tell Syd about how good it felt to kiss her. How surprising the whole thing was. How in one single second it was like all these questions I hadn't even known I was asking were being answered with the word *yes*. I want to talk about the way, after Syd slunk back into the tent, I pulled out my phone and texted Kit Molina: **I'll do it.**

But of course the one time I actually want to reveal what's happening inside my head, Syd won't let me get a word in edgewise. Three hours pass in a blur of Syd rambling and me trying to put together sentences in my mind:

I think we need to

I think I want to

What if we just

And before I know it we are pulling up to the club and Syd is tumbling out of the car, almost before it stops, like an action hero. I sigh and pull my phone out of my pocket, looking for a text from Kit. There's nothing there.

I sit for a while in the front seat, leaning my head against the steering wheel. My tattoo itches and stings. I run my thumb over the screen of my phone, knowing that I need to call Dad. There's no way we are making it home tomorrow. It should bother me more, this inevitable collision with the truth, but for some reason it doesn't. For now, I'm here, and that's enough.

The Darlas pull up twenty minutes later and tackle us into another group hug. We'd texted them from the car that we were coming, and Julia had said: Fuck yes my back is dying. And Jasmyn wrote: YES but also are you sure it's ok logistics wise? And Sunny had written: They're adults! And Jasmyn replied: I don't want to think about Geo road-tripping at 18 with a bunch of 40-year-olds! And then the group chat had devolved into a back-and-forth about being forty and having kids and growing up, so I'd written, Aren't you all in the same car? and turned off the notifications. Charlie texted me separately: You're playing tonight right? And I'd said, OK.

By the time we are all set up and waiting in the greenroom, Syd is already rip-roaring drunk. It's a state I've been in many times before but for some reason, here, with the Darlas, the specter of my mother so close, it doesn't feel right. She slinks out to the bar and comes back with another drink that smells like rubbing alcohol, and when I say, "You want to slow down a little?" she sneers at me, turns on her heel, and marches right back out.

That *here* feeling starts to wobble and disappear, like the top part of the road in a heat mirage when we are driving on the highway. I check my phone again. Nothing but a text from Dad: **See you tomorrow.**

When I'm onstage, the music is like mud. I'm off tonight and everyone knows it. Julia turns around after the third song and whispers, "Are you okay?"

I just nod and lean down to adjust my pedals so she can't look too closely at my face. This has never happened to me before. Always, *always,* the music just comes.

I'm starting to get this feeling like a cartoon character who has run right off a cliff without noticing, and then suddenly they notice and just before they start plummeting toward the earth, reality sets in. I've gone really, really far out on a limb here.

Worse, I suddenly can't be up on stage without thinking of my mother, without feeling like she's right next to me, trying to play her guitar, swaying and smelling like vodka, like Syd. And every time I look at Julia or Charlie or Sunny, that question I've pushed deep down keeps bubbling right up to the surface, covered in anger, thick and hot: *How could you have let her do it?* I grit my teeth and push through the rest of the set. I have to focus. I can't let the band down. I hit every note, but there's no feeling.

After the show, Syd has clearly forgotten about feeling insulted by my comment because she corners me at the end of the hallway, a dangerous look in her dark eyes. I'm feeling awful enough to be leveled by it, to let go of the fact that neither of us can say what this is and that we could be heading for disaster, to turn the tables and flip her around so that I'm pressing her against the wall with the full weight of me. She smells like jasmine and honeysuckle and everything I never knew I always wanted. But when she lurches up and kisses me, it's sloppy and tastes like liquor. My hand, which is trailing up under the back of her skirt, stops. My lips stop.

Syd pulls back, a question in her eyes.

"I can't do this right now," I say, and then I push through the back door and into the parking lot.

In the morning, at our sticky hot campsite just outside Austin city limits, Syd at least has the decency to look a little sheepish.

"Sorry about last night," she says, her voice raspy and sweet. She's looking down at where her hand is wrapped around her water bottle, not into my eyes. I stare at her long dark eyelashes, at the freckles on her nose. I can't get over the way that every single part of her is the same, but the sum of the details is somehow wholly different. I can't look at her black heap of hair without wanting to bury my face in it.

"It's fine," I say, unable to think of anything else. All the words that were ready to burst out yesterday have scattered. "We should hit the road. It's late and it's eight hours to New Orleans."

"New Orleans?" Syd says, raising her eyebrows. "I thought we were going home."

I smile, a peace offering. "At this point we won't make it back in time no matter what we do."

Syd takes a long sip of water. "Amoeba took me off the schedule for July," she says. "So I guess I'm also free."

"Shit, Syd," I say, feeling instantly guilty for not thinking more about how this trip might be messing with her life. "I'm so sorry, I didn't realize."

She shrugs. "It's okay. Let's just not talk about it."

My phone vibrates at my side.

Dad: What time will you be home tonight?

I don't write back. I still haven't figured out what to say.

"Ugh," Syd blanches, unaware of my inner turmoil. "I don't think I can handle the car right now. Can we get coffee first? My treat."

I look at Syd, with her messy hair and red morning cheeks and sorry eyes and kissable mouth and I want to just forget about everything else but this.

"Sure," I say. "Let's go."

We eat a breakfast of four-dollar croissants and six-dollar coffees at an outdoor cafe where the kitchen is an airstream trailer and the tables are surrounded by succulents that look like they came straight from San Francisco. Syd winces as the barista runs the credit card. "We okay?" I ask.

"I think so," she says, recording the transaction in her notes app.

I keep checking my phone, looking for a text from Kit. Nothing.

"Why do you keep doing that?" Syd asks.

"No reason," I say, sliding it back into my pocket.

"So we're back to this then," Syd says, stirring her coffee and looking out at the street. I'm instantly annoyed that she's accusing me of avoiding anything after the past twenty-four hours.

"Same as it ever was." I shrug, quoting our old favorite Talking Heads song.

Despite the frustration, I want to cross the space between us, to touch the back of Syd's neck or the pale, freckled top of her shoulder. But Syd has clearly set up some kind of epic, impenetrable force field. I can't figure out how to cross it.

Then she surprises me by sweeping her crumbs up with a napkin and grabbing my hand, motioning with her head toward the street. "C'mon," she says. "Let's walk around for a minute." It's getting late if we want to make it to New Orleans in time for load-in, but with Syd's hand soft in mine it's hard to say no to anything.

We wander through the heat of downtown Austin, counting cracks in the sidewalk like we used to. It's quiet between us, the ghost of what we did two days ago looming in the middle space between our bodies.

My whole life with Syd, before we fell apart, she was the one propelling us forward, forcing me to dye my hair black in third grade, to ride my bike all the way down our steep hill without using the brakes, to listen to the Clash, to dance, ask questions, talk to people. I'm not sure what to do now that we are walking side by side, Syd just as spooked and slow as I ever was.

We pass a bar with a giant cowboy boot-shaped sign over the door. Flyers taped to the glass advertise happy hour, trivia night, a show headlined by a band called the Jolly Ranchers. I slow down a little to pause for a moment in the shade. Syd turns away from me, looking off down the street.

I clear my throat. I guess, this time, it's up to me. If we are going to figure this out, I have to be the one to take the risk.

"Hey, Syd," I say, tugging on her hand. "We need to talk."

"Cass," she says, looking straight ahead. "We really don't."

I study her profile, the sharp nose and soft mouth. This feels delicate. I have to be so careful and slow if I'm going to even have a chance.

"Syd," I say. "I—"

"Hey, look!" Syd starts walking again, faster than before, and somehow, despite my being almost twice her size, I have to jog a little to keep up. And then she stops dead in front of a shop window that's covered in tapestries. A neon sign that says PSYCHIC hangs in the window.

"Syd," I say, wiping at the sweat on my brow. I'm pleading.

"Come on," she says. Another dare.

I look down at my watch. My tattoo is still stinging under my shirt. "We have to talk. And go back to the car. We're going to be late if we don't."

"We have plenty of time," says Syd, despite not having looked at a clock all morning. And then she opens the door and disappears inside the shop.

I stand on the sidewalk for a few minutes, sweating and shaking my head, wondering how things have gone so sideways. Why can't Syd ever just hear me when I try to tell her no?

I wait for a while to see if she'll come out. She doesn't. Resigned, I step inside. It takes my eyes a moment to adjust to the darkness after the blinding white Texas sunshine. The windows and walls are covered in scarves and tapestries, and the only light in the room comes from a wooden lamp that's shaped like a wave. A counter and shelves on one side of the shop display various crystals, tarot decks, and jars of herbs, and a low table surrounded by white cushions fills the space near the window. Syd is leaning against the counter, chatting with a person who looks like they could be one of the Darlas—white, somewhere in their forties, with long, stick-straight blond hair and a nose ring.

Syd has chosen black lipstick today, applied in the sun visor mirror, and she is wearing black from head to toe; she sort of looks like she should be the one behind the counter, not this cheerful-looking blonde with giant, clear-rimmed glasses.

"You must be Cass," the person says, smiling like I'm a long lost relative. "I'm Rainy. She/her."

I frown at my name. Of course, Syd has probably told her my entire life story in the ninety seconds they've been alone in here.

"I heard you guys are broke," Rainy says. "But I've got some time before my next appointment and I'd be happy to give you a free reading if you'd like."

I start to say, "I'm good," but Syd steps on my toes and says, "Yes, definitely."

Rainy raises an eyebrow at me and says, "Are you sure?"

It feels like resistance is futile. Especially as Syd grins and says, "Cass will go first."

I'm annoyed but past the point of struggle. I nod and walk over toward the cushions, just wanting to get it over with.

Rainy grabs a ragged-looking deck of tarot cards from under the counter and plops down across from me. She begins shuffling the deck, which is black with white suns on the backs of all the cards.

"I'll just do a quick spread," Rainy says, scanning my face. It feels like she's looking right inside my head. Like she can hear my heart picking up speed. "It seems like you're in a hurry."

Syd, still leaning on the counter, raises her eyebrows and says, "Wow, you're good."

But Rainy just shrugs and says to me, "You've checked your watch twice since you walked in the door."

"Sorry," I say, not sure why I'm saying it. "We just have a long drive ahead."

Rainy nods and says, "Got it."

She starts talking about the tarot, the Major Arcana, which she explains is an archetypal story for the journey through life, and the Minor Arcana, which are split into four suits like playing cards. She tells us that the cups represent the heart, the swords the mind, the wands passion, and the pentacles the earth and physical world. Rainy's voice is soothing, like she knows that I feel like I'm crawling out of my skin.

She stops shuffling and hands me the cards, which are a little larger and heavier than playing cards, worn soft at the edges. "A musician," she says, noticing the callouses on the fingers of my left hand. Then she smiles and says, "Shuffle, and then pick one."

I look down at the table and start moving the deck through my hands. I shuffle and shuffle, trying to figure out how long is long enough. All I want is for this to be over, to be back in the car, heading east, driving away.

The cards are cool and I keep seeing little flashes of color peeking out behind the black. Eventually, when I feel like maybe it's been enough time, I pull one out and lay it down.

The card has a yellow sky and a person in a flowery outfit with a kit bag, who looks like they're about to step off a cliff. It doesn't feel like a good start.

"The fool," Rainy says, smiling. "You're on a journey. But anyone could have told you that. Pick another one."

I start shuffling again, feeling awkward under Rainy's and Syd's gazes. I lose my rhythm and a second card falls out of the deck and lands on the table. A queen, sitting on a throne next to the sea. It's upside down. "Queen of cups," Rainy says, raising her eyebrows. "In reverse . . . interesting. Okay, pick one more."

The back of my neck is starting to feel prickly and hot. I want to just get up and leave but that would be awkward, so I reach into the deck and pull out one more. This one looks ominous: a blindfolded person sitting on a bench and raising two swords, crossed in the air.

"Two of swords," she says. "Interesting. Okay."

"You keep saying that," I grumble.

"Don't be grumpy," says Syd, who has made her way across the room and is now perching on the windowsill near my right hand. She's watching closely, obviously thrilled to be granted this view into my future, my inner world.

Rainy laughs. "It's all right," she says. "The cards are not for every-one. We can stop any time you want. But honestly, this is a great spread. Do you want me to tell you about it?" There's something careful in her voice; she knows how weird this is for me.

"Okay," I say.

"Well . . ." She pauses. "It seems like—the fool card says you're on this journey, following your mom's band, Syd told me about that, but there's more to it too, isn't there? There's something about yourself that you're trying to discover. And the fool is telling me that you're on the right path. Whatever you're doing, you're doing it right."

Whether or not Rainy has any kind of psychic gift, that one can't be true.

Rainy stops, bites her lip. "I mean, there will be ups and downs. The fool's journey goes through the entire Major Arcana. The lovers"—she eyes Syd—"the world. Death. All of it. It will bring you to your knees. But it will also bring you to yourself."

She pauses, as if to let the words sink in. I look at Syd and Syd looks at me, and for a moment everything—love, anger, resentment, grief—hangs in the air between us.

Then Rainy touches the center card. I notice the way the sea laps at the queen's feet. "And your mother, well, wow."

My mother.

It hits me like a ton of bricks.

"She must have been amazing. The queen of cups is creative and eccentric and pure of heart. But the way you've drawn it, it's reversed. That means there's some resistance there. Some kind of entanglement. Maybe some darkness." I try to keep my breathing slow and steady, to maintain an air of nonchalance, but she's looking at me like she can see it all, even the things I can't.

"Ah," she says, nodding. "So that's what the journey is about."

Syd's gone quiet next to me. I can't tell how I feel about her being here, or about any of this. Under the table my hand starts to tremble.

Rainy's quiet for a long time, touching the card on the table, right at the spot that would be my mother's face. Above our heads, the air conditioner clicks on and cold air comes down the back of my neck, making me shiver. I feel a pressure building in my chest, like I'm right at the edge, like something is about to break.

"Do you . . ." Rainy says, hesitantly. "Do you want me to try to contact her? I can do that sometimes."

I don't know what to say to that; I'm a little stunned. My brain is still stuck on the queen of cups. I feel like all of this is happening way too fast.

"I don't think—" I start to say, but Syd looks at me, insistent.

"Cass," she breathes. "You have to."

I look back at her, not sure what to say. She gestures toward the door.

"I can go," she says, "if you want."

"No. It's okay. Stay."

I close my eyes. Push it all back down. This is stupid. I don't believe in tarot or psychics. I don't believe in ghosts. I might as well take the path of least resistance.

"Fine," I say to Rainy, trying to convey how little it matters to me.

She studies my face again and nods slowly. "Just give me a second," she says, closing her eyes.

I expect her to light some candles or incense or start chanting but instead she just takes a few deep breaths, and I watch as a calm settles over her features. "Can you tell me your mother's full name?" she says.

I think, This is it? No flashing lights, no eyes rolling back into heads. Just the three of us sitting in the dim light of the shop.

"Iris Madeline McCarthy," I say. The words feel strange in my mouth and I wonder if I've ever actually said them aloud.

"Okay," she says, and then she's quiet for a moment. "Does she have long dark hair?"

I nod.

"Wild eyes?"

Syd whispers, "Definitely."

"Okay," Rainy says, folding her hands in her lap. "I think she's here."

This isn't real. I tell myself. None of this is real.

Rainy closes her eyes. "Is there anything you want to ask?"

What a fucking question. I almost choke on it.

"I should warn you," Rainy says, "she's been gone a long time. So she's not exactly how she used to be. She's a little more . . . distant, maybe."

I'm quiet for a long time. The air is cold; the air conditioner is still blasting. I know my mother isn't here. I don't believe in things like this.

But what if she was? What if she's been there this whole time, my whole life, just watching me struggle, watching Dad fade into nothing?

I realize that Rainy and Syd are both looking at me, waiting for me to say something. *None of this is real*, I think again. Still, I ask it, the question that's been pressing on the back of my eyelids every time I try to go to sleep.

"What happened?"

Rainy is quiet for a moment, like she's listening for a sound, a signal. Then, "Are you sure you want to know?"

I nod. *Just a couple more minutes*, I think. *It's almost over.*

Rainy closes her eyes, exhales. "It seems like . . . I think she's saying . . ." She takes another deep breath. "She just got to a point in her life where it felt like she got stuck. You know?"

I nod again. In my mind I'm inching toward the door.

"She's telling me that you have it too. That feeling. Like you love your life, your people. In some ways your love is your greatest gift. But there's another part of you that could just walk away and leave everything behind. It was like that for her."

Rainy opens her eyes; she looks a little hesitant, like she knows she should stop but she can't help it.

I take a breath. *You're okay.* "But she couldn't leave," Rainy says. "So." She clears her throat. "She left in her mind."

"Oh," I say, suddenly realizing with absolute certainty that I need to get out of here. Two words begin to repeat like a riff on my loop station pedal, *She left she left she left she left she left she left she left she left she left.*

Somewhere in this room, Rainy is still talking. "She says, or . . . it seems like she's . . . she wants you to know something about the music. She says that the music is the thread that connects you . . ."

I can't really hear anything after that because a hot wave of panic rushes over my entire body. I stand all the way up from the floor in one jerky motion, almost knocking over the table. The two of swords flutters to the ground.

"I have to go," I say. "I really have to go."

I run out the door, down the street, all the way back to the car. I can hear Syd's red cowboy boots clomping down the pavement behind me but I don't turn around.

I'm sitting in the driver's seat, head resting on the wheel, trying to calm my breathing, when my cell phone buzzes with one text, then another:

Kit Molina: I'm so sorry Cass, we ended up finding someone else for the tour.

Kit Molina: I still want you to come in when you get back!

I read it only once before shoving my phone into the glove compartment and slamming it shut with enough force to make the whole car shake.

Syd opens her door and slides in next to me, wheezing and searching through her purse for her inhaler.

"Cass," she says, once we've both caught our breath. "Talk to me."

I turn the engine, silently, and pull out onto the street.

When we hit the gridlock traffic on the outskirts of New Orleans seven hours later, it's so late that the sun is already sinking. We've missed load-in and sound check and it's starting to feel like everything is finally beginning to unravel. At the corners of my mind, a dark, muddy sludge is oozing down.

Syd and I haven't spoken, or rather, I haven't spoken, except to work out the logistics of texting Julia and finding our way to the club. Syd's been playing music and commenting on the scenery but I can't really hear it. All I can hear is that one riff: *she left she left she left she left she left she left.* It's so different from the way I heard Gram describe it once, to a neighbor: "She was taken, too soon." Somehow Rainy's description feels more accurate.

By the time we reach the traffic jam, the words in my head are clanging louder and louder. Underneath them is the heavy bass line of disappointment, of failure, of Kit's text. I should have said yes. I should have just fucking said yes the minute she asked. But I didn't because I never do. Because I'm a coward and a loser and I'm never going anywhere.

The sky looks like it's on fire; the pollution of the city has made everything bright pink and orange above the swampy line of trees by the side of the road. Inside the car, the air is hot and stuffy. Syd keeps fiddling with the AC but nothing seems to affect the blazing heat blasting through the vents, right at my face. The volume in my head gets louder still. Syd rolls down the window, letting in the smell of exhaust.

And that's when the front of the car starts smoking. A cloud of grayish black billows out, smelling like burnt plastic and oil. Immediately, all of the anger and emptiness trapped inside me surges to the surface in a great big, "FUUUUUUUUUCK."

"Cass, pull over," Syd says, her voice unusually calm.

"Thanks, Captain Obvious," I reply, turning on my blinker and inching across the lanes of traffic. There's a glut of cars and they all try to move to let us over but it takes forever because they are all a little bit stuck. The front of the Jeep continues to let out a steady stream of suffocating smoke.

A drop of sweat rolls down my forehead as I finally pull onto the shoulder and turn off the car. Now that the engine is quiet, everything else is suddenly very loud. Beyond the hissing of the radiator and the disgruntled screeching of all the cars limping by, it sounds like a million bugs are chirping right outside the window. About a hundred feet ahead the road turns into a causeway, crossing a giant stretch of water that's probably filled with alligators. The smoke begins to slow but the air is still thick and humid.

"Cass, say something," Syd says.

I close my eyes. "What the fuck are we going to do?" It comes out sharper than I mean it to. Or maybe I mean it to be sharp. Maybe I want it to hurt a little. This, all of this, feels like some big game that Syd pulled me into. The traffic, the psychic, getting drunk at our show, the tattoos, the kissing, the Darlas, everything. And now I'm so fucking far away from where I started and I don't recognize myself at all. *How did I get here how did I get here how did I get here how did I get here.*

Syd takes a breath, like she sees my anger and is carefully trying to navigate her way around it. "Do you have roadside assistance?" she asks. She glances nervously around my car. Both of us know we can't afford a breakdown like this.

"I can't use it," I say. "They'll contact my dad."

She sighs. "Maybe it's time to contact your dad."

"No," I say. "No way."

At that exact moment, as if to prove Syd right, my phone starts vibrating in my pocket: Dad. I ignore the call but it rings again. And again. And again. When I reject the call a fourth time, I get a text:

WHERE ARE YOU.

And that's when I remember that today is the day I'm supposed to come home.

"Fuck!" I yell, punching my fist against the steering wheel. Syd jumps in her seat. "Fuck fuck fuck!" I pull up my text thread with Jake, trying to think of a way to cover this, but I can't. It's done. The finality of it all sinks into my stomach, bringing with it a wave of nausea.

Syd says, "I'll call a tow truck company, then." And she lets herself out of the car.

I stare down at the screen of my phone until it goes black again, trying to think of something to say. I can't let my dad just wait for me, thinking something happened, that I'm dead on the highway somewhere like Mom was.

Don't worry, I write. **I'm safe.**

The phone starts vibrating again. Three more calls. And then:

Not when I find you.

I'm with Syd, I write.

Syd isn't even your friend anymore, Dad writes back.

Touché, Dad. Touché.

Look, I say. **My car broke down and I'm waiting for a tow truck and I can't really talk right now. I'll call you in the morning.**

I sit there, closing my eyes, waiting for a response, afraid of what he'll say. But he doesn't write back, which is almost scarier.

It's hot in the car, so hot that my face, neck, and back are all sweating profusely. My hair is glued to my cheek. I get out and walk around to where Syd is perched on the guardrail, looking down at her phone.

"Tow truck will be here in two hours," she says, looking annoyed.

I'm still shaking with anger, so I don't say anything. She searches my face, like she's looking for a way in. When she sees that there isn't one, she shrugs to herself and turns back to the highway. I squeeze my eyes shut, trying to block out the world.

"Holy shit!" Syd says, just as I feel a whooshing gust of wind directly over my head.

I open my eyes to see three pelicans landing gracefully on the hood of my car.

Syd stares for a few seconds, with her mouth wide open. The birds just stand there, as if untroubled by the burning plastic smell, moving only their heads to peer around them. They are large, with gray-and-brown feathered bodies and long white necks. Syd starts furiously typing into her phone.

I see a man in a Baltimore Orioles hat climb out of his car and start filming.

"Brown pelicans," Syd says excitedly. "I think these are juveniles." She keeps reading. "They were on the endangered species list for almost fifty years." Syd carefully takes a few steps toward the Jeep. "Wow, this is so amazing."

I don't say anything. I just sit there, hands gripping the guardrail, watching the giant birds preening on my car as the last bit of light leaches out of the sky. The hood is no longer smoking, but the air is full of exhaust. More people, seemingly resigned that traffic is going nowhere, have gotten out of their cars to look at the birds.

Syd turns to me with a goofy grin. "Maybe this is some kind of sign. Maybe it's Zelda. Maybe she wants us to—"

"Would you stop?" I snap.

"Stop what?" she says, as if she can't see how bad this is.

And the fact that she's pretending she doesn't understand is the thing that pushes me over the edge. For two days she's been joking and deflecting. And meanwhile, I've been slowly imploding, all these small disasters converging into this one moment. It's like this whole time, the void has been steadily filling up with anger and emptiness and now the entire thing is about to rupture outward, turning my entire body to confetti, sprinkling bits of my guts all over the cars on the highway.

"Stop pushing me!" I yell, my hands pulling at my hair. "Just fucking stop."

Syd looks like she's been kicked. Her sad brown eyes are somehow even sadder.

"Okay," she says. "Jeez."

On the hood of the car, one of the pelicans extends its wings outward and makes an awful screeching sound.

"No. Not okay." I shake my head. "This is not okay."

Syd lets out a frustrated breath and crosses her arms. She's quiet for a while. Two more birds fly down onto my car, each landing with a thunk. I could almost laugh at the absurdity of the moment, the utter outlandishness of these giant creatures flapping around on my ruined Jeep, but I'm too frustrated. I take my glasses off and start to clean them on my shirt. Finally she says, "This is way better than the alternative."

I put my glasses back on and look around, confused and frustrated. "What are you talking about?"

She narrows her eyes. "If you weren't here, you'd be in Yosemite with Hannah and your bros, wearing Patagonia and reminiscing about all your best high school moments."

Somehow, her response makes me even angrier. My palms itch, my chest tightens. I stand up, and then sit back down again, my body not sure where to go. Then everything comes exploding to the surface. "This," I say. "This is why."

"This is why what?"

"This is why we aren't friends anymore."

Syd flinches.

"No," she says. "We aren't friends anymore because you ditched me. You made friends with the cool kids and never looked back."

I shake my head, furious. "That isn't how it happened." I stare at the flock of pelicans nodding their heads up and down. "You act like it was all my fault, but it wasn't. You ridiculed everything I wanted to be a part of. Who cares if I wanted to hang out with Hannah or Jake or go to a party? There's nothing wrong with that, but you made me feel like I was the world's biggest sellout every time I talked to anyone who wasn't you."

Syd looks stunned. I watch as she cycles through several expressions: surprise, hurt, then finally anger. Her mouth opens and closes, her fingers flex against the case of her phone. "Because they're assholes," she finally says.

I cross my arms. "They're my friends."

"They treated me like garbage." She looks away, her jaw set.

Guilt seeps into my stomach but I push it down. The people around us have gone back to their cars and once again traffic has started inching forward. The pelicans are still milling around on top of the Jeep.

I close my eyes, and for a moment, the past comes into full focus. A million eyerolls and sarcastic comments. The feeling of being pushed beyond my boundaries, again and again and again. "You always wanted me to do everything just like you," I say. "But not everyone wants what you want."

"What does that mean?" Syd says. In her eyes is another dare. She wants me to go too far, to cross the line, to say something I can't take back.

"Not everyone wants to lie to their parents," I say. The pelicans, the traffic, the humidity, all of it disappears and I just keep digging into this anger. "Not everyone wants to get tattoos and talk to dead people and just . . . embarrass themselves all the time. Not everyone is like you. I'm not like you."

Syd's face hardens then. All the way. It's like we are back in the middle of senior year, when she wouldn't even look at me if we passed each other in the hallway. For a second all I can feel is regret.

We hear a loud, raucous flapping sound and the pelicans lift off the car in one unit. Syd's face falls as she watches them fly away. Then she turns back to me, eyes suddenly angry, snakelike under her heavy black lashes.

"No," she says, her voice shaking. "You're not like me. If you had it your way, you'd be back in El Sobrante, sitting on the couch with your dad, never going anywhere or doing anything or being anyone. You are a fucking coward."

I can't deny it. I *am* a coward. I have two texts in my pocket to prove it.

But I can't look at Syd anymore, knowing that she knows. So I get up and walk off down the highway, following the stream of red brake lights until I can't hear Syd's angry breathing anymore.

35
Sydney

I STAND FOR A WHILE, STUNNED, watching Cass walk away. I don't think I've ever seen him get angry like that and I'm not sure how to feel about it. Is he right? Was it really all my fault? Suddenly I feel like I'm the one who can't see the past clearly.

I stare at the roof of the car, where the pelicans were waddling around only a couple of minutes ago; it's now abandoned and covered in bird shit. My first endangered species sighting and somehow I messed it up. We've missed the show. The car is fucked. I'm hungover and lost and I've never felt so alone in my life.

I think about the panic of the past two days. How, ever since Cass kissed me in the desert, I haven't been able to think a single coherent thought. I'm embarrassed at how I acted last night, getting too drunk to work the board, letting Cass kiss me again, watching him walk away.

Between Liam W. and Robbie, there have been a lot of guys. A lot of hot fumbling in closets and basements and cars. A lot of reaching under T-shirts and pulling up skirts, ramming knees into gearshifts and knocking teeth behind closet doors. There have been a lot of hickeys and stubble burn and secret bruises that I like to press on when I'm alone. Because I really, really like kissing. And, as it turns out, ever since Danny McKenzie went down on me in the back of his mom's Subaru Forester, I really like sex too.

My favorite part is right before it all begins. We've snuck away from everyone else, from the party or the game or the movie. We haven't kissed yet but we know we are going to. Anything, everything is possible. They might taste like lemons or have soft hands or make a little gasp right before the end. And I might be one of the only people who knows it.

The part that I don't like is after it's done, the way the magical film of closeness dissolves into the scrambling of clothes and tossing of the condom and the awkward conversation: "This was great, but . . ." *Don't tell anyone.*

Nobody wants to actually be seen with a weirdo like me.

Anyway, the bad part, the *after* part, is why I didn't have sex with Cass in Marfa. Even though I wanted to. I *wanted* to. I think I've wanted to since I found out what sex was.

I just couldn't bear seeing it on Cass's face, the realization that we are utterly incongruous. The way we can never, ever fit.

So I did what I always do. I panicked. I pushed. And then he went and said it anyway. *Not everyone wants what you want.* It hurts just as much as I thought it would.

"Ma'am?" The tow truck driver's voice startles me back to where I'm sitting in the moonlight on the hood of Cass's car, in a repair shop parking lot that is empty except for us. Cass is inside the car, not talking, just like he's been for the past several hours.

The tow truck driver has a friendly face and a red beard, and small pink ears that stick out from his head like a spectral tarsier.

He looks a little pained when he says, "Your card's been declined."

Fuck.

"Really?" I say, even though I believe him.

In my head, I'm trying to do the math, except that math is my mortal enemy. And just like an enemy, she's betrayed me again. I thought for sure we had at least three hundred dollars left. But apparently, no dice.

"Shit," I say. "I'm so sorry. I thought I had more than enough. Hang on. Let me call someone."

"You know what?" he says, tilting his head to look down at me. It's a look my dad gives me sometimes, when he wanders into the kitchen and I'm sitting there doing my homework and it's like he's remembering he has a fourth daughter, like he's remembering he actually likes me. "Don't worry about it. Just be safe, okay?" He adjusts his cap. "Do you guys need a ride anywhere?"

I shake my head. "No," I say. "We've got it."

Julia shows up at the lot forty minutes later, wearing an incredible dress with parakeets all over it and long, jangly dagger earrings.

"I'm so sorry," I say, shame burning up my cheeks. If there is such a thing as rock bottom, I've reached it in the past half hour of sitting silently next to Cass inside the car.

"Me too," says Cass.

Out here, the crickets are loud. They sound giant, like they might be the size of your hand. She looks both of us over from head to toe. "It's okay. Our set ended a while ago and we were just hanging out," she says, and then, "Come on. You two can stay with us tonight."

She takes us back to her friend Dusty's house, which is half falling down but also beautifully ornate, with wooden carvings on the door and giant blue shutters next to the windows. She makes us tea and feeds us grilled cheese sandwiches and doesn't make us feel bad for being fuckups. If she notices the loaded silence between me and Cass, she doesn't say anything. When we are settled into our sleeping bags on the living room floor, Julia raises an eyebrow at me and says, "Want to talk?"

It doesn't feel like an actual question; it's more like a command. "Sure," I shrug, and follow her out to the backyard. It's dark out here but the moonlight paints everything silver, the patio furniture and neat square of grass and flowers that look like they would eat you alive.

I flop into a chaise lounge and lie back, looking up at the stars. For a moment I'm transported back to the closet, to my "talk" with Mom. Even though I don't want to, I miss her a little.

"Thanks for getting us," I say, still feeling mildly embarrassed. The last time I saw Julia I was too drunk to properly plug in her microphone.

"Of course," she says, settling into a patio chair next to me and closing her eyes. "You're part of the crew now. No Darla left behind and all that." She yawns. "We'll go back and check on the car in the morning."

"Okay," I say. I'm still watching the stars, which are so much more self-contained than they were in the desert, where they seemed in constant, shivering motion.

"You ran out of money, huh?" Julia says.

"I guess you're not paying us enough," I joke. It feels a little forced.

I wonder why it's me out here and not Cass. Julia and I have never really had a heart-to-heart like this.

"Probably not," she muses. Then she straightens up in her chair. "But seriously, tell me what's going on."

"Well," I say, closing my eyes. "We didn't exactly plan this out."

"That seemed like it might be the case." She lights a cigarette, and the tip burns orange in the silvery darkness. I think about asking for one but it feels like that would be pushing my luck. She looks at me and says, "Go on, then."

And the whole story tumbles out, starting with graduation. Julia just sits there in her chair, eyes closed, nodding and weaving some magic truth spell while I spill my guts. Robbie, the internship, Mom, Cass. When I get to the part about the desert, I stop short.

"Hey," Julia chides. "You were just getting to the good part."

I shake my head. "It's not good. That part is never, ever good."

"What do you mean?"

"It's just . . . I'm just . . ." But I don't have the words. Or I have them, but I don't have the guts to say them out loud.

"I see," Julia says. Then she's quiet for a long time. "You know, Syd, whatever it is that you think you are, it's not true."

I laugh, and it tastes bitter on my tongue. "This is starting to sound like an after-school special."

"Don't do that," Julia says. "I see what you're doing, and just . . . don't. You are amazing. You're eighteen years old and you can run a soundboard just as good as a forty-year-old Deadhead." She flicks her cigarette, and ash sprinkles to the ground. "The world is full of shit-heads," Julia continues, "but you are a fucking gem. You tell the truth and you're funny and kind and unapologetically yourself. Cass is lucky to have you. The world is lucky to have you."

I consider her words in the quiet that follows. For one second, I allow myself to imagine what it would be like if they were true.

Stupid.

I push the idea down and sit up, narrowing my eyes.

"Look," I say. "I appreciate the pep talk. But really, I just need to get some sleep."

"Okay," Julia says, stubbing out her cigarette. "Sure."

She stays outside in the moonlight while I slip back through the kitchen door.

Two days later we pull up in front of a farmhouse on the outskirts of Athens, Georgia. It is four in the afternoon and the air feels heavy, even though night is still hours away. The house, the only one in sight, is still half built—a giant Tyvek wrapper covers half the roof. The front yard, if you can call the piece of land that just spills into all the other pieces of land a yard, is full of chickens that are roaming in and out of flower beds. A big barn sits behind the house, just beyond a field with three giant white horses grazing in the grass.

"We're here," I say, my voice flat. It's the first thing either of us have said in two whole days, ever since Julia paid for the car repairs and left us with cash and instructions to meet the band here once everything was fixed. It doesn't seem like Cass's dad has returned any of his calls. My mom has stopped calling too. It feels like some weird tether has been cut and we are truly off on our own.

I've been thinking a lot since our fight in New Orleans. I've been remembering. It's so strange to have a defining moment in your life suddenly recast, all the various meanings shifting. I think I can see it now, the way Cass must have felt at times. I think I finally understand.

But it doesn't change anything, because one fact remains true: Cass left. He left. And he will leave again. This has to be over now, before something else gets broken.

When I turn off the engine, Cass, predictably, doesn't say a word. He just slips out of the car and takes off walking down the long dirt road, through a long hallway of trees that seems to never end. I walk up toward the house, where the Darlas are waiting. After two days of silence, I wonder what it will be like to be around other people.

The front door is open, but the house is quiet. I step inside the main room, slipping off my shoes. Everything inside is made of dark wood, and light filters in through giant windows, through the leaves of the trees outside. The ceiling is at least two stories tall and a loft hangs above my head.

"The show's gonna be in here," a voice says behind me. "Cool, right?" Charlie is standing at the top of the stairs, next to a white person with dark eyes and a full sleeve of tattoos.

"This is Syd, our sound guy. Syd," they say, turning back to me. "This is Frank, one of my oldest friends."

Frank reaches out his hand and shakes mine vigorously, a friendly smile revealing a mouthful of crooked teeth.

"I hear that you're good at what you do," Frank says. "Which is good because we've never had a show here before and have no idea how to do it."

"Don't worry," Charlie says. "We rented a PA. Everything's behind the house. I'll show you once you've had a chance to hang for a bit."

I feel intense relief that the Darlas still trust me, after everything that's transpired in the past few days. And also a thrum of excitement—tonight at the board it's just going to be me.

For the next hour, I sit on the couch with Charlie and Frank, drinking iced tea and listening to the history of the Darlas. They met here, in Athens, where Cass's mom is from, while Charlie, Julia, and Sunny were at UGA. The three of them were out at a Hope Sandoval show one night and became friends. Iris was a guitar prodigy and a senior in high school and she used to busk on the street after school. Sunny spotted her playing in front of the Morton Theater one afternoon. The Darlas were looking for a lead guitarist for their band, and everything fell into place. Once school ended, the four of them moved to San Francisco to record an album with a small record label there. Then Iris met Craig, and Cass was born, and Iris, well . . . that's where the story ends.

I have so many questions, but it doesn't feel right to ask them without Cass here. I keep watching the door, waiting for him to creep in. He should be the one hearing this, not me.

36
Caspian

WHEN WE GET TO ATHENS, I walk and walk and walk down a long and curving country road lined by trees and tall grass and horses. I don't stop for a long time because I can't stand being still with myself. Knowing what a loser I am. My mother may have been a disaster but at least she did things. At least she was honest.

I am the opposite of honest. A liar. A coward. A boring, ridiculous person. This experiment in being something different has been a spectacular failure.

By the time I get back to the farmhouse, party preparation appears to be in full swing. The backyard is crawling with people setting up tables and kegs and amps, and for a moment I think I'm going to be able to sneak in unnoticed. But then Julia spots me and hugs me and drags me over to a circle of people who are casually watching several children chase each other through the trees.

"This is Cass," Julia says, before I have a chance to say anything. "Iris's son."

It might be the first time anyone has ever introduced me like this, and it feels strangely good, to be claimed like that.

I nod, and everyone seems to start talking at once.

"Wow. You look exactly like her."

"Same eyes."

"Your mom was amazing."

"The best guitar player I've ever seen."

"She made the best chocolate cake."

"She wrote the funniest postcards."

For the rest of the night, I am unable to escape stories about my mother. It's like, after eighteen years of nothing, she is fully formed, right in front of my eyes. She is a real person who spent six months wearing black after Nina Simone died, who fixed flat tires and made spaghetti sauce from scratch and knew how to ride a unicycle. It feels like my skin is on fire. I wish I could leave and I wish I could never leave. I wish I could talk to Syd.

When I think about what happened between us in New Orleans, my stomach turns. The things that I said weren't untrue; I'm glad that for once I was honest, that I faced the truth head-on. But the tone of it, the intensity, was all wrong. For days I've been trying to think of a way to make it right. But Syd has been impenetrable. Something about our fight feels final.

I look over and there she is, chatting with Charlie in her sparkly dress, casually adjusting a wire. Her hair is up in a messy bun and she isn't wearing any makeup at all and she reminds me of her old self, the one who used to sleep in my bed and howl at the full moon.

I suddenly feel the barest longing to walk right up to her and sling my arm across her shoulders, to tuck her under my arm and smell her hair. Like I might have with Hannah, except I know that if I did that with Syd I would actually feel something. Everything. But when I catch her eye, she frowns and looks away.

That night, in a room full of my mother's friends, a room full of my mother, I play my best show ever. I feel like I've opened my veins and the music is pouring out, growing more intense with every heartbeat, like I'm swimming in it, drowning in it. I mix my own music with Mom's, I become a part of her again. Every fucked-up feeling from the past few days, all of the people I've let down—Kit, Dad, Syd—I weave them all into my song. I'm sorry, I say. I love you. When I look out at Syd, her eyes are glazed over with tears.

And then, just as we are coming into the swell of the last song in the set, my song, I get a feeling, a tingling in my left ear, a skip of my heartbeat; I miss a note, but quickly pull myself back into the flow. I look up and search the crowd, trying to figure out what it is. And that's when I see him, tucked into the back corner, arms tight across his chest, face white as chalk, shoulders rigid with anger. My dad.

37
Sydney

TONIGHT MIGHT BE THE BEST SHOW I've ever seen. It is like the Darlas and Cass are actually raising the dead. Like the music is so good that it's called Iris here and everyone can feel it. The air in the farmhouse is thick with sound. Like heavy smoke, it curls around the room; we breathe it in.

My eyes are riveted to Cass—to his square fingers, which I now know the feel and weight of on my skin, and to his wide mouth, which is hanging partway open, and to the perfect curl of dark hair that falls between his brows. I want him. And the fact that he could never really want me the way I am cuts me right down the middle.

Watching the show feels like torture, and somewhere in the back of my mind I wonder if I can go on like this. Four more shows between here and New York. Four more quiet days in the car, four more nights of this exquisite pain. But then there's the fact that I am somehow part of it now, that I had a hand in the crystal-clear tone of the guitar and the fuzzy, hazy vocals and the perfect sound that comes from all the sounds melting together.

So I keep myself from falling apart. I hover over the board like all the other sound guys did, making minuscule adjustments like Dad showed me, guarding the music until the last chords have washed over the stunned and speechless crowd. But when the thunderous applause begins, I make my escape. I can't be here with him for another minute.

I turn to sneak out the back door, but there's a soft squeeze on my shoulder. A familiar squeeze. I turn around to see my mother.

She has tears in her eyes and one hand over her mouth and when she finally speaks, all she can say is "Wow."

I don't know what to say myself. I'm too shocked, so I stand there awkwardly as she looks me over. I wonder what she sees. Then she says, "I had no idea."

About what? I think. *About everything?*

Then the moment is broken by Charlie clapping a hand on my back and saying, "Perfection, Syd. Fucking perfection. You are a genius."

And despite my mother's assessing look, which has been known to shrivel me down like an earthworm in the sun, I feel proud. Mom holds out a hand and says, "I'm Jenn Greenfield, Syd's mom."

Charlies eyes go wide as they say, "Oooooh." Then, "I see a resemblance. It's in the cheekbones."

Mom finally seems to come back from her orbit, face tightening just a bit as she says, "If you'll excuse me, I need to talk to my daughter."

I follow her out, feeling my elation start to deflate in a slow and steady stream. We push our way through the sweaty crowd, past the small cluster of people smoking next to the back door. I think I catch sight of Cass's dad, body tight like a rubber band, walking off down the driveway.

People reach out to high-five me, to tell me what a great show it was, but I don't really hear them. My head is too full of a million questions: *How are they here? How did they find us?*

Finally, Mom stops just at the edge between the darkness and the back porch light. She watches me and I watch her. The shadows on her face look harsher out here, her features sharp and small. I wonder what she looked like when she was my age, but I also find it hard to believe that she ever was my age, that she would ever understand what it feels like to be impulsive and fuck up all the time.

Mom pushes back the loose strands of hair that have fallen around her face and says, "Syd."

I spend about ten seconds trying to figure out how bad this is. And then I remember that, legally, I'm an adult now. Even if I have no job, no money, no place to live. She can't drag me back without my permission.

I straighten my shoulders and say, "Why are you here?"

That seems to make her remember just how mad she is. She runs a hand over her hair again, smoothing it down. "Why am I here? Why are you here? You skipped your graduation. You bailed on the internship I went out of my way to get for you. You stopped talking to me. You disappeared, Syd. Do you have any idea how scary that was?"

I cross my arms, roll my eyes. "I've been texting you this whole time." Even as I say it, though, I know it wasn't enough.

For a moment Mom looks like she might actually explode. Her body shakes from the effort of holding all her anger in. But then she brings her hands to her temples, massages them a few times, blows out a breath.

"I don't want to fight with you anymore," she says, her voice defeated. "I just want to try to understand."

I turn away, toward the black night and the hot, heavy air. My oldest, most hopeless feeling returns. Mom will never understand me. "Don't you feel like it's a little late for that?" I say.

She puts her hands on my shoulders. "Come on, Syd. Please."

I sigh. "Let's just go."

I look for Cass as we walk out to Mom's rental car, but I can't see him anywhere. Even though I know that he and I are over, it feels strange to be spending the night apart. I miss him so much more than I thought I would. We spent years without talking and I barely noticed, but now, after two days, I actually feel a physical pain, right in the center of my chest.

It's quiet in the car as Mom drives us back to her hotel in her tiny rental car. I can tell Mom's mind is whirring, but she doesn't say anything.

We reach the nondescript hotel room with its navy blue bedspreads and fake flowers, both of us exhausted. When we are showered and pajamaed and tucked under the covers, watching a show about animal rescues, I ask Mom, "How did you find us, anyway?"

We seem to have reached a silent truce, just for the night.

She sighs. "Julia called Craig. When your car broke down and you ran out of money." She combs her fingers through the wet, dark blond strands of her hair. "Seriously," she says. "What were you thinking?"

I sigh, burying my face in my hands. I'm so tired. "I don't know. I just felt lost." Mom turns off the TV but keeps looking straight ahead, as though she's still watching it. "And the stupid thing is that I wasn't actually lost at all."

Mom huffs. "I find that a little hard to believe now that you've reached your credit limit."

I ignore her sarcasm, gather my confidence, sit up straight against my pillow. "I have an internship," I say. "An apprenticeship. I set it up months ago. It starts in two weeks."

Mom looks baffled. She shakes her head a few times, as though trying to make her vision line up. "What are you talking about?"

"I have a sound apprenticeship at the Fox Theater. It's actually really hard to get." I take a deep breath. "I'm really proud of it."

Mom's outrage seems to break at this. "Why didn't you just tell me?" she says.

I give her a look. "Because you're you. And it's a sound internship at a music venue in Oakland and I thought there was no way you would possibly understand."

Mom gets a crushed look on her face. After a long, heavy silence she says, "You're probably right."

I cross my arms, wanting to feel some kind of satisfaction at her admission, but all I feel is a little hollow sensation in the center of my chest. It's the spot where I've held years of frustration, but with all the bite gone, it's just empty.

"I'm not like you," I say. "And I'm never going to be."

"I know," she says, finally turning toward me. Her eyes are sad and sincere. "I love that."

"You don't," I say, quick like a flinch. "You never did."

"Syd," she says again, and she reaches for my hand, but I pull it back under the covers.

"I'm tired," I say. And then I turn out the light.

WHEN I FINISH THE SET, DAD is gone, disappeared into the night so completely that it feels like he was a figment of my imagination. I look all over the house but he's nowhere.

I pack up the equipment methodically and bring it out to the van, trying to avoid eye contact with all the people who try to talk to me after the show. From across the yard, I see Syd and her mom drive away and I get a strange lump in my throat.

I'm walking back to the car when Julia catches up to me and says, "Cass, that was amazing."

"Thanks," I say. And she's right, it was. But already the show feels like it was a hundred years ago. The bubble of good feeling, the bubble of my mother, feels like it has burst forever, and the emptiness left behind is almost unbearable.

"I saw your dad," she says. "Is everything okay?"

"What a question." I laugh awkwardly, trying not to show how crushed I am. She laughs too, but there's no joy in it. Then we stand there for what feels like forever, not saying anything. Finally, she reaches over and pulls me into a hug. She smells like incense. I have to bite down hard on my cheek so I don't cry.

I sit for a long time in the front seat of the car, alone with the crickets and the heavy feeling of failure and impending doom. I think about the night with Syd in Texas, her soft lips and warm body and tangled hair and perfect sounds. I think about her long fingers on the soundboard, the way she closes her eyes in concentration and the dark slash of her lashes seems to shut out the whole world. I think about all the times she crawled through the hole in the hedge at the back of our houses, tugged me by the hand right into danger. Of all the things I've found on this trip, Syd is going to be the hardest to give up.

Eventually I must fall asleep because when I open my eyes the sun is starting to turn the sky a lighter blue. My knees are tucked up to my chest and my back is aching. There's a hard knocking on the window and I look up to see Dad, his face as solemn as an old oak tree.

"Wake up," he says. "We're going home."

He drives us in the Jeep to the hotel where Syd is staying with her mom, and he waits while Syd and I go through the contents of the car, separating our things. I pack everything that's mine, which isn't very much, into my thrift store backpack. Then I load my guitar into Syd's mom's rental car so she can drive us to the airport.

The whole time, I wish that Syd would look at me with that mischievous glint in her eye, would whisper *They haven't even seen the tattoos yet.* But she just moves around me like I'm not even there.

Somehow, without me, a plan has been formed. Syd and her mom are going to finish out the tour and then drive back across the country. They'll bring my car back in two weeks, just in time for the Darlas' last show in San Francisco. My dad has decided that we'll fly back this morning. Aside from the logistics of our trip home, he hasn't said anything to me since my wakeup call. Like the coward I am, I haven't uttered a word to him either.

Syd follows us to the airport in my car, so her mom can bring the rental back after she drops us off. The whole time I keep twisting around in my seat, looking back at her through the rear window. This ending with Syd feels all wrong. I have to fix it somehow. I need to apologize and make things right. As we pull up to the curb I jump out and run up to her open window. Her cheeks are pink in the Georgia heat, her hair pulled into a floppy topknot with wisps falling all around her face. Her lips turn down at the corners and she doesn't meet my eye. I whisper, "Syd," leaning into her, breathing her in, already missing her so much it hurts.

But she just pulls away and says, "Don't." Her face is unreadable under her sunglasses but I can tell that whatever this was, it's over.

As we fly back across America, the plane eating up the miles that took us days to cross in the car, Dad never breaks his stony silence. He reads a book, he adjusts his air-conditioning vent, he's polite to the flight attendant, he falls asleep. And with each quiet gesture something starts to grow inside me. Something angry.

I've lived most of my life with Dad in silence. But I'm not a silent person anymore.

The thing inside me grows louder and louder until the sound of it is overpowering. It grows as we walk through SFO, it grows as we find Dad's car, it grows as we drive all the way back over the bridge, down our street, into the driveway. And when we get inside the house, it finally opens its mouth.

"We can't do this anymore," it says. Suddenly I feel like this house is so small, the living room with its sagging shelf and shaggy carpet, the sad staircase and the records all smushed together and covered in dust. It feels like if I stay in here much longer the smallness of it might crush me to death.

Dad just puts his bag down by the door and begins pacing across the living room.

"Say something," I say, and this time the voice is mine.

Dad throws his keys onto the coffee table, runs both hands through his hair and down his face.

"I found the cash under your bed," he says. "I was looking for a drill bit and I found almost four thousand dollars."

Oh, fuck. I adjust my backpack on my shoulders, my sudden burst of courage receding.

"So I decided to come and get you in Yosemite. And do you know what I found?" He turns to look at me and his face is flushed. "You weren't even there."

He sits down at the end of the couch, staring at me like I'm a ghost. "Do you know how scared I was, Cass? Do you know what that felt like?"

I open my mouth. "I—"

"Are you dealing drugs?" he says then, turning away to look at the kitchen doorway. I can see the tension in his neck.

A pinched laugh bubbles up from inside of me, from where I am still just waiting in the doorway with the night at my back. How ridiculous is it that my dad saw me with the Darlas and he still can't figure it out? I almost wish I was dealing drugs. That would be so much less loaded than explaining what's really going on. But, fuck, I am sick of this. I am so sick of being a coward.

"No, Dad," I say. "I wasn't doing drugs. I was playing music at the BART station."

Before I can hear what he has to say next, I turn around and walk back out the door, down the road. I get all the way to center of town before I realize that there is really nowhere to go.

39
Sydney

THE NEXT THREE DAYS PASS, A little awkwardly at first. Mom and I fall into a routine—coffee and podcasts in the morning, music and gas station snacks in the afternoon. We don't really talk much about what we're doing. It feels too out there to even bring it up.

I know that Mom is taking two weeks off from work, which is pretty much unheard of. She's brought a suitcase of casual clothes, jeans and T-shirts that I almost never see her wear.

I don't hear much from my siblings, which feels strange. Normally, they would jump at the chance to weigh in on my mistakes. Mom must have called them off. Dad texts me: Don't tell Mom but I think you are the coolest.

When we're setting up for the show each night, Mom watches me with an intensity she usually saves for studying the files of tricky patients at the kitchen table late at night. She hands me cords and asks questions about the equipment, like she's trying to understand it all just as well as I do.

After the shows, we sit around with the Darlas listening to their stories, and one night, when Mom's had a few too many glasses of wine, she tells me about her early twenties in Salt Lake City, before med school, hitchhiking up the canyon every morning to wait tables at a ski resort after staying up all night with the other ski bums. It feels like she's trying to come back to me. So I let her.

At a rest stop in Virginia, I call Robbie. He answers with a sort of half groan, but his voice is sweet when he says, "Hey, Syd."

"I'm sorry for breaking up with you in a text," I blurt out. "I mean, I did want to break up with you. Do want to." I run a hand down my face. This is so awkward. "I just wish I didn't do it in such a shitty way."

Robbie laughs, quietly. "I can't say the delivery didn't suck, but it's okay. I get it."

I look over to where my mom is putting gas in the car, shaking her hips to the country music playing from the outdoor speakers. "You do?"

There's a long pause. I can hear Robbie moving around his room, can imagine him trying to find a shirt, tugging on a sock. "I mean, not really," he finally says. "But I'll be okay."

"Good," I say. It feels a little sad, knowing that this is really the end.

"Good," he says. He clears his throat. "I should—"

"Yeah."

"Okay, take care, Syd," he says, voice soft. And then he hangs up the phone.

An hour outside Washington, DC, Mom says, "What is going on with you and Cass?" I can tell she's been working up to it; she's been raising and lowering the volume of the stereo for the past hour. Still, hearing his name feels jarring.

Mom gives me a worried look. "You two haven't talked to each other in years, then suddenly you're running away together." She frowns. "And you haven't said a word about him since I got here."

I turn and look out the window for a while, trying to find a way to describe what exactly happened—how for a moment it almost seemed like we were meant to be, and then how quickly it all unraveled. In the end, I just say, "It was a fluke. I think it was more about Iris than anything else."

Mom stays quiet, even though I can tell it's hard for her. By now, she knows me well enough not to ask any more questions.

The next day, we are crossing the border into Maryland, listening to Fleetwood Mac. Everything is overwhelmingly green and Mom is singing at the top of her lungs. It feels like a perfect moment, and it almost is, except that something inside me still feels off.

In the space between songs, I turn to her and say, "I've been having panic attacks again."

I hadn't been meaning to tell her that, but once it's out, I feel relieved.

Mom looks worried, but not disappointed, not like it's the end of the world and I'm ruining everything. "Thanks for telling me," she says.

"Yeah," I say.

"Do you want to start seeing Dr. Michaels again?"

I think about the hours spent in the depressing Berkeley office, staring at the beige walls and not really saying anything. "Maybe I could try someone else."

"Of course," she says. "Anything."

• • •

In Delaware, Mom asks me about college. "Maybe you can apply in the fall for next year," she says.

"Maybe," I say. "But I'm going to be pretty busy with the internship."

"Okay." She takes a deep breath, a yoga breath, and taps her fingers on the window. This morning we have matching messy topknots and Mom is wearing her glasses. She looks happy and relaxed.

"I'll think about it," I say, even though I know I won't. I don't want to go to college any time soon, but I know it might take Mom a while to get it. And that's okay. She's trying.

Then, on the fourth day, we get to New York City. We drive into the Holland Tunnel, and when we emerge, the buildings tower over our heads, blotting out the sunlight. People are everywhere, flowing down the sidewalk like a river, veering into the street at seemingly random intervals. Everywhere there is honking, talking, shouting, chaos.

We meet the Darlas in Brooklyn at a tiny club with a red doorway and a chalkboard sign out front. The sidewalk glitters like it does at home and the air vibrates with energy and noise. Mom leaves me to have coffee with a friend, and after sound check I wander the maze of streets until I feel dizzy.

The heat in New York is different from anywhere else we've been. There's a grit to it; it sticks to my skin. It smells like everything, all at once. There is every kind of person here too. Weirdos, tech bros, fancy suit-and-dress people, groups of kids my age hanging out at the park looking so much cooler than I ever could.

I almost open my phone to text Cass, *Wish you were here.*

It feels like he belongs in this city, busking on this glittery sidewalk with the whole world walking by. But it still hurts way too much to even think about Cass. So I walk back to the club, I watch the show, I pretend it's just as good without his green guitar.

In the end, I decide that I don't want to disappear into this city just yet. It seems like a good place to run away to, the perfect place to get lost, but as I help Sunny lug her bass amp out to the van, both of us cursing and sweating and laughing, I realize that's not what I want. And after all these days on the road, I think I might be ready to go back home.

We say goodbye to the Darlas, who are splitting up for the next week until the last show of the tour at the Great American Music Hall in San Francisco. Everyone hugs, even my mom and me. Charlie gives me a lucky rabbit's foot keychain to match my tattoo and Sunny gives me a piece of black tourmaline and Jasmyn and Julia ruffle my hair like I'm one of their kids. Mom and I walk all the way back to our hotel, across the crowded Brooklyn Bridge. And then, the next morning, we turn the car west and drive.

40
Caspian

THE NEXT TEN DAYS PASS VERY quietly. Somehow, impossibly, Dad and I slip back into our old routines without really talking about anything. I catch him staring at me sometimes when I walk through the living room as he's eating his dinner, or when he walks past the open door to my room, like he wants to say something but can't. It's frustrating. I could break the silence but I don't feel like I should have to. He's my dad. He should be the one to fix this.

I return to work at the hardware store, stare at my registration paperwork for school, look at Kit Molina's number in my phone, at her last text message with its empty invitation. When Jake stops by the hardware store, I tell him I'm grounded, even though I'm not.

I try to get through the week, try to get numb again, but it's a lot harder than it used to be. All I can think about is Syd and the Darlas, drifting across the country, making music. Without my car, I can't even get to the BART station.

At night, I sit on my bed and hold my guitar. It barely makes a sound without the amp but I move my fingers anyway.

On the Monday after I get home, Gram comes for a surprise visit. She brings turkey-and-butter sandwiches and drags us into the backyard to eat at the rusty wrought iron table and says, "Jesus, you two are even more talkative than usual."

Gram looks young for her sixty-seven years. She wears a polar fleece and khaki pants and hiking sneakers every day, even in the summer. Her salt-and-pepper hair is always swept up in a neat bun and her skin is sun-browned with lots of laugh lines. She loves to garden, hike, fish, and ride her bike on the trails near the water. Whenever something troubles me, she says, "Go for a walk," as if fresh air can fix any ailment.

When Dad gets up to clear the table, Gram leans in and whispers to me, "What the hell is going on?"

I just let out a sigh and say, "Everything. And nothing."

When Dad gets back, Gram says, "Cass and I are going for a drive."

When I'm safely ensconced in the front seat of her red Prius, winding around the chaparral-covered curves of San Pablo Dam Road, Gram turns to me and says, "Okay, Caspian, time to talk."

Maybe it's the fact that she's the first person I've really spoken to after over a week of deadly silence, but I open my mouth and tell her every last sordid detail. Even the part about the psychic and kissing Syd in the desert. By the time I finish, Gram is pulled over by the side of the road, blinking her eyes and staring into the middle distance.

"Cass," she says, her voice breaking, "I am so sorry."

I look at her. "Why? You have nothing to do with any of this."

Gram puts her head in her hands. And then she begins to cry. Gram never, ever cries. I look around, bewildered.

Then she says, "We shouldn't have kept her from you." She shakes her head. "It wasn't right."

I stare out the window, at the cars whizzing past and the red-brown gravel at the side of the road. I tell the truth. "It wasn't."

Gram reaches across to the glove box and grabs a small packet of tissues. "Your dad was devastated when she died. So scared and lost. I didn't know how to help him. I think the only way he felt like he had any control was to keep you away from all of it, especially the thing that killed her."

I shake my head. "Music wasn't what killed my mom."

She smiles ruefully. "I know."

I reach over and take Gram's hand, which is smooth and warm with blue raised veins and papery skin. She squeezes tightly. It kicks up a swirl of confused feelings.

"I think I need to talk to someone," I say. I clear my throat, feeling awkward. "Like a therapist."

"I think that's a good idea," she says. Then she straightens up and says, "You need to call that producer, right now."

She watches while I make the call and leave the message, my voice awkward and my words meandering.

When I'm done calling Kit, Gram takes me on a hike up Wildcat Canyon. We sit in the shade of a live oak tree while she tells me every story she can remember about my mother.

"She was such a wild young thing, like an alley cat. Scared the hell out of me when Craig first brought her home." She shakes her head, as if it were all happening right now. "But she grew on me. She was kind. She had this charm about her; it was hard not to get swept up in it."

I think about me and Dad and our utter lack of charm, how sorely we are missing someone like that in our lives.

The rays of the sun get longer, melting through the gnarled man-zanitas, and Gram gets up and brushes off her knees. "Come on," she says. "I need to go talk to my son." All the way back down the trail, she keeps reaching out and grabbing my hand, as if to reassure herself that I'm still here.

A few days later, I pull up in Dad's truck at an abandoned-looking factory building in East Oakland with a brick facade that is covered in many layers of white, signs painted over and over and over. Some-where inside this building are the offices of Mourning Light Records. I ring the buzzer, my palms sweating. Kit appears in the doorway, wear-ing a faded David Bowie T-shirt and work pants. Her eyes crinkle at the edges when she smiles and claps a hand on my back.

"Cass!" she says. "You finally made it."

It's been three weeks since we met, but it feels like a lifetime has passed since then.

I follow her down a maze of hallways until we get to the office, which is also a mixing room with a vintage soundboard and reel-to-reel tape machine at one end and a beat-up couch at the other.

She introduces me to two people who are sitting on the couch going through a stack of papers.

"This is Gene," she says, gesturing toward a person with a long white wizard's beard and a striped button-down shirt. "And Penel-ope."

Penelope nods, pushing a few strands of short blue hair out of their face. They are wearing all black, with beat-up low-top Doc Martens on their feet. "Hey, Cass," they say, as if they already know who I am.

I clear my throat. "I brought my guitar, but I don't have an amp right now."

"No worries," says Kit. "We've got one in the other room. Hang on."

While Kit goes for the amp, I stand awkwardly in the center of the room, my guitar case between my feet.

"Is that your pedal board?" Gene says, pointing to my Makita case.

"Yep," I say, trying to smile but feeling like a weird clown.

"Love it," says Gene, and then they look back down into their paper stack.

When I finally get set up it's a little awkward, me standing by the soundboard and Kit, Gene, and Penelope all staring at me from the couch.

"Just pretend we're not here," says Kit.

"Sure," I say, laughing a little.

It's hard to find my first note in here because it's so quiet. No street subway sounds, no birds or garbage skittering in the wind. But still, I close my eyes and tunnel deep and start to play. Almost immediately I get caught in this melody I've been thinking for days. It reminds me of Syd, soft skin and moonstone eyes and total oblivion.

I don't know how long I play for, but when I'm done I look up to see Kit grinning. "See, guys?" she says. "I told you."

Penelope looks up at me and says, "How would you like to make a record?"

41
Sydney

MOM AND I DRIVE BACK ACROSS the country in a straight line along Route 80 so she can make it back in time to not be fired from her job. In the past ten days, things have become easy between us. Mom plays me all her favorite music and I play her mine and we fill in the center of our Venn diagram, bit by bit. For the first time since I can remember, she looks at me like I'm a person and not a problem.

On our last day, in Reno, we sync up with the route that Cass and I drove that first night, winding through the mountains and crossing the border back into California. Something inside me aches as we drive through the dense forest, smelling dust and pine. It feels like it's been years since Cass and I drove this road in the middle of the night, Cass's face impenetrable in the darkness.

I've tried not to think about him since we left Georgia but now it feels impossible not to. I remember the way he looked at the very last show, his eyes closed, lost in the music. And I remember him at the airport, sad and desperate, the way he leaned in the window of the car, his lips almost touching my cheek. It was torture, being that close to him. I wanted to give in; it would have been so easy to turn my face and let him kiss me.

But still, even though I think I understand why Cass said what he did, I feel hurt and angry. The idea that he could find me embarrassing is painful. I've always thought that Cass understood me. The entirety of De Anza High might have been laughing behind my back, but Cass was always on my side, even when we weren't friends anymore. Now I'm not sure what to think.

When we cross the Carquinez Bridge, over the northeastern end of the San Pablo Bay, something in my heart falters. Home: the smell of the tide, the squawking of gulls, the soft browns and golds of the grassy hillsides in early summer. I remember how it felt almost three weeks ago to wander the streets of my hometown, desperate to get out of here. And now?

Now I don't know. The desperation isn't there anymore. Something has softened. I don't feel transformed, exactly, but I don't feel the same, either.

When we pull in the driveway, Dad is waiting, sitting on the top porch step. He's wearing his day-off clothes, cargo shorts and a flannel, even though it's Thursday. He's got a layer of red-gold scruff on his cheek. I forget to be cool and I run to him, throwing myself into his arms like a little kid. He spins me around and kisses my cheek. "Welcome home, kiddo," he says. "I missed you."

"Me too," I say.

He pulls back and grins at me. "And also, you're in deep shit."

I duck my head. "I know."

He puts on his most serious face. "It's going to take an awful lot of yard work to pay off that credit card. In fact"—he pulls a pair of garden gloves out of his back pocket—"you probably should get started right away."

• • •

That night, I sit on the couch with my sisters, watching *Real Housewives* and eating ice cream with peanut butter and granola on top. They still have not said a word about my tremendous nosedive into reckless behavior and high-interest debt. I'm starting to think that maybe they somehow don't even know. Or maybe, as usual, they have been too wrapped up in their own lives to care.

"This is boring," Anna says, braiding strands of her blond hair in front of her face.

"Is it?" I ask. I kind of feel like I could do this forever, sitting still, not moving. "I think I'm actually having fun."

"You've changed, little one," says Grace.

I shrug. Out the living room window, through the low branches of the redwood tree, I can see the lights of Caspian's house glowing softly.

"Syd and Cass sitting in a tree . . ." sings Anna, Grace joining in halfway through.

"Shut up," I say. And the look on my face must be crushed enough that both of them stop immediately.

42
Caspian

WHEN I GET HOME FROM THE studio, Dad is waiting in the living room. We haven't seen each other since Gram left last night, after the two of them talked quietly for a long time in the kitchen. He looks at me standing there with my guitar in one hand and his old drill case in the other and lets out a long breath, like he's not quite ready for what's coming. I take off my shoes and set down my things by the door and sit down on the couch, so that we are side by side, both of us looking straight ahead at the shelf of records.

"Look," I say, breaking the long silence between us. "I'm sorry I didn't tell you where I was. It's just"—I search around for the words, and for once they are right there, exactly where I need them—"there are so many things I didn't feel like I could tell you."

He nods along, as though grateful that I'm speaking so that he doesn't have to.

But then I say, "Why didn't you ever tell me about her?"

He goes still, stays quiet until I'm almost not sure if he's going to respond. Finally he says, "A lot of reasons, Cass. A lot of reasons."

His usual cryptic nature, his calm quiet, grates in this moment.

"Didn't you think that I might need her? Didn't you know that there would be parts of me that you couldn't understand?"

Dad laughs a little, a dark laugh, because none of this is funny.

"I guess I hoped there wouldn't be. I was scared. And hurting. Your mom—it was hard, even before she died."

I stand up and start pacing back and forth across the room, unable to keep still in this house that now feels so still. Too still.

"You should have told me," I say. "You should have let me know her."

He looks at me with wide eyes, like he is startled and overwhelmed, like he doesn't know how to deal with a son who talks and asks for things. His face and hands are weathered from years of working in the sun but his hair is thick and dark brown. He suddenly looks very young, and I remember that he was only twenty-two years old when I was born. I imagine him when my mother died, not even twenty-five, alone with a baby in an apartment in Oakland.

Finally, he says, "I know." It feels like it takes a lot for him to say it.

I stop pacing, halfway between the table and the door. "Anyway. This is who I am. I'm not Mom but this part of her is part of me too."

I look at Dad. At six feet, two inches, he usually towers above everyone, but sitting there on our old couch he looks so small. He sighs deeply. I wait for him to say something else. Something that will make this right. But he doesn't. He just nods and says, "Okay." And then he walks into the kitchen for a beer.

I stand there watching him leave, trying to tell myself that it's enough. I'm about to start up the stairs when he leans his head back into the living room and says, "I love you, son."

And I nod and say, "I love you too."

The next morning there's a knock on the door, and there, standing on the mat, is Sydney Greenfield. My heart lurches up into my throat at the sight of her oversized black T-shirt and messy hair, her long, bruised-up legs in cowboy boots, her dark lashes and bare lips and angry brown eyes.

I *love you*, I think. "Hey," I say.

She clears her throat. "Hey," she says, voice raspy.

Then she holds up my car keys. "I brought her back in one piece."

I grin. "Thanks."

She looks over her shoulder to where the car sits in front of the house. It's covered in dust, a little bit of grime from each place we've been.

"Might need a wash though."

"Definitely."

There's an awkward pause. Everything I've wanted to say since New Orleans comes rushing back, all at once. I reach for her arm, my fingers encircling her wrist.

"Listen," I say. "I'm sorry—"

She tugs her hand back out of my grip. "Don't worry about it," she says. Her eyes slice into mine, in a way that makes me feel like I'll never get a second chance. Embarrassed, I lift my hand up to my hair.

"Anyway," I say. "I owe you a couple thousand dollars."

She shrugs. "Let's talk about it later. I need a nap."

"Are you going to the show tonight?" I ask as she slinks back down the stairs. "I can't believe they're playing the Great American."

"Wouldn't miss it," she says, without turning around.

When she's gone, I go out to my car and take out the amp that's been buried under blankets in the back for years. I bring it into the house, past my dad, who is watching a baseball game. He looks at me and raises his eyebrows, and I raise mine, and that's it. I walk up the stairs, into my room, and plug it in.

I play the guitar, at full volume, all afternoon. One riff, over and over, in one million different ways.

Syd. She's all that I can think of. What an idiot I was to leave her behind.

For the first time, I admit to myself that the distance I placed between us was intentional. At sixteen, Syd scared me. She was different. Loud. She knew how to be herself. All I wanted was to be numb, and she wouldn't let me. So I pushed her away, even though she was the only person who ever really knew me.

43
Sydney

BEFORE LOAD-IN AT THE GREAT AMERICAN Music Hall, the Darlas take me out to a four-o'clock dinner. We go to a dumpling place on Clement Street and order way too much food and the whole thing feels surreal, to be here with them on my home turf. I'm sitting in a booth, squished between Sunny and Charlie. The San Francisco July afternoon is cold and cloudy, and it's warm and cozy inside the restaurant.

Everyone starts giving toasts: *To forty times around the sun; To the band; To Syd; To Charlie, Sunny, Julia, Jasmyn, Iris.*

"Thank you all so very much," I say when it's my turn, holding up a glass of orange soda. "You guys fucking rule."

"Aw, Syd," Charlie says. "You fucking rule."

I lean my head onto Charlie's shoulder. "What will I do without you?"

"You think you can get rid of us?" Jasmyn says.

"Good fucking luck with that," Charlie laughs. "Our musical careers are over, so we have to live vicariously through you."

"No more shows?" I ask. The idea of the Darlas not playing anymore makes me so sad.

"Meh," says Julia, "I think we're done."

"Yeah," says Charlie, "I'm fucking exhausted."

"Sorry, Syd," Sunny says. "Looks like you and Cass are gonna have to take it from here."

The mention of Cass makes my stomach ache.

Jasmyn reaches across the table and squeezes my hand, like she knows. "We got you," she says.

The last show of the Darlas' reunion tour starts just like any other, with Jasmyn playing a long, low, distorted note. I am sitting behind the board of the Great American Music Hall, one of my all-time favorite venues, watching a guy named Axle make tiny adjustments on the levels.

I try not to, but I keep staring at Cass, who is standing in a shadow, bent over his guitar. He looks so perfect, just like every time he plays. Like everything about him that has puzzled me our entire lives suddenly makes sense.

Yesterday, on Cass's front porch, feeling his fingers around my wrist, my heart cracked right down the middle. No matter how much I want to feel nothing for him, I can't. I feel everything for Cass; I always will.

I look down at the audience below us and spot Craig, who is wearing a button-down shirt and bolo tie, holding a brown beer bottle in his hand. He's perched at the bar next to Mom and Dad and Anna and Grace. It's weird having my family here; I'm not sure if I like it. But they are trying and so am I.

"Twenty-one" melts into "Clover." The familiar set is like a favorite record—predictable now, and comforting. I feel overwhelmingly sad that this is the last time I'll hear it. I try to soak in the music and the lights, the magic pull of Julia behind the microphone, the steady heartbeat of Charlie on the drums. I try to pretend that it's my first time and I don't know what's coming next.

But then, just before the last song, Julia grabs the microphone and says, "You might not know it, but we have Iris McCarthy's son here on stage with us tonight."

The interruption to the usual flow startles me.

The crowd starts cheering and hooting and Julia says, "Cass, get over here."

Cass grabs his guitar by the neck and walks out into the spotlight. He is actually smiling, an adorable, lopsided, dimply grin, which makes me wonder what the hell has happened to him in the past ten days.

Then he steps up to the microphone and says, "If it's okay with you, I'd like to play a song of my own tonight." He runs his hand nervously through his hair and the crowd goes wild. My own heart starts to race and jealousy pricks under my skin.

But then he clears his throat and says, "This song is for the person I love." He looks right at the sound booth, right at me, his eyes two heavy, sad moons. My heart actually stops in my chest. "Sydney Greenfield, this one's for you."

I've always wondered what it would be like to have someone write me a song. I always thought it would be Robbie, and that it would have silly lyrics and rhyme *Sydney* with *smokes like a chimney* or something like that. But this. This is nothing like that.

There aren't any words at all, just sound. So much sound. And Cass's face, smooth like a seashell under the lights, looking right at me.

I don't know why but tears are streaming down my face and I don't even care whether Axle thinks I'm an idiot or not. Because Caspian Forrester just said that he loves me, is playing me a song that sounds like outer space.

When he's finished, he gives a salute, laughs a little over the roar of the crowd. And then I start running.

I tear down the steps, past the mezzanine, into the lobby, out the front door and into the freezing cold of a San Francisco July night. The air is wet and it sinks all the way into my bones, but I just keep on running, down the block, past all the late-night wanderers, on and on down O'Farrell Street.

I have to get away from here, I think. *I have to get away from Cass.* I can't let him break my heart again.

But he's right there, on my heels, a block away, then half, yelling my name.

My lungs start to burn and I finally come to a stop at the corner of Jones Street, doubling over and fumbling in my back pocket for my inhaler. Cass catches up to me and skids to a stop and we both stand under the streetlight, trying to catch our breath in the fog. I'm shaking. I turn away from him, back toward the venue, the round bulb lights that twinkle in the distance. A soft, warm, quilted jacket drops onto my shoulders.

"I'm so scared," I say. I bury face in my hands. "And I'm never scared. I don't know how to do this."

"I know," he says, right behind me. "It's my fault. I am so, so sorry."

And then I start to cry again.

"You were right," he says. "I was a coward." I can feel him moving closer, his presence tall and steady at my back. "For a really long time. I thought—

"My mom—

"My dad—

"I don't know. I was stupid and scared and I just wanted to stop feeling so much." He rests one big hand on my shoulder. "That was a mistake." He takes a deep, sad breath. "Listen. What I said to you in New Orleans was wrong. The truth is, you aren't like anyone else. But I'm so glad you're not."

"I'm sorry too," I say. "You're right, I shouldn't have pushed you so hard. That's not my job. But I still can't—" I look around, trying to find the words to say what I'm feeling. "I'm still so mad at you." I can't let this anger go; it feels like the only thing holding me to the earth.

Cass watches me carefully, like he's afraid I'll run away again.

"It's okay," he says, letting out a shaky breath. "Just please, come back to me."

I look up into his dark brown eyes and I feel terrified. I wanted so badly to go, to get lost, to never let anyone hurt me ever again. And now I'm back at home, standing on the street with the person who ripped my heart out.

Cass leans his forehead down to mine. "Please," he whispers. His voice sounds unbearably sad.

My heart stutters in my chest as I flail around for the right answer. I need a sign, a promise from the universe, but I know it isn't coming. This one is on me.

Then, somewhere outside of the circle of Cass and me, maybe across the street, a person walks by, singing.

And then I think, Fuck it.

I reach up for Cass's glasses, sliding them off and folding them neatly in my left hand. Then I push up onto my toes until I'm right there, my lips a millimeter away from his. "Okay," I say. And then I press my lips to his.

I mean the kiss to be soft and sweet. A promise. A beginning. But we are in the middle of this; we both know it. Cass threads his fingers into my hair, walking me backward until I feel the cold scrape of bricks on the backs of my legs. His kiss is hot and wild. He tastes like cinnamon gum. He kisses me until I can't breathe.

A car drives by fast, someone yelling "Get a room!" out the open window. Cass pulls back, out of breath, and raises his arm, giving them the finger. I start to giggle, almost hysterically. The air is cold enough to make my fingers sting.

Just before he kisses me again, I pull back and whisper, "Cass?"

"Yeah?" he says, his hands warm on the side of my face. I can feel his heart thumping through the front of his button-down.

"That was a really good song."

THE MORNING MY INTERNSHIP STARTS, I wake up to a text in my Darlas group chat:

Jasmyn: Give em hell little one.

It's 9:03 a.m. I am lying in my childhood bed, in the room I shared with Grace and Anna until Levi moved out when I was ten. The sunlight filters through the gap in my black swiss dot curtains, making a wide stripe across my Whales of North America poster. I am home.

I text the group: **Def.**

Because they seem to get a real kick out of it when I abbreviate.

Then I get a text from Mom: Good luck today! Also, please mop the kitchen this morning and bring the garbage cans in.

One from Levi linking to an article from the *Wall Street Journal* about the benefits of taking a gap year before starting college.

I text back: **I'm not taking a gap year, doof. This is my actual life.**

I guess it's too late at this point to go back to sleep, so I kick my feet over the side of the bed and sit up, giving my arms a long stretch.

Today is the day.

When I step out my front door I see Cass, waiting for me in the gravel driveway between our houses. His hair is sticking out of the bottom of his bicycle helmet, and his eyes are big and sleepy. He catches sight of me and the smile that stretches across his face is pure sunshine.

"Race you to the diner?" he says.

He walks over to where I'm standing on the steps and tugs the bottom of my shirt until our bodies are flush, pressing a soft kiss to the edge of my mouth. Then he whispers, "Unless you're afraid I'll beat you."

"Hasn't happened yet," I say, snaking my hands up around his neck.

Caspian reaches up and sets my sparkly teal helmet carefully down on my head. "Is that a yes?"

I grin. "You're on."

After breakfast, Cass drives me to the BART station. I'm nervous, so I leave a little too much time for my commute and end up at the Fox twenty minutes early. I circle the block three times, looking at the old brick building from every angle, trying to let myself soak in every ounce of history that's taken place inside of its walls. I watch the way the afternoon light bends across the uneven rooftop; I listen to the music of the birds and the wind and the cars on the street. When it's finally time, I take a deep breath, walk under the marquee, and make my way inside.

I'M SITTING IN AN OFFICE AT the edge of campus, at the back of a building that's nestled in a grove of eucalyptus trees. It's the third week of school; I'm in the two-hour break between Music Theory 101 and Calc Three.

Across from me, in a chair that's angled halfway toward mine, sits Dr. Mendoza, a school psychologist. It's our first visit, and neither of us has said much of anything for the past ten minutes.

My eyes trace the lines of the Turkish rug, the potted plants, the sunlight slanting across the carpet. My palms are sweaty. I'm not sure how to do this.

"Why don't you start by telling me why you're here," Dr. Mendoza finally says, tossing me a line. Her face is serene, half smiling, eyes kind behind round wire-rimmed glasses.

I laugh a little. "I feel like that question isn't the easiest to answer."

"Why not?" she says.

I rake a hand down my face.

"I'm not very good at talking," I say.

"That's okay," she says, leaning back in her chair. "We've got time."

I think about the question, about everything that's happened in the past couple of months to bring me to this place, the day I found out about the Darlas' tour, finding Syd and then losing Syd and then finding her again, the night in Georgia where I played my guitar in front of everyone, even Dad. And then before that, all those years of emptiness and quiet. There's too much to tell, no clear beginning. But I'm here to sort it out, to feel better. I have to try.

She waits, and I wait. The second hand moves slowly around the face of the clock on the wall. And then I close my eyes and say, "My mother was a musician."

Acknowledgments

THIS BOOK WAS LARGELY WRITTEN DURING the first year of the pandemic, and I'll never forget walking along the San Pablo Bay every day with my husband, Andrew, and my son, Angelo, watching the birds fly over the water, and then coming home to try to write it all down.

Thank you to my wonderful agents, Taylor Haggerty and Melanie Figueroa—without you, none of this would be possible. I am so grateful for your consistent support and unflagging enthusiasm for my writing, and your expert, patience guidance through the sometimes overwhelming world of publishing. And many thanks to the entire team at Root Literary—you all are amazing!

Thank you to my editor, Kelsey Murphy, for helping to hold the vision for my books and lovingly pushing me to be a better writer. This book is so much better because of you.

A big thank-you to the team at Penguin Random House and Viking Children's Books for helping send this book out into the world, especially Jen Loja, Jocelyn Schmidt, Stephanie Sabol, Robyn Bender, Pete Facente, Gaby Corzo, Gerard Mancini, Alexandra Aleman, Ginny Dominguez, Vanessa Robles, Nadine Britt, Amy White, Lisa Schwartz, Amanda Cranney, Cherisse Landau, Marinda Valenti, Sola Akinlana, Kristy Gilbert, Kelley Salas, Ken Wright, Tamar Brazis, Ellice Lee, Emily Romero, Christina Colangelo, Bri Lockhart,

Jessie Clark, Danielle Presley, Shanta Newlin, Elyse Marshall, Lizzie Goodell, Felicity Vallence, Shannon Spann, James Akinaka, Alex Garber, Bezi Yohannes, Carmela Iaria, Trevor Ingerson, Summer Ogata, Rachel Wease, Judith Huerta, Venessa Carson, Felicia Frazier, Debra Polansky, Trevor Bundy, Talisa Ramos, Allan Winebarger, Todd Jones, Emily Bruce, Mary Raymond, Mary McGrath, Colleen Conway, Dandy Conway, Jill Bailey, Andrea Baird, Maggie Brennan, Nicole Davies, John Dennany, Doni Kay, Steve Kent, Carol Monteiro, Stacey Pyle, Kate Sullivan, Nicole White, and Rachel Jacobs.

Thank you to Nicole Rifkin for creating the beautiful illustration of Cass and Syd on the cover. The pink moon is the cover art of my dreams. Thank you also to Lucia Baez for interior design and Theresa Evangelista and Deborah Kaplan for cover design.

Thank you to Terry Yerves for sharing your expert insight into sound engineering and the Fox Theater. Thank you to Lisa Cron of *Story Genius*—your book got me through a serious block in the middle of this one. Thank you to Nina LaCour and the Slow Novel Lab for helping me find inspiration.

Thank you to Martina Papinchak, Edith Thornton Cohn, Gwen Mesco, Kate Spencer, Emily Barth Isler, Samantha Speiller, and Amelia Coombs, who read early drafts and pieces of this book and offered feedback and advice. Thank you to all of the writers in my Write! Write! Write! group; I wouldn't be able to keep going without your support.

Thank you to all the musicians in my life, past, present, and future. Especially to the babes of July, the band that inspired the songs and lyrics for the Darlas: Jasmyn Wong, Claire Plumb, Hannah Weiss, Lily

Rachles, Andrew Sweeney, and Jeff Moller. And to Sarah Simon and Sam Berman of MMR, my first and forever-love band. Also, there could not be a book about the Darlas without my amazing friends Lee, Marisa, Shelby, and Erin.

Thank you to Andrew and Angelo for living life with me and for supporting my dreams. I love you both so much. And an extra thank-you to Andrew, who provided me with innumerable obscure musical references for this book. Thank you to my nieces, Mia and Ellie, and to my nephew, Jack, for providing the most thoughtful insight into what it's like to be a young adult. Thank you to all of my family, for your support and love.

Finally, thank you to all of the booksellers, librarians, bloggers, and readers out there. You are what makes my dream of writing possible.